THE
CLINIC

BOOKS BY CARA REINARD

THE
CLINIC

CARA REINARD

bookouture

Published by Bookouture in 2024

An imprint of Storyfire Ltd.
Carmelite House
50 Victoria Embankment
London EC4Y 0DZ

www.bookouture.com

Storyfire Ltd's authorised representative in the EEA is Hachette Ireland
8 Castlecourt Centre
Castleknock Road
Castleknock
Dublin 15, D15 YF6A
Ireland

ISBN: 978-1-83525-259-8
eBook ISBN: 978-1-83525-258-1

The hand that rocks the cradle is the hand that rules the world.

W.R. WALLACE

PROLOGUE

It's a shared want, like love or sunlight.

I could probably live without it, but the thought leaves me cold and dead inside.

Motherhood is a gift, they say.

And she's my cross to bear, grasping at the same rays of light.

It makes me wonder if she's my greatest blessing or my biggest curse.

Why do I get the feeling that what leaves me empty, brings her joy?

And that whatever secret she's keeping with him will end us both?

ONE

EMILY

BARREN

The first time anyone breathed the word—*barren*—in my ear, I was studying abroad at Cambridge, in England. I went hiking with a gorgeous fellow graduate student named Louie on the edge of the Yorkshire Dales National Park on an expanse of land called Riggs Moor.

The grounds here are absolutely barren, he said, in a chirpy voice I found delicious.

I liked Louie because of his spontaneity, a quality he shared with my college ex-boyfriend, Ben, who I'd left thousands of miles away.

My romance with Louie, a hot flame that burned out on the back of a hillside in the most desolate part of England, was almost as short-lived as my first experience of the word.

In my late twenties, the word—*barren*—took on a different meaning. After I was diagnosed and moved home to the States, the harsh treatments to cure me diminished my fertility. My only shot at having biological children was to freeze my eggs.

And today, on my thirty-sixth birthday, barren means something entirely different.

I'm thankful for each new year, but it's the wicked meaning of the word that gets to me now.

And there's a special place in Hell for those who ask the unmarried childless woman of a certain age the questions—*So when do you think you'll settle down and have kids? Your biological clock is ticking, you know?*

We know.

Believe me. We know...

TWO

EMILY

UPGRADE

My birthday dinner is inside of a bar, jampacked with more men wearing black and gold hats backwards than should be legally allowed, and it's only pre-season.

Outside isn't much better. Sweat and smoke and leering drunk eyes beneath a shabby tent dressed up with a string of Christmas lights all year around—that's Redbeard's, Pittsburgh's hole-in-the-wall bar on the top of a mountain.

Laurel, my best friend, takes in her surroundings like she'd rather be anywhere else, but she let me choose the venue tonight—her mistake.

The waitress slops down our over-flowing mixed drinks on the table.

"Why did you pick... this place for your birthday dinner?" Laurel asks.

"I know something is going on. We always celebrate my birthday on the weekend and you insisted on the actual day this year."

Laurel looks as though she's been stung. "You're right... So, what? You torture me by bringing me here?"

I smile brightly. "Exactly. You know I don't like surprises." This couldn't be more true. I'm a scientist. I prefer my life in measured doses.

Laurel shakes her head, laughs, and sticks her middle finger up at me. "I hate you!"

"You love me." I point at her vodka tonic. The runoff is dripping down the side. "Here." I throw her a drink napkin and she dabs at her glass, but she won't look at me. Something is wrong.

"Kids okay?" I ask, a bit worried.

"Yeah, they're great," she says. I know I would've heard about it long before now if this were about them.

"What's going on, Laurel?" I ask.

"Emily, it's... Ben."

"*Oh.*" I don't have to ask which Ben she's referring to, because there's only one—Ben Holiday. My college ex, and sadly the man with whom I had my last serious relationship—nearly fifteen years ago. He somehow found the heart beneath Emily the clinical scientist; the real me. When I think about Ben it makes me miss both of us. My ex-boyfriend, and the girl I used to be with him.

Laurel flashes her long lashes at me. "He's going to be in town."

My eyes are on fire. But it's not from the cigar smoke. Ben is coming home and I'm the last to know.

"He's having... relationship trouble. I don't know much. I overheard his conversation with Zach."

I bite my lip. "What kind of issues?" This is interesting. "What're Zach's thoughts?" I ask of Laurel's husband.

"Zach's just happy to hang out with him, but he hasn't invited me to come with them... for the meetup," Laurel says.

"Have you seen him? Seen *them?*" This is the million-dollar question. Ben has been off the radar for a decade. He's anti-all-things-social-media. I heard his wife was religious and considers social media a sin, or something. Although, I always receive his grand updates from Laurel via Zach.

"Hey, Zach talked to Ben and he just returned from Vail on some epic ski trip."

"Zach heard from Ben and I guess he caught like three gigantic swordfish in Mexico!"

"You're not going to believe this, but Ben just completed his first Ironman."

It's not my fault I haven't gotten over Ben. Everyone makes him out to be some kind of Herculean, mountain-leaping enigma, too mysterious to make an appearance on Facebook or Instagram.

"Is she... going to be with him when he visits Zach?" I ask.

"I don't think so. I asked Zach if I should plan a dinner for the four of us, and he said that he needed a guys' night to talk to Ben at the bar alone."

Betrayal digs deep at the thought of my best friend having dinner with Ben's wife. The four of us—Laurel and Zach, and Ben and me—used to be inseparable. "Are you sure you heard Zach right? What did he say, exactly?" I couldn't be more curious.

"He said maybe time apart from her will help you figure things out." Laurel shoots me a sly little smile.

Ooh, this is good. Maybe they won't figure it out.

Divorce happens around this stage in a marriage.

It's got that whole itch attached to it—seven years. I should know how long it's been. I drink myself to sleep nearly every year on the eve of their wedding anniversary. "What do you think could've happened?"

I'm hoping Laurel's holding out—that she knows more than she's revealing, because the suspense is killing me.

"The only other thing I overheard once was that Ben

wanted to have kids right away and she didn't. That was a long time ago, though."

A light bulb clicks on. "Why doesn't Ben have kids yet? He wanted a mob of children, and he's thirty-five, and how old is this woman he married anyway?" The questions tumble out of my mouth like they're on a conveyor.

"I think around the same age. He doesn't talk to Zach about those kinds of things. His wife is super active. I guess she likes to hike and kayak and travel, like him, you know? Maybe she doesn't want to give up her freedom?"

"That's the dumbest reason I've ever heard for not having children," I say.

Laurel flashes her gorgeous blue eyes at me again.

"Well, come on," I protest, "she won't have a baby with him because she'd rather take a hike? I'd tell her to take a walk." I know it's unreasonable to be upset with Laurel, but she's got me all fired up. *Why didn't you tell me the minute you knew he was coming home?!*

Laurel laughs, but her forehead pinches together like this conversation is stressing her out.

She's given a reprieve as our food is plunked on the table with force, and my mind skitters to Ben. Maybe he's tired of suburbia with the missus. Maybe he even misses—*me*.

I pluck a wing off the plate and sink my teeth into it, observing Laurel's white, limp fries. She prods one with her fork and it hangs on the silver tine like a wet noodle.

"That's why you order the wings when you come here," I inform.

"Message received. Hopefully, we won't be dining here again anytime soon. Time for an upgrade—in all things, Emily."

I exhale, because we both know she's talking about Ben, but she can't outright say it. Not after how we broke up. Laurel shares some responsibility there. My breakup with Ben has thrown off the entire trajectory of my life. We could've had kids early, before I got sick, if I hadn't ended the relationship.

I want a baby so bad it hurts sometimes, and talking about them all day only makes it worse. Forget talking about them, pouring test tubes into petri dishes and creating them with my own hands makes it downright excruciating. All because I was waiting for the right guy.

But Ben was the right guy, the only man I'd ever thought of having a child with, and I just let him go...

THREE

EMILY

MOUNTAIN

My townhouse sits on Mount Washington's Grandview Avenue, the cream of the crop view of Pittsburgh's skyline, the homes an incongruent smattering of every type of architectural design possible—gothic revival, art deco, Victorian, a swanky high-rise condominium, a four-story, vertically constructed modern masterpiece—all crammed next to one another in a hulking conglomerate of buildings. My favorite house on the mountain is constructed of stone with evil-looking dragon figurines guarding the entrance—black fencing, overgrown vines.

An old witch lives there, I'm sure.

But she can't possibly be worse than Chelsea Asad.

"You're miserable! *Miserable*. Slob." The echo of Chelsea's voice streams through the open windows.

According to Chelsea, Jasper is—*a freeloading, lazy bastard who refuses to work*. Ironically, from what I've gathered, Chelsea has never worked a day in her life. Jasper likely stays for their three-year-old daughter, Clementine. I was sure, once

Clem was born, that they'd move from our adjoined building, view-side of the steep cliffs. But there Chelsea is, still.

I sit on the balcony and wave at her.

I do this sometimes so she realizes I'm there.

And so she stops screaming at her fucking husband.

One of the only sacred moments in my day is when I can sit on the balcony and drink my morning coffee before I report to the clinic.

Chelsea waves back, but continues to complain—*If you don't find a job by the end of the month, you can find somewhere else to live!*

I yawn, because I've heard this threat more times than I care to count in my seven years living here. A trust fund baby, Chelsea can afford to make the threat. Jasper's eviction has yet to occur.

Jasper catches my eye next, and we've shared so many wayward glances, he's long past embarrassed. More amused—a sharp edge that's been worn down to a nub. Although, his nub is apparently sizeable by the way Chelsea screams in pleasure during their lovemaking.

She also keeps the window open for those overt vindications of control over her husband.

Sometimes she walks onto her balcony afterward, silk robe flapping in the wind that always seems to catch at this altitude, exposing her naked body to the city, still slick with Jasper. I think she struts out there so I'll watch her. The way she fake-inhales her cigarette gives away more than she thinks.

Chelsea's not my type, though. Jasper is.

Dark and brooding, brown hair and eyes, washboard abs. Likes to stain antique furniture on the balcony with his shirt off in the summertime—*Jasper*.

We're quiet people—Jasper and me.

Sometimes we both sit on the balcony, together, in silence, sipping our cocktails or hot drinks. We might offer each other a nod, at ease in each other's presence. He's caught me in little more than my underwear before, but it's never motivated me enough to change. *It's just Jasper.* We're like roommates, in a way.

Then Chelsea returns, enters our sacred space, destroys our bliss.

There's usually immediate discord, something for Chelsea to complain about—*why didn't you take care of the bills... arrange the childcare... order the repair?*

Chelsea's presence embodies a bundle of nervous energy, even on the balcony, a place that should instill wonder with the city and its twinkling lights just below. She often leans too far over the edge in a way that makes me uneasy.

There're the days I crave my peace so badly that I imagine pushing her right off the ledge.

I visualize the way her body would smack off the rocks, which ones she'd likely hit first. Living here for so long, I've memorized each one, the way they cut and jut from the side of the steep hill. Perhaps, she'd bounce far enough over to the right to get tangled in the tracks of the red incline cable car that moves up and down the side of the mountain—an archaic transport system still used.

Chelsea would certainly die from that type of fall, but it could be an *accident*.

I hate that the thought enters my mind on a regular basis. But we can control our thoughts no more than we can surgically detach our feelings from our body. I'd like to alter how I feel, but as it stands I can't help but think how unfair the world is that vile women like Chelsea Asad are blessed with children, and I'm all alone—and barren.

Far too often, Clementine appears scared from all of the shouting. She shouldn't be around all this. She'd be better off...

With a mother like me.

FOUR

EMILY

911

I feel a vibration in my purse and grab for my phone. It's my office manager, Lisette.

Lisette: Can you come in early? #911

Not a #911. Again. I just had one last week.

Emily: Send it to me

I hear my email ding with the electronic patient chart—immediate. A #911 must be treated as so.

Lisette: You're up

Lisette's well aware of our code words too. She's paid twice the amount of any office manager to understand the covert language Batey has devised for us.

I scroll through the chart on my phone, scouring for the

reason Batey is thinking about denying treatment for the hopeful couple on the schedule, and I quickly find it. The patient has had more than three previous miscarriages.

Most IVF clinics will accept money from anyone who wants to try their services, provided the patient is a healthy, viable candidate—but we're not every clinic.

Money isn't Dr. Magda Batey's main motivator.

She's all about the success rates.

Being the best.

Logging in the highest birth rates in the country.

Receiving invitations to speak on panels for her expertise.

But that also means turning down couples like the ones in this file, and squashing their dreams of becoming parents. And when she can't deliver the news herself, she taps me on the shoulder to assist her.

The hardest part is admitting to myself that I crave it too—being the "best" in the country at what I do. If I can't have a man's love or a family of my own, then I'll be the most regarded person in my field.

The title is addictive—*the most renowned embryologist in the United States.*

I plod in my ugly Crocs to the room of doom we've quaintly named the gray haven of tranquility. It took me two days to regulate after delivering the bad news to the last couple, just the previous week. I knew I'd upset them, but my emotional response was delayed—then lingered.

Even though Dr. Batey receives the credit for the miraculous acts that occur at our clinic, the real conjuring of life occurs behind closed doors, in a highly regulated laboratory led by me.

Dr. Batey might be the physician to implant the embryos, but I'm the one to care for them throughout the transfer.

They are my babies before they're hers—or theirs.

I take special care of them and feel a real loss when they don't make it. It doesn't seem to faze Dr. Batey. It's just an opportunity to try again, gouge them for more money. Because, it isn't Dr. Batey's time, money, hopes, dreams at stake, and if they don't conceive, her success rates drop.

Even though this practice is hers, this lab is mine.

It's the only thing in this world that truly belongs to me.

And until I have a baby of my own, I treat every specimen with the greatest of care, because I know someday it will be my turn, and I'll want someone else to do the same thing for me.

I'm lost in thought as I prepare for my meeting with the couple. My vision is slightly sabotaged with fear and panic, but I can't miss the couple rushing toward me.

"Emily!" I hear my name being shouted, and it's surreal. I know that voice, but it doesn't belong here.

I figured the next time I saw Ben, it would be like a Hollywood moment, where the background music stopped, and everything else froze in the room except for me and him. We'd be vacuum-packed in a self-contained bubble of nostalgia no one else could see or permeate, and we'd stare at each other as long as we'd like, examining every little detail that might've changed since the last time we saw one another.

I'd have my hair perfectly done up and I'd be wearing something signature and fresh, like an off-colored pea coat or a fitted black dress. I'd think stupid, silly things like, *Did he always have that little wrinkle around his smile line?*

And he might tell me I look—*just the same*—the way people who haven't seen me in a while tend to say, and I would wonder if he was paying me a compliment or an insult like I did with the others.

But it's not like that at all.

I'm in a white lab coat and I'm sweating profusely, and we're definitely not alone. "Ben, hi," I manage.

"I thought I might run into you. I mean, I knew you worked here..." Ben rambles as they near me. *She's* holding his hand, but I can't focus on her right now. They're fuzzy images, imaginary people. He's just a mountain-climbing enigma. This can't be real.

"Yeah, I'm here..." is all I can utter. I place my hand on my forehead.

Ben stares at me funny, but I only notice his pensive dark eyes for a second before I look away. I can't read Ben's wife's expression, because my line of vision hasn't found her face yet. I concentrate on the patient chart in my hands instead.

Allyson and Ben

Profile: Allyson Holiday

How did I miss the last name?!

Allyson: 37
Occupation: Marketing Analyst
Marital Status: M
Previous Children/Miscarriages: 4
Surgeries in the last year: n/a
Allergies: n/a
Please list any medical conditions (including diabetes, high blood pressure, high cholesterol, heart disease, etc.):
_____n/a_____
Reason being seen: Patient has had four miscarriages.
Patient has religious reasons for not consulting IVF sooner

This can't be happening, and I cannot take this case today.

"We'll catch up at Laurel's Labor Day party if you can make it, but right now we're late to meet Dr. Batey," he says so casually, I want to faint, die, and throw-up all at the same time. It's as if he's run into an old pal from college. Like I'm just a girl he split a beer with once in a bar. And I have no idea what party he's talking about. Apparently, I didn't get an invite.

"I don't think she's going to be able to meet with you today," I say in a rushed tone, now curious about the girl who's made him forget me.

"What do you mean? We're only five minutes late," he says.

I still can't concentrate on his wife yet, but I can feel the anxiety in her swaying movement. According to her file, she's religious, and this IVF-business is wrong, and they've finally made the decision to go through with it anyway, and secure the very best doctor they could—and she's bailed on them.

I stare at the file—four miscarriages.

Ben has lost four babies.

This woman standing halfway behind her love and protector has tried to create a child with him four times and failed.

"If you're comfortable with it, Ben, they actually asked me to handle your case today. I'm the head embryologist at the clinic." I finally make full eye contact with him. I'm a professional, after all, and this is what I do when I meet with a new couple.

And he is—*just the same*, only different in the most beautiful, grown-up-Ben way. His hair is shorter, but still longish for a male. His body trim and taut, his smile still ever-present. Ben has one of those skinny black ties on with a white checked dress shirt and Harry Styles-esque tapered jeans. He's totally an art teacher; a hot art teacher.

I'm not ready to look at her yet.

It probably seems like I'm ignoring her on purpose, but my analytical brain can only examine one thing at a time, and I haven't had my fill of Ben yet.

"That should be fine. Ally?" Ben says in question form to his wife. All that I can make out in my temporary blindness is that Ben's wife has on trendy glasses, sort of like mine. I don't like that she wears glasses. That's my thing.

When she doesn't protest or say much of anything, I lead the way back to the gray-violet room of tranquility that will be anything but calm today. They follow me with quiet footfalls. I don't hear the clicking of heels behind me, which tells me she isn't wearing them.

We enter the room and I study their chart some more as they settle into armchairs. I vaguely see Ben's wife picking up pamphlets out of my peripheral vision. She's probably looking for some papers to hide behind too.

I attempt to focus, but my eyes blur again. I'm gathering that jittery feeling in my chest I sometimes get right before I become tearful. Crying would be the worst possible scenario here.

"Good morning, my name is Emily Daugherty and I am the head embryologist at the clinic..." I page through the file again even though I know what it says. I'll probably relive carbon copy images of it in my sleep. "It says here that you're interested in having your fertility evaluated, and possibly undergoing IVF, and my job is to discuss the general protocol here, and see if you have any questions."

I look up and finally focus my attention on Allyson. Well, Ally, because Ben prefers to give cute nicknames to his loves. I like how Ally sounds way better than Em.

"M", the thirteenth letter of the alphabet.

"Ally", an adorable name shared by one of the first stars of *The Bachelorette*.

Alley is also where you dump the trash.

Stop it, Emily.

Ally hasn't said a word, but I can tell she's almost ready to speak by the way she edges her neat black skirt to the brim of the seat of the cushioned chair. Her legs are long and toned; she must really like to hike with those legs—wrap them right around Ben's...

"I have some questions," Ally says, and now I'm honing in

on her whole face, the place I was trying so hard not to go. *Ah damn*, she's adorable with her Jennifer Garner dimples and full lips. Ally has brown eyes like Ben, and long dark hair that falls well over her shoulders. It's fastened and swept back to the side with a jeweled hummingbird barrette that looks antique, an interesting piece.

"Okay, go ahead," I say.

She pulls out the notepad from her purse-like tote bag, and that's when I really begin to hate her. Ally starts going through the very reasonable, intelligent questions I always expect but never receive from the overly emotional patients who stride through these doors.

"The seventy percent success rate is the highest I've ever seen, and I'm just wondering if that implies seventy percent of all patients you treat become pregnant through your services or something else?"

Great question. You are smart. Batey would loathe you.

"The seventy percent success rate is in regard to those embryos that are implanted. If an extraction doesn't pull any viable eggs, and we don't attempt implantation, Dr. Batey doesn't count those cases toward her success rate. She considers those failed extractions."

"That's kind of skewed, don't you think?" Ally's brilliant eyes stare back at me through her black-rimmed glasses.

Yes, I do.

I suddenly have a burning desire to know what Mrs. Holiday does for a living.

"I don't make the rules. Are you in the medical field by any chance?" Surely, Zach would've told Laurel if Ben had married a doctor. Wouldn't that be swell?

"I'm not. But I'm very good at technical research. I'm actually a marketing analyst. Research is my life."

Research is my life too.

"I see... It must've been hard to move with a job you obviously loved so much," I comment.

"Oh, I can work from home, so I didn't have to quit," she says, sharply.

"How great for you. The success rate information is more of a Dr. Batey question on how she determines the exact number. You can ask her more about that at a later date. She has a full caseload, and if she doesn't think she can help a patient, she has the right to refuse her services."

They both startle at that comment. Ally looks as though she's been choked, the muscles of her throat pulling back in anguish.

Ally's put in the work, physically and emotionally. She's obviously torn about the process because of her beliefs, but she knows from her research that we're the best, and if there's one clinic she'll consider trying, it's ours. I feel her desperation in that moment. A desperation I share, but I'm not sure I can help her. Batey will lose her mind if I don't follow her orders.

It's best if I try to contact Batey, explain the situation, that I know these people and would like to give them a chance at the clinic. Maybe we can keep their numbers out of the data... somehow.

I glance at my phone. "I've received an urgent message. I'm so sorry, this is terribly unprofessional, but I have to step outside for just a moment."

Both Ally and Ben eye me suspiciously, maybe because my phone didn't ring or buzz. It could be on silent mode, but I'm guessing Ben knows I'm lying.

Ben nods at me and I scamper out the door, not entirely sure I'll be returning if I can't deliver this couple the answer they deserve.

FIVE

EMILY

I dial Batey's cell, but it goes straight to voicemail—*Shit.*

I'm shocked when I turn around and find Ben right behind me. I jostle my phone and toss it in the pocket of my lab coat. Ally must still be in the consult room. "Hey, Ben... did you need to use the restroom? It's right..." I point down the hall.

"Cut the shit, Emily," Ben says.

Whoa. I lose my footing for a moment. The handrail steadies my wobble. "What do you mean?"

Ben continues, "I know you were going to tell us you can't treat us. And now you're hiding out here, just like... when you were hiding from the investigators in Cook's case in college. Never were good at confrontation."

Cook. Professor Ivan Cook.

I freeze in place, my mind flashing back. Logically, it made sense to tell the professor he was showing early signs of Parkinson's disease. The tremor in his hands, his suddenly rigid posture, the teeny, tiny handwriting on my graded paper—all classic indicators.

I didn't know he would fall into an Internet black hole, decide to self-medicate, take too many pills—die.

It wasn't my fault. I didn't kill him.

But... I did give him the leftover pain pills from my father's surgery.

He'd thanked me discreetly for letting him know my thoughts, pleaded with me not to share my findings with the dean, and asked me if I had anything to help him with his pain until he could get to a doctor. I was a college kid and had access to stuff—*wink, wink. Nod, nod.* He didn't.

I was prematurely diagnosing patients back then, without a degree. I thought I was so smart, even though I wasn't. And I wanted to be the kid who had connections, even though I was far from it—a science geek with too much curiosity, at best.

After Cook died, Ben helped me sneak into his ramshackle house in Point Breeze roped off with caution tape. We found the pill bottle with my father's name printed on the label and disposed of it. Ben wanted me to turn myself in, a simple mistake, but what I did carried a prison sentence with it for drug-induced homicide.

I wouldn't go down like that for a man I didn't really know.

Especially one who never gave me above a B in class, or any other female for that matter. Sexist egotist. He could lie down and push up daisies. And I wasn't going to be punished simply for being educated. Ben said he couldn't live with himself if the situation were reversed, and here we both are—alive and well, and faced with more moral dilemmas and consequences, once again.

"What're you saying, Ben? This is not how I wanted our first conversation to go, after all this time." I admit how disappointed I am. I've built Ben up for years in my mind and he's being just plain cruel.

"I'm saying I want you to do your job. The one that was so important that you traded everything for it."

By everything he's saying—*him.* He was my everything, but

he's also admitting I was his everything too. I can barely breathe as he says the next words.

"I did things for you that still keep me up at night. Do this for me. Help us, Emily."

He walks away, back into the consultation room, leaving me breathless. And without much choice.

I reenter the room a bit of a mess. So much to unpack in that little hallway chat, but I can't do it right now. "I'm so sorry for the interruption."

Ben sits there, expectant. Nervous. "That's okay."

He called me out, and maybe it's time somebody did. It strikes me hard that maybe it's time for me to adjust some of my own standards too. Do I have to cow tail to all of Batey's demands? Even when I don't agree with them? Even when they break my heart? I know enough of her secrets. Maybe I can make her bend on her practices the way Ben tried to make me rethink mine.

And I may not have a husband who loves me, and while that might be ideal, maybe I don't need one. Allyson wishes that she'd be blessed with a baby the natural way, but maybe I should give up on the idea that Mr. Perfect will arrive, and take matters into my own hands like the brave couple before me.

"Do you have any other questions... before we get started with the evaluations?"

Ben smiles freely now. His left hand grips Ally's right one, and I can tell it's because he wants this so badly. I wish I had someone to hold my hand like that. But... just because I don't doesn't mean I can't have the same thing as them—a baby.

Seeing him sitting there makes me realize there truly is only one Ben Holiday. And waiting around for another comparable match, one who would crawl through a crime scene for me, and keep my deepest, darkest secrets, is like hoping lightning will strike the same place twice. I do owe him. More so than that, I want to help them.

Ally fingers the crucifix that's strung around her neck with her other hand, her face a sad pit of confliction. There's a creased pamphlet on her lap. "It says here bleeding can be normal throughout the process, and as you can see in my chart, I've had miscarriages. How will I know the difference?" she asks.

Ben loses his perma-smile at the word *miscarriage*. His knee, that likes to bounce around when he's in a seated position for any length of time, stops. If I could climb inside Ben's head, I'm sure I could feel his hopefulness for the loss of each one of those children he never got to bounce on that jumpy knee. He's imagined their faces.

Wondered if they were boys or girls. Tried to visualize whether they'd look like him or Ally.

"During the egg collection, light spotting or bleeding can occur because the doctor has to stick a needle through your vaginal wall in order to retrieve your eggs. But it's very light. After the transfer, you may have the same symptoms," I explain.

"I see," Ally says, tightly.

"The staff will do a thorough examination, and they will test Ben as well. You'll get the full workup."

I've answered Ally's questions, and we're almost done with the most horrible consult of my life when the worst of Ally's comments comes out next.

She still holds the pamphlet in her hand. She keeps setting it down on her lap to play with her crucifix charm. "I know I have a lot of questions, it's just this is all research-based stuff, and that's my thing. And if there's a science to this, then I want to get it right," she proclaims.

Science is my thing too, Ally. And that's when I really understand what's happened here.

That's when it hits me like a hypodermic needle to the eye.

Ben has married a girl just like me—a research-based, chic-glasses-wearing, flat-shoe-donning, intelligent woman.

"You'll be made privy to every step. We're very thorough. I will let the nurses know you're ready for them," I say, quickly. Then, I exit the room before they can say another word to me. There will be no final greetings or well wishes to the Holidays. Because I cannot spend another minute in the room of tranquility with the love of my life and the exponentially better version of myself.

Ben made it clear that I traded him for my career, and this is where we stand now. Little did he know, it wasn't something, it was someone. Another man—but my fascination with him had nothing to do with love.

SIX

EMILY

CAMBRIDGE

13 Years Ago

The University of Cambridge is nestled about fifty miles north of London on the River Cam. I remember standing there with my mouth agape, staring at the institution that appeared more like a series of small castles than a college.

The medieval-looking buildings were Tudor meets Gothic Revival. Ancient spindles poked out of the triangle-shaped rooftops like stick pins praying to the sky, their tippy tops getting lost in the swab of swishy white clouds. There was a stone barricade around the outside of the university, fortifying the perimeter of the learning institution. Those who were inside were the chosen, the protected—the coveted.

But it wasn't the ostentatious presentation that grabbed me. The university was one of the most credited medical research facilities in the entire world, specializing in the area of embryology—my research specialty of interest. And the wing I was standing inside of that very moment had started it all.

"Can I help you?" A man appeared before me with snow-white hair and spectacles. Just another normal professor-looking guy in a gray tweed sport coat.

"Hello there... I'm studying embryology. Was just looking for some information on the studies of Sir Robert Edward." I thought I was going to get busted and thrown off the campus because I wasn't a student or a properly registered visitor. This wasn't the kind of place you just went and hobnobbed around. I was counting on my air of youthful innocence to save me.

"Really? Are you a post-graduate student here?" he asked.

"No, I just completed my undergraduate studies six months ago."

"Pity," he said, shaking his head.

"Why do you ask?"

"Because I could really use a grad assistant. Mine just quit."

It was then that I recognized the earnest eyes behind the spectacles and almost fell to my knees. I'd never bought into religion. I was too enraptured with science to believe we didn't evolve from anything other than the animal species. But if there was a God, this man before me was it, and this was my moment with him.

"Are you... are you Sir Robert Edward?" I asked, startled and mesmerized at the same time. I pushed my own glasses up my face even though they hadn't slid down. He took a step back at the wobbly young American girl in the cargo pants who'd just gone moony over him.

"That, I am," he said, proudly, straightening his old spine.

"Well, if you'll still have me, I'd be honored to be your grad assistant."

"But you're not a graduate student here," he said.

"I'll apply. How about my position is conditional on my acceptance?"

During my interview with Sir Edward, I cited every clinical result from each study he'd ever been involved in right down to the year it was conducted, and afterward he made sure that my application was expedited. And when I was accepted, he pulled the necessary strings so I'd get the position. He agreed—no one was more deserving of the job than me.

It was the moment my new door opened, and a glorious one at that, but it would forever seal the other one shut—The Ben Door.

There were only two things I loved in this world: Science and Ben.

I realize now, I chose Science over Ben that day.

I hadn't at the time, but that's what occurred.

I called Ben the day I was accepted. I wasn't sure why, because I hadn't spoken to him since I left.

Now, I know. I wanted to see if he was still waiting for me.

"Hey, Em. How're you?" he asked. His voice made me sad. I should've been nothing but elated, but Laurel had left for home by then, and the excitement of my trip had run out of gas. Hearing Ben's voice made me hurt. Made me miss him.

"Still traveling, living the dream. How're you?" I asked. There was noise in the background, lots of people talking and glasses chinking together. He was still bartending at Mario's Sports Bar on the South Side. I could hear the newscaster for the Pittsburgh Penguins blaring in the background.

Home. I missed home too.

"Working now, let me step in the hallway." I heard him say to someone, sounding flustered, "Hey man, cover for me."

Then—deafening quiet. My hands were suddenly sweaty at the fact that he could now hear me properly.

"Okay, is that better?" he asked.

"Yeah, Penguins 'N That?" I joked.

"You got it." He sighed.

"Sorry, am I calling at a bad time?" I asked.

"It's okay. Actually, I saw Laurel last weekend... um... drunk. And I was surprised you weren't with her.

She said you didn't come home. I kind of expected you to be back by now." He tried not to sound let down, but I could tell that he was.

"Well... Ben, I've scored the most amazing opportunity. You're not going to believe it."

"What's that?" he asked.

"The scientist who conceptualized the test-tube baby and head of the Embryo Project asked me—*me!*—to be his graduate assistant at the University of Cambridge. So, I'm going to grad school in England. I just found out today that I got in. They have an accelerated program where I can also get my PhD. Can you believe it?" In a way, I was still trying to compensate for what happened with Cook in college. *See, Ben, I'm putting all my energy toward helping others—not hurting them.*

But I don't think he saw it that way.

There was silence again. More than silence. An emptiness that stretched across the sea that separated us and blackened the world. "Th–that's great," Ben finally said. But he didn't sound excited for me at all.

"Yeah, so I start spring semester and I'll be here another two years or so." I gritted my teeth.

"Two years?" he asked, exasperated.

"Yes... So, how are *you?*" I asked again. But what I really wanted to know was if he had found anyone else yet. And whether this information was enough to keep him hanging on.

"Good for you, Emily. I haven't had any luck getting a teaching job around here, so I'm looking at possibly moving south. Hooch found one in the Carolinas and he said I could stay with him while I interview." Jaden Hooch was one of Ben's friends, but the idea of Ben following him to a different state was uninspiring. Ben loved Pittsburgh. It never dawned on me that he might not be there when I returned.

"Well, you gotta do what you gotta do to get the job, right?

Look at me, I'm studying at Cambridge. I still can't believe it. You'll get something, Ben. You're an amazing artist."

"Yeah, well, Em, lots has changed since you left. The market is so bad, no one can get a job. Laurel had to take an internship at a department store, and Zach found a part-time accounting position, but there are no permanent positions available to any new grads. Good time to be in school, though, I guess." Ben sounded solemn and foreign, like life had beaten him down already. But I knew things would eventually pan out for him, because people like Ben didn't fall flat.

"That's too bad. I'm sure I'll have a hard time too when I get back, since my field is so specific, and there are fewer fertility clinics than schools, department stores, and advertising agencies, you know?" I tried to relate.

"Hey, man, we need you back out here. It's going into OT, people are getting crazy," I heard someone echo-holler.

"I gotta go, Em. Good luck in England. Take care, okay?"

"It was so nice to talk to you, Ben. I hope you land a great job."

"Sure, see ya," he said.

And those were the last words he'd spoken to me. But it was a lie. He wouldn't see me like he said. He was just gone. Until now.

Present Day

"Emily, there's no cancels for next week, but I'll squeeze you in Monday morning if you come in early. Six-thirty a.m.?" Tessa, my favorite nurse, startles me out of the past.

"Great, thanks so much, Tess," I say. I'm at my desk, and I should move into the lab, but my thoughts have paralyzed me.

These are going to be a hard few months. The last time I

had my shots, my stomach was littered with tiny bruises, but it felt more like a hundred bee stings. At least I know what to expect, but it's going to be difficult going through it with just my mother.

My father was around when I had my shots the first time.

I'll miss his hugs too. Everything is different since he passed away. Colder. If I don't make a move now, my life will just continue on this path of solitude. My mother is getting older. I don't want to end up all alone.

Tess hurries away with her charts, and I try not to chew on the inside of my mouth too harshly at the fact that Ally's scan is today and mine isn't until next week, but then I remind myself —I run this place. So much of my life has been out of my control.

None worse than when I was sick.

The scars left behind on my chest are a constant reminder from that time period.

It's not the surgical wounds that stick with me though, it's the emotional ones.

Batey informed me less than five percent of women who survive breast cancer with the type of treatment I had are able to conceive naturally afterward. What a punishment, it seemed. To lose your breasts and your chances of having a baby at the same time, as if your womanhood was taken in one fell swoop.

Assisting other women struggling with fertility is both rewarding and slow torture. Every day I watch others fulfill their dreams of starting a family when I'm stuck trying to nail down the first step—a committed partner.

Batey is the one who insisted I freeze my eggs.

The scars from the double mastectomy have healed since then. Implants have been inserted, which Laurel says are a "bonus" but they're far from it. It took three surgeries, but my breasts still sit like awkward oranges with a large space in between.

The scar from my port is a constant reminder of my pain—my journey—a little line below my collar bone, above my left breast. When I rub it I think about the days during chemo where I used to dream about what my life would be like if I'd made different decisions.

If I had a husband's hand to hold during that time.

I rub the scar now.

My mother retired early from her school nurse position to take care of me, and I'll be forever grateful to her for that. But never was there a day I felt so pitiful and alone than in between my second and third surgeries—nipple-less, my skin withered, my head bald—and fully aware that on that very day Ben was marrying someone else.

SEVEN

ALLY

EXPOSE

"Is there another clinic we can visit instead?" We're back in the car, but I still feel like someone has pulled back a sheet on an exam table exposing my naked body. And the rest of the world gathered around to watch—even Emily—Ben's ex.

Ben explains, "This is the one that will get us the best results. I knew Emily worked there, but I pictured her more behind the scenes. I'm sure we won't have to see her again once Dr. Batey is feeling better."

Ben, the eternal optimist. His positivity isn't doing the trick this time.

I only know three things about Ben's ex, Emily Daugherty—she's a cancer survivor, she's Ben's college sweetheart—and she broke his damn heart. None of this history makes me want to trust her with my future family.

"She'll be working on our case, one way or another. *Your ex.* You can't expect me to be okay with this. I've compromised so much already..." Agreeing to start the fertility shots in North Carolina and then moving here was a mistake, and I knew it.

We haven't put the house on the market yet. Ben says we can wait until I'm ready, but I never will be.

He shakes his head. "Give Laurel's party a chance. Once you meet Emily, outside of the hospital, you'll see she's harmless. She loves her work. She'll do right by us."

"Why would you want to go to a party with your ex?" I don't understand my husband. He wants to change everything about our entire lives—insert new people—and he just expects me to march right along.

"Because... all of my old friends will be there. From school. She's one of them."

And I'm not. I'm an outsider. "So, you don't think that will be awkward for me to show up at a house where everyone knows your old girlfriend is handling our fertility treatments?"

"That's not the way it was supposed to go. We don't have to tell anyone," he says.

"Well, it's how it's going, Ben. And it's not like your chatty little circle won't figure it out." I stare out the window at the gray cloud cover that smears the cityscape. It seems an appropriate canvas for my new life. I never had the circle of friends Ben did in college. I lived at home and attended community college for two years before transferring to a main campus, and by then everyone had already formed their friendship groups.

"The last seven years have been all about living where you grew up. What you wanted. I miss home..." He says this like a little boy who's been at sleepaway camp too long.

I miss home too. This all feels like a test. A test of my commitment to him. To God. A test of my marriage. "We never even talked about moving before a few months ago. You kept your job interview from me. And now this..."

He grabs my hand. "I know. I'm sorry I didn't tell you about the interview. I didn't think I would get it." His voice threads with glee and drowns out the apology.

"Keep one more thing from me, and I'm moving back to Charlotte," I tell him.

He withdraws his hand and it's the first time I've ever made a threat.

I will leave you if you keep anything else from me.

He needs to understand this. There's only so much I can take. He was going to accept this new teaching job whether I came with him or not.

I'll move back after the school year is over, and then we can figure it out.

It seemed like such an impossible solution. As if I was really going to live separately from my husband for months and depend on school breaks to keep us together. We were barely hanging on as it was.

"I didn't see it as a secret. I was just taking a chance on a job I didn't think I'd get and kept it private." He grips the steering wheel. I don't want to start a fight, but maybe I should.

"That's a convenient way to look at it. I'm sure if I did the same, your perspective would be totally different. What if my job didn't let me relocate, Ben? I love my job. And it pays really, really well."

"It all worked out. One of the reasons I took a stab at the position is because of the salary hike. No reason to harp over problems that will never come to be." He brushes me off so easily.

"That's not even the point. It's a complete lack of consideration for how I might feel. The move. You made a rash decision and didn't include me. Your wife."

He drums his fingers on the steering wheel and sometimes his undiagnosed ADHD is more than I can handle. "You know I can be impulsive sometimes. You used to love that about me." He smiles, sweetly, but good looks only go so far. "I just had to take this opportunity, Ally. And you got to keep your job. So let's not argue over something that's not an issue. I promise I won't keep anything else from you again."

"You're lucky they let me work from here..." I'll let those words hang there, although I know Ben hasn't felt lucky to be with me in a long time.

"It's an adjustment, but I want us to try it together. We can always move back if it doesn't work out. But in a way, I think it's all meant to be—even Emily getting involved. She's the best. And so is the clinic," he says.

Is she now? My skin crawls at that comment. I'm sure he's referring to her work acumen, but what else is Emily the best at? My mind travels to untoward places; Emily's cupid-shaped lips trailing my husband's twenty-something neck.

She seemed sharp and small, and capable and quick—like a little torpedo.

Ben doesn't quite crest six feet and I bet her small frame molds nicely with his. I shake the thought away, but she did seem stealthy, the way she slipped in and out of that room without notice. And I don't like that.

What kind of woman leaves Ben?

Lord knows I couldn't. Even after he left me first, and moved home.

And especially not after my conversation with my mother. My father thought another woman was *best* too.

EIGHT

ALLY

SUITCASE

A suitcase by the door.

That's how I remember him leaving us.

It was an old leather wheelless bag, the kind that was distressed with age, the cracks blond and dirty. He probably inherited it from his father who also left my grandmother in a time when people didn't divorce.

My father's side of the family is rife with separation. My mother said it was because they didn't have God in their life.

My father and mother attended mass every Sunday. And their relationship still didn't survive.

Our small ranch in Shelby, North Carolina, was surrounded by trailers. We didn't have much, but until that point, we had each other.

When I asked my mother what happened to our family, she said that Daddy had fallen in love with someone else. He broke his marriage vows, a complete disappointment. I hated my father after that. And I also didn't trust men either.

In my mind, all relationships had an expiration date, and

sometimes people hold on long past theirs. In new relationships, I'd often think—how long will it be before he tires of me and leaves?

My defense mechanism when I was younger was to break up with men first, before they had the chance to ditch me. The moment the relationship went soft, the initial swoony period over, I'd cut bait.

It wasn't until I met Ben that I tried to really make a relationship work. It's like my mother used to say—your true love isn't about finding the man you can live with, it's about finding the man you can't live without.

I didn't understand what she meant until I met Ben.

He told me about his own parents who'd been married for a number of years, and how he aspired to have the same type of relationship as them; and I believed him.

But every man has his limits.

And now that there's this other woman, and we're having issues, I wonder.

Is he thinking of Emily at this very moment? Their past? Their chance meeting again—now? And maybe it's not by chance at all? I don't know Emily's relationship status, but I didn't see a wedding ring on her finger. She might be one of those women who doesn't wear one, seeing as how she deals with samples of bodily fluid all day, but something inside me screams otherwise.

That she's alone by choice. Or because she can't find a proper partner.

And that maybe... just maybe... she still wants mine.

I pick up the phone, because a drive is much too far to reach her. Another thing about this place that makes it hard to adjust. My mother's never been more than a few miles from me before.

"Hi, Mama."

I hear her scrambling around on the phone, probably trying

to find a quiet space in the store to take a call. "How's it going, June bug?"

I smile at her old greeting for me. Who knew an ugly little beetle that ate through plants could sound so cute. "It's going... Ben's ex is working at the hospital. Where I'm having my procedures..."

"Ugh. Well, he married you, sweetheart. Not her."

"I'm not sure that matters much anymore."

She chuffs into the phone. "The sacrament of marriage means quite a bit. To Ben too." Mother still blames herself for the way her own marriage ended, I can tell. "You need to support your husband to save your relationship, Ally. Don't let that woman bother you."

Man is head of the household, she said, a phrase I didn't buy into much as a liberated careerwoman. And as someone who brought in the lion's share, it was hard to call Ben the head of our family, although I did my best to respect him like he was.

"It's hard when I don't even want to be here in the first place. And now *she's* here..."

"Don't make the same mistake I did. Ben's a good man. If you don't stand by him, he will find someone else. You can't make it easy for her."

"I won't," I tell her. My mother's words twist in my gut for many reasons. Maybe because I know there's some truth to them, and I don't like the idea that I'm replaceable. Ben was the one I decided to commit to, after all. I let all the other men in my life go. One who meant even more to me than he does...

Mother never did recover properly after my father left. She didn't date anyone seriously and she wore her divorce like a dirty sash strapped across her chest. We'd walk into church, just the two of us, and she'd hang her head low before the opening prayer even began.

It was a sorry existence, and one I wouldn't have for myself.

I was raised to be a strong, fierce, financially independent woman.

Education was placed first.

And I am every bit the strong, Christian woman she raised, but my faith is being tested, and while I'm willing to stretch myself to meet Ben's needs, I'm not sure I can include another person in our relationship—Emily Daugherty.

NINE

ALLY

POPLAR

The kneeler at the new church digs into my shins as I pray for the hundredth time for something God has not delivered us. Ben prays with me, something we've always done together, but I'm running out of Hail Marys.

And hope.

Everyone's well wishes have begun to feel hollow.

"All in God's time."

"Trust God's plan."

"God will bless your family."

Except He hasn't blessed us.

It's the end of mass at our new church.

Tiny wafers were ingested, and churchgoers said their peace. We make the sign of the cross in a room full of strangers, and walk down the center aisle together. From the outside, we probably look like a happy couple, but I can't stop thinking about how Ben screamed at me after our last fight.

Every time I attend mass I'm reminded of it. Church is where I go to help me forgive my husband.

Please God—just press the erase button in my head and let me forget those vicious words he said to me. What's the lesson here? What am I supposed to learn from this?

Now that some time has passed, looking back, I see how wrong Ben was.

He was so upset with me. Disgusted, more like.

I can't shake it; the image of Ben holding a plastic container in his gloved hands.

I don't know if I can ever look at him the same, without picturing his hands wrapped in latex. He was going to do something no man or woman should ever have to do—take a sample of our unborn to the hospital and have it examined. To figure out why this keeps happening to us.

The little one was smaller than my others, barely formed.

I wouldn't let him touch him or her with his gloved hands.

"It's God's will," I told him. I didn't cry. Not that time. I cried after the first three and then seemingly ran out of tears.

I was backed into a corner between the shower and the toilet—trapped.

"No, it's not! There's something wrong with you." The pointedness of his statement. The way his finger lacerated the air and made a tip targeted at the center of my heart. The heat on the end of his words, how they translated to—*this is all your fault, and you're not enough for me*—I feel every ounce of them.

He later apologized and said what he meant was that there could be a reason for why the babies didn't make it and we should figure out what that is.

But we can't return to the time before the moment those words left his mouth.

We reach the outside of the church. The stifling August air chokes me.

"Let's go to breakfast," Ben says.

I nod, because we always have breakfast after mass, a tradition, but I can't just settle into our old routine in this rustbelt town like another tie on the railroad. I'm not even sure who we are anymore.

A couple who dances around ovulation charts and daily prayers.

It wasn't always like this. We used to have fun—Grand Teton was our last big trip. I'd plan our adventures for weeks ahead, but we don't take them anymore.

Once we decided to start a family and we learned I was "at risk," life became too careful for excursions.

With every pregnancy I wonder—is it all too much for him?

Is he going to leave me and find a woman who can give him a proper family? *Just like my father.* After he ran off with the other woman, he started a new family—I've never met my stepbrother and sisters.

Ben's dressed in his Sunday best this morning with his own artistic flair, the undersides of the cuffs of his button-down shirt a purple paisley, his dark hair parted down the middle and hanging softly in two thick waves.

We sit at a pancake house, but I can already tell this place is not as good as the ones in Charlotte. They don't even have grits on the menu. What a joke.

A sticky summer day makes me all the more agitated, and I gnaw on the inside of my cheek thinking about how I was dreading going through my second trimester in this heat. How silly of me to think I'd make it that far.

We order our food, and then Ben comes out with it. I know something is weighing heavily because he was shifty during church. Last night we made love, but he might've well been in the other room.

Probably because our townhouse rental feels very much... like a sublet unit. Cold and uninviting, the paint white and dull. Our bed is the same one we've slept in for the last decade, but the room is smaller.

Everything is a muted version of the beautiful home

we left, decorated without the warm touches of us, like the portraits of all of our vacations lining the wall. There're still in boxes and I can't bear to put them up here. We have nothing to remind us how happy we once were.

"I need to know if you're going to the party." The way he says *you're* tells me he's going with or without me. A common theme lately.

"It's not for another few weeks, right? I haven't even thought about it."

"Laurel texted me for a headcount," Ben says.

I'm tired of hearing about Laurel, Emily's best friend. "How can two people make such a difference? Just tell her we're a maybe."

The waitress takes our drink order and when I ask her for sweet tea she informs me they don't have that here—in this region of the country. The waitress and Ben laugh and grin at me. Who wants to live in a place that has bland old tea? *I hate it here.*

"Laurel goes all out. Knowing her, she's making gifts for the guests and monogrammed napkins, or something." Ben cheeses at me like this is an admirable gesture, but it makes me want to meet this woman less. Over-doers don't impress those who never had the means to keep up.

"Can't wait," I say.

Our food is served, and I'm disconcerted, washing it down with tea I have to poison with fake sweetener because the sugar packets here are old and clumpy.

"Come on, Ally. We need to surround ourselves with people other than just me and you. Things have been so tense. You'll like Zach and Laurel."

What he means is if we're never having children, we need friends to fill that void. That just the two of us aren't enough anymore—and never will be.

"Laurel doesn't sound like my type of girl." *Monogramming is so tacky*.

"Cat and Seth will be there too," he says of his other random college friends he speaks of sporadically, people he expects me to automatically love just because he does. Ben has a guy trip once a year with Seth and Zach, and that's the space I've always placed them in—the guy trip bucket. I could've gone the rest of my life without meeting them beyond my wedding day, and been just fine.

"That's nice. Is Cat also an overachieving crafter as well? Should I show up with gifts for your friends?"

Ben laughs. "No, no. Cat is laid-back. She's a stay-at-home mom. Three kids. Has her hands full."

"I'm sure we'll have something in common," I quip.

His smile slips off his face.

My fork hits the plate. I haven't found a healthy space in my life for food these days. When I'm pregnant, I eat for the baby, because the baby needs protein and vitamins. But when I lose the babies, I feel like I can't make room for food. Punishing myself, perhaps, because the nourishment I provided wasn't good enough to keep them alive.

"We need a change, Ally."

I stare out the window, panic settling in at the unfamiliar backdrop. Discontentment consumes me like a flame.

Ben digs into his pancakes.

"We've never talked about moving here. My family is in North Carolina. This feels so underhanded. And this new clinic. *Wrong*." I whisper the last part. It feels a sin even talking about it, especially right after mass.

God created man.

Science did not create man. Period.

I was conflicted even going to a clinic in the first place, and now, after finally becoming comfortable with my first doctor,

Ben makes me switch to another—and she didn't even show up to meet us!

"I never got checked out. It could be something with me," he says.

Ah yes, too busy interviewing to make his appointment. Another sore spot in our marriage. It would've been grounds for war, but as much as Ben says it could be him, we both know the truth—it's me. Ben's sperm makes babies. It's my womb, my vessel, that cannot carry them to term. I don't need a doctor to tell me that.

"I'm not sure about this place and all its cutting-edge claims. I was comfortable with Dr. Williams," I say of my old doctor.

"No one can perform a medical procedure on you without your consent. Who knows, maybe once you hear what they have to say..." Ben's become his own Web MD, researching everything he can to fix me.

My losses mean more to me than they do to him. I can't get over the fact that he was reducing them to mere tissue to be dissected in a lab. In my mind, they're all my children who never got the chance to be. I even gave the first three a permanent resting spot.

The others are buried in my old backyard behind the house I refuse to put on the market.

Ben doesn't know that. I was alone the first three times I miscarried. They always occurred while he was teaching, or on his way to and from his classroom of kids. While I sat alone on cold ceramic weeping the loss of mine.

I knew I'd have to interrupt him at school to tell him. And I couldn't handle the questions or the drama from his close-knit colleagues that would follow—what was the family emergency? Is everything okay?

I didn't want the teachers in our school district to know about our loss(es). Thankfully, I was at home when the miscarriages occurred.

We have a lovely yellow poplar tree in the backyard. The trees are a vital source to the furniture industry, the poplar's hearty wood used as core material for parts and frames. My unborn children rest in the ground near its strong roots.

Some days, I stared out the window and imagined the three of them playing beneath the shade under the protection of the tree.

I can't tell Ben this or where they're at. Knowing him, he'll try to dig them back up for his genetic quest.

And I certainly can't stay in Pennsylvania.

What if our home is purchased and the new owner renovates the yard? Uproots the tree?

What if the homeowner digs *them* up?

I'm sick inside just thinking about it.

And I'm angry for apologizing for something that's completely out of my control. Something that's tearing us apart.

When I saw Ben rushing in with his gear, I had to get rid of it—down the drain. And that's what I'm most upset by. He robbed number four of a spot beneath the tree with the others. I'll never forgive him for that. The baby was already gone. I didn't want anyone to poke and prod what was left of him or her. The idea made me shake.

"I'm just asking you to meet me halfway here. This isn't working. We're stuck. Just being here... feels right. A step forward."

By *this*, he means—*us*. We're not working. And I'm sorry to tell him, he's the only one who thinks this feels right. "I start suffocating the moment I wake up here. I can't breathe. Literally. The air smells polluted," I tell him, and he frowns at me.

I feel like it's a fair statement compared to all of the other thoughts rolling around in my head.

He pushes his empty plate away. No trouble eating. He's a man with no guilt. "Part of the reason you feel this way is because of your mother's strong opinions against IVF."

I cross my arms, my sundress pulling at my breasts, swollen from all the hormones I've been injecting into my body for my husband's benefit. "I won't keep things from my mother."

"Maybe you just need a little distance from her. It won't feel so wrong if you aren't guilted into telling her every little detail about our marriage," he says. "You can at least try, Ally. That's all I'm asking."

"That's what I'm doing here..." Doesn't he see that? He doesn't realize how hard it is to fulfill his requests. Or how close I am to walking out the door and hightailing it back home—*my real home*—because this doesn't feel like us.

We used to be a strong couple. We were bound physically. Spiritually. There was a strength about us that I didn't think could be broken. When we started out we were as solid as the red rocks and as bright as the sun.

TEN

ALLY

PRICKLY

2017

We sit to grab coffee and prickly pear ice cream in the little strip that makes up downtown Sedona, Arizona, and you smile at me as the grounds seem to hum beneath us. You're so hyped up from our hike to Cathedral Rock that you can't seem to wait to do our next one.

"I feel like I can float here. This place makes me want to paint and do cartwheels at the same time."

What a statement of pure happiness. I can't hide the shared excitement. Ben's enthusiasm is addictive. He's somebody everybody wants to be around, and I'm so lucky he's mine.

"It's the vortexes." I flap a tourist pamphlet at him that he refuses to look at. Whenever I ask Ben to read something, he tells me to draw him a picture instead. "I'm more visual," he usually responds. Which is code for, "I hate reading." We're opposite that way, and I love that about us.

I love us.

"A vortex?" He laughs at me. "Are we not on planet Earth anymore? I'd believe you if you told me that."

We squint through the sun and gaze out into the mountainous ranges in the distance. The red dusty tops surround us in a warm hug. This place feels good. It's the perfect spot for our anniversary, a trip that signifies many more adventures ahead.

"For reals," I tell him. "There's supposedly four vortexes in Sedona. Cathedral Rock is one of them. That's why you probably still feel a little high. The vortexes radiate energy. That's why people come here to meditate, recharge, and create. It's a very spiritual place."

Ben smiles at me, and I know he feels this at a different level than I do. When I close my eyes, I can almost palpitate the low purr of life all around me. To Ben's intuitive being I'm guessing it's more like the roar of an engine.

"This place is total Zen. We should come here every year. The guide said there are some easier trails for kids. I saw a bunch of families hiking."

I smile at his comment, even though we decided to wait to have kids. I saw how burdened my mother was her entire life, never venturing out of our hometown. I want to build a solid foundation with Ben first. Plus, I didn't grow up like him. He and his family traveled quite a bit, and I've been nowhere but North Carolina for the better part of my life. I want to see things...

"Eventually," I tell him. "Let's go to Chapel of the Holy Cross and pray on it."

Ben lights up with glee, because the church built into the mountainside is on his wish list too.

He leaps from his seat, never very good at sitting still.

We drive to the inclined walkway that leads to the Catholic church and hike the rest of the way. I'm brought to tears by the magnificence of it, the gigantic cross and glass windows that seem to sprout from a cropping of red rocks.

Vanloads of tourists wait in line to see the holy structure.

Ben's mouth drops open in wonder. "I have to take a picture for my mom. She'd love this."

We enter the church, and the first order of business when we walk in are candles to light, prayers to be sent to the Heavens—with a small donation, of course.

We light one for Mama Della, Ben's grandmother. And I light one more—for divine guidance, with a little prayer attached—*please don't bless me with children quite yet...*

It's a moment I think about more than I should. Maybe I somehow knew once we tried to start a family, things wouldn't work out. Perhaps, I wanted to preserve our beautiful couple-dom. It can't be my fault this is happening, but we both own our poor reaction to how we've handled our situation. How we've fallen since.

There's a danger in only seeing someone's positive side. Ben's led a blessed life—full family, private education, free ride to college, a group of friends who'd lie down in oncoming traffic for him.

I had none of those things. I was tested in life long before he arrived. I thought that by being with him, I could drink in some of his luck.

But I never could've predicted what would happen when he was handed disappointment.

It's me—I'm the biggest disappointment in his life.

And I never dreamed he'd turn on me.

Or that I would turn on him—because I can't stand that I'm the one who brings him down. The only good thing about this move is that it will be harder for him to find out what I've done.

In my eyes, his dark turn is much worse than mine.

ELEVEN
EMILY

HOLLOW

I pull up to my childhood home in Brentwood, a working-class borough on the industrial strip of Route 51, south of the city of Pittsburgh. Like most of the homes in the area, my parents' house is an older brick split level.

It isn't large by any means, but the above-ground pool in the backyard made me the most popular kid on the block—the only thing that made me the most popular kid on the block.

I give my mother a warning knock before grabbing the doorknob. I hesitate just a moment before turning it, contemplating how I'm going to tell her about my decision to have a baby on my own—a decision I came to following my run-in last week with the Holidays.

After our consult I was sure of two things:

Ben moved back home to start a family, probably so he could be closer to his.

And I didn't want to wait one more single day before I start my own.

It's time to stop wishing and waiting for the right man to

come along, and take the IVF plunge by myself. I've always wanted a baby.

I have a stash of perfectly healthy frozen eggs.

And if Ben is having babies, then I can have babies too.

I pull the door open.

"Emily, is that you?" I hear my mother echo.

"Yes, Mother."

Her shadow appears down the hallway, first, then she rounds the bend, earbuds in. She's a self-help podcast addict— *The Widows' Club, Starting Life in your 60s, Living and Letting Go.*

That last one is dedicated to me, I'm sure.

"You look pale. Even for you." Mother swipes the back of her hand over my cheek. A retired nurse, I swear she's been doing that since the beginning of time.

"Gee thanks, Mom."

"Happy birthday! I made your favorite. Oh, and here." She grabs a giftbag off the kitchen table and hands it to me. I pull out a fuzzy blue crop sweater I'll never wear and open the card to find inspirational words for a new year, and a gift card for a mani-pedi.

"Thank you. I need to get my nails done." A pedicure will feel especially nice on my sore, swollen feet once I'm pregnant.

"I'm just finishing up." Her blonde-bobbed, nimble body floats to the eat-in kitchenette where sunlight streams through the windows, highlighting the empty chairs. Everything in this house seems hollow since Dad passed away, even though it's been years. When I look for reasons why I haven't accomplished all of my life goals, I can't point to my parents.

They gave me everything they possibly could.

Dad was an underwater welder who worked on the many Pittsburgh bridges. It was a unique job and when I was a little girl I imagined him a merman with scuba gear sawing through metal, which is mostly accurate. He was my hero, and at the end of his life, after a long battle with ALS, all he wanted was to be put out of his misery—and I had the opportunity to be his hero.

Not all superheroes wear capes.

Although, I know my mother doesn't view what I did the same way.

"Dinner's ready. Sit," she says.

We walk over to the table, set with gold-lined china, the good stuff, and take our places. Dad's empty chair fills the room. We both pretend not to notice it.

"And how's work going?" She walks over with a dish of baked chicken, carrots, potatoes and green beans. Not my actual favorite, but anything homemade tastes good. "Is that woman still working you to the bone?"

"She's keeping me busy." Batey will need a talking to if the #911s continue at this frequency. It's not just the emotional turmoil that comes with delivering the bad news, it's the fact that her selectivity with taking on new patients is becoming more visible. If Ally had questions about their success rates after one visit, it's only a matter of time before a disgruntled, rejected couple reports them for medical malpractice.

"Anything new at the clinic?" Mother is spooning out my dinner, fixing my plate, as if I'm five. After I moved out, she stopped doing this, but when I got sick she started back up again and hasn't stopped.

I let her. We're both still healing.

"Actually, Dr. Batey has expanded our genetics division to include gender selection, which I'm excited about."

"Now... what's that?" she asks.

"The male determines the sex of the baby. So, if a couple decides they want a boy or a girl, they can use our services to make that happen. It's called Microsort. We sort out the sperms' male or female component."

"So what happens if you accidentally make the wrong gender?" Mother asks.

"It can happen, but I'm going to try to make sure it doesn't. If it does, we'll dispose of the unwanted gendered embryo or freeze it for later use."

My mother, who remains complacent ninety-eight percent of the time when I discuss work, startles at my comment. "Well, that seems a little wrong, don't you think?"

When the clinic broached the introduction of gender selection I had those thoughts myself, but I provided the answer that was given to me at the facility, which made it okay—at least for me. "There's actually genetic factors that make certain genders more prone to hereditary diseases than others, such as hemophilia and muscular dystrophy. So, if you're a carrier or have a strong genetic predisposition to one of these disorders, this procedure makes sense. There's all kinds of gender-related diseases that make these procedures relevant."

She nods. "Fascinating. I'm so proud of you, Emily. Dedicating your life to your work."

I flinch. I'm sure she doesn't mean to say that my work is all I have, but it's how I take it. It seems like the perfect segue for my big news.

"That's something I want to talk to you about. I might be dedicating my life to something else soon." I try to sound hopeful.

"Ooh... have you met someone?" Mother asks excitedly.

"No, but I've decided to have a baby on my own, and I need your support if I'm going to do it." I swallow my green beans, hardly able to look up, for fear she'll disagree with me.

"Well, what do you mean on your own?" Mother's rigid in her chair, playing nervously with the oversized charms on the chain around her neck. She's stopped eating and places her silverware down on her gold-lined plate.

"I've tried dating, and it just hasn't worked out for me. I'm getting older, thirty-six now, and I only have so much time to safely carry a baby to term. The eggs I froze before my treatment are aging too. With each year, their viability wanes. And I'm ready for a baby… now," I declare.

Mother offers a tight-lipped smile. "So, you're going to, what, be inseminated?" she asks.

"I have frozen eggs at the clinic. They're my twenty-eight-year-old eggs. There's a much higher chance of pregnancy with them if I do IVF," I say.

"Of course, I'll support you in anything you decide to do," my mom says, "but what's brought this on?"

I clench my jaw, because I can't tell her the real reason. "Another birthday. My age. I'm well-established financially. I assume you'll help with babysitting, which is what I needed to ask you about. I just want one baby. I'm sure I can handle one baby. Just like you, Mom."

Mother bristles at my last statement. "Perhaps, after you have this one, you'll meet a man and have another," she says.

She's reaching for the moon.

"Let's just concentrate on this one," I say.

"Right, right…" she says, patting my hand. "It's just that I always regretted not giving you a sibling."

I regret that she made that decision too, but apparently her post-partum depression was so bad my father had a vasectomy shortly after my birth.

"How do you pick the father?" she asks, still puzzling. She pushes her plate away, food half-eaten.

"I go through a sperm catalog and basically choose," I say.

"Like from just some guy off the street?" she asks.

"From a sperm donor. The catalog lists their occupation, education level, skin color, eye color, etc.," I explain.

"Who're these donors? Can't you ask someone you know? Like someone in the community?" She points out the window. "A neighbor or something?"

"Mom, really?" I laugh. The thought of my mother choosing my sperm donor is just creepy.

"It makes me worried... not knowing who this person is and splitting genes with them. Hey, there's this new guy I met at yoga your age," Mom says, earnestly, and my fake smile is so plastered on, it's hurting my face. "He's on the creative team at one of those new tech startups in the Strip District. Harrison is his name. Want me to introduce you?" she asks.

"No, I'm done dating. My last relationship didn't work out because I think I wanted a baby more than a husband. I've been considering this for a long time, and I've made my decision."

"Harrison was an art major. You like those types," she pushes.

She didn't have to go *there*. "Oh yeah, he moved back by the way," I say quickly.

"Who did?" Mom asks.

I lock eyes with her, nervous. *Why did I open my big mouth?*

"Ben moved back to Pittsburgh with his wife."

Mom spoons some more potatoes onto her plate, hurriedly, almost angrily. Then she shoves them to the side. "So, that's what this is about?"

"It's not. It's really not. It's just the timing," I insist, shoving my plate away too, a stand-off.

"Where did he move to?" she asks.

"Cranberry."

"Oh, really?" Mom asks, surprised. "Must have some little ones."

"Not yet."

"Interesting," she says.

"It is," I say, more determined than ever to be placed on the IVF schedule right away. It would be great to beat Ally to it. I hate being that way, but she got Ben. I want to have my baby first.

"Okay, well, I'm on your side, Honey. Do you have to start those awful shots, then?" Mother asked. "Like when you had your eggs extracted?"

"Yes. That's the other thing. I may need someone to help administer them." Over the years having my mother as a nurse has come in handy. I tried not to abuse the privilege, but she did always sneak me Tylenol from her purse when I begged for it at school.

"We'll figure it out. My schedule is open to you," she assures me.

"Laurel's going to help me pick out the donor. I called her on the way over here. She was really excited. She said we can order salads, split a bottle of rosé, and pick out my baby daddy," I joke, but Mother doesn't laugh. She's probably never heard the term "baby daddy" before.

"Well, don't I get a say in who our grandchild's father is?" she asks.

"I can bring over a list of the final contenders."

"Whatever you want to do, Emily, it's your choice," she says. "I just have concerns about... well, you know I struggled after I had you. And last time you were under stress, with your father..."

She can't say the words.

We don't speak them.

I look out the window at the sunshine flowing through, envisioning that it's him, in a better place. Pain-free. I know my mother thinks what I did—ending his life prematurely—was wrong, but it was a request he'd made to me before he got really sick. It was his final wish that when he became incapacitated and was no longer able to form thoughts, create movement, he'd be helped to end the agony.

I had the tools at my disposal to make his suffering go away, forever.

It was horrible to watch him deteriorate.

My mother would've been happy to nurse him into his grave, but I couldn't stand by and witness it, knowing his final requests were to do just the opposite. This was different from when I thought I knew how to treat Cook. I was educated. Wiser. It wouldn't be an accident, but a well-thought-out endeavor.

It's a point of contention between me and my mother.

No one else knows about it, and we've dealt with it our own way, but now her insinuations about what kind of mother I could be because of my previous decisions are making it even worse.

She's afraid I'll have post-partum depression like her.

She's afraid I'll harm my baby—like I killed my father.

"May I be excused?" I ask, because I can't sit here with her anymore. That last comment was a lot to unpack, and way too much for an afternoon dinner.

"Fine," she says, rather icily.

I climb the stairs to my old bedroom where I used to sit on the window seat and dream of living in a faraway place. The entire house is filled with ornate stained-glass windows my dad welded in himself, but my bedroom is the only one that features a creature, a bright pink and green butterfly in the right-hand corner. Those were my nursery colors, pink and green, and though the wall colors changed through the years, the gorgeous window remains.

As I trace the wing of the insect, one of amazing transformation, I visualize new things on the horizon for me. I can almost see a little crib in here, a wooden rocker, my mom shushing a baby to sleep at night. We'll sit at the kitchen table after the baby is asleep and she'll make me tea from her collection.

"White tea or black tea, and do you want me to drain the leaves so you don't get too much caffeine? It'll keep you up," Mother will say.

She'll forget all about the day she walked in on me shooting toxic chemicals into my father's IV.

Those memories will be replaced by new ones.

Thoughts of death will be replaced by life, and then she'll be able to look at me again like the daughter she's always loved.

We'll finally have something to talk about other than my health, work, and my non-existent love life. We won't have to tiptoe around what happened in this house. It won't feel like an abandoned tomb when I walk through the door anymore—not when my baby's squeals will fill the space with giggles and happiness.

One baby will be enough for me. I can raise my son or daughter partially here, just like I was brought up, and send them to the best private school around. I'll shower my child with every bit of love I have. I'll do my very best to raise them all by myself.

Ben coming back into town is a good thing for me.

Even years later, he's helping me put my life into perspective, making me dream again. Maybe our babies can meet and become friends—or even fall in love.

Wouldn't that make a perfect made-for-TV movie?

My mind is already searching my mental celebrity database for movie stars who could play our parts, and I can't think of anyone appropriate for Ben, but people say I look a little like Reese Witherspoon, heart-shaped face and all. I sigh loudly and think it quite possible I'll never find a real man, because I live my life entirely through microscope lenses and celebrity magazines. I'm determined to create my own happily ever after though. No matter what I have to do to get it.

TWELVE

ALLY

FINGERPRINTS

Ben leans against the quartz countertop, coffee resting against his taut chest. I can smell the sawdust from the newly installed wooden cabinets. The white walls and gray subway tile backsplash are airy and fresh. I want to picture a smattering of tiny fingerprints there too, but I can't. I miss my old house too much.

The décor here is so white, it feels almost clinical, like that damn hospital I have to visit today.

My home in Charlotte has beautiful window treatments with tiny blue flowers on the lace trim. My mother made them for us.

"They just planted the bushes outside. Everything is so new," Ben states the obvious. I only nod and make wide eyes at him.

I already know I can't be happy here, but I'm letting him try this new job out. Maybe I can get pregnant here—and then I can finally move.

It's one thing to live apart from me.

Ben won't live separately from his child. He made a decision to move without consulting me, and I can do the same. Only next time, he'll be trailing behind me, asking to come along.

"I have to visit my new classroom today," Ben says.

"Oh?" He lied about the first time he—*visited his new employer*. He said he was going home to see his parents and left out the part that he also had a job interview. What else has he lied about? "I have a scan today at the clinic. I told you about it," I say.

He looks at me dumbfounded. "I thought you said you didn't need me for the scan. You already had a scan at the last clinic. If I'm not mistaken, it's the same kind. I was there for that one."

He doesn't get it. These are all new doctors and nurses. It was beyond uncomfortable getting used to the first set to undergo a procedure against my religious beliefs, and this time around isn't any easier. "I never said I didn't want you to come."

He sighs. "There's going to be a lot of appointments, right?" He waves his phone at me. "I have it on my schedule that I'm going in to be evaluated with you next week." His calendar app is up, as if that clarifies everything.

"No, you didn't put it in your calendar that I had an appointment today." It's a statement, not a question. He just stands there, gaping at me dumbly with his kidlike JanSport backpack slung over his shoulder. I want to yell at him that he's supposed to be teaching children, not pretending to be one, but I won't. It's not his appearance that angers me. It's his actions.

"I have to go in, Ally. I told them I'd be there. School starts in two weeks," he says. "I wish you were more excited about this opportunity for me. It's a fantastic district. Benefits are great." He still won't look at me. He knows he's wrong. It doesn't seem like a sufficient answer for missing my first doctor's appointment.

"Your health benefits were great back home too." I'll keep referring to Charlotte as home, because it is.

Ben's stellar health insurance is one of the only huge plusses of his job in education. When he wanted to buy expensive paintbrushes for his students and the school wouldn't cover the costs, I let him use our joint account to fund the expense, because I always told myself, what he lacked in dollars he made up for in heart.

I'm currently losing on that investment.

"I made sure to enroll us when I signed the paperwork." He smiles, pleased with himself, and hoists his bag further up on his shoulder, a definitive move that seems more about him leaving than me struggling while he's gone.

"Why're you being like this?" My sadness has morphed into fury. I don't really care about his insurance coverage. I needed him today.

"What do you mean? I have to go into work, Ally?"

I shake my head at him. He doesn't get it. "Since when has your job been more important than me?"

Ben stops packing his things. These are fighting words. "Your career was the most important thing to you, for years, and I sat back and cheered you along. Now that you're at a senior position, I'd hope you'd do the same for me." He looks up then, irritated.

"It's not that I'm not happy for you. I just wish you could've found an opportunity at home."

"The money isn't the same there... But I guess it doesn't matter to you. Because I'm just a lowly teacher." He slams his coffee mug down. "Forget about all the time I'll be able to spend with our child in the summertime while you're working. We have a pool right there." He points outside, and one thing this community does have is a stellar pool. But in Charlotte we were a hop, skip, and jump from Lake Norman, and only a few hours away from the beach. Seems a poor substitute.

"I didn't mean that your job wasn't important. I just meant it seems more important than me at the moment."

"Sure you did." He walks toward the door. "Let me know how your scan goes." The door shuts quietly behind him but it's still somehow deafening.

It leaves me chillier than when he told me he was moving to Pittsburgh with or without me. Will he not come with me to the clinic because he's afraid they'll tell us I'm a lost cause? That—we're—as a couple, unable to conceive?

Ben said that if this doesn't work, we don't have to try again, but I don't believe that's a solution. I can't imagine a life where Ben and I just pander around each other for all of eternity without a family, the only dirty fingerprints on that backsplash, our own. We won't make it. Ben wants to have a child.

I want to have a child.

It will always be this thing that's missing in our lives.

My work phone sends an alert that a call is due to start in fifteen minutes. I choke down some coffee and try to forget that my husband would rather set up a classroom to paint with eighth graders than accompany me to one of the most stressful doctor's visits of my life.

THIRTEEN

EMILY

BALCONY

It's earlier than usual for me to be out here. Hotter too, but I can't sleep.

I'm outside in my boy shorts and tank, my first cup of coffee in hand. There will be more cups before I can fully operate for the day.

One which holds so much more promise than the last.

The sun beams warmly on my skin.

Cars and pedestrians bustle below, the city already lighting up into full view although it's barely 6 a.m., and still dark outside.

I push my hand over my flat middle, my belly button a tiny circle. I think about how it will stretch and spread with life in the coming months. I feel my way around the balcony, sashaying with my pretend pregnancy bump, thinking how much room my body will take up once I'm with child.

I hear a slight chuckle and glance over my shoulder to find Jasper watching me parade around like a confused peacock who's lost its feathers.

My mouth drops open and I set down my coffee cup on my mosaic accent table.

"What're you doing?" he asks.

And... *he speaks*.

We've never actually had a conversation before. The sound of his voice is smooth and strong, like his abs. This morning Jasper is shirtless, a pair of well-worn PJ pants on the bottom. I can't help but think, the two of us combined would make a full outfit.

My first instinct is to cover myself.

"Don't do that," he says, a wolfish grin on his face.

I let my arms flop at my sides. What's the point? He's already watched me for a good five minutes now.

"You shouldn't sneak up on people," I say, a little peeved he didn't announce himself sooner.

"You realize I live here, right?" He laughs again. "This balcony is part of my house. I'm not sneaking up on you. I'm sitting on my front porch." He flips his hands around to display the view of the city, the same reason I bought my place.

I feel like a fool. He has every right to be sitting or standing exactly where he is—on his property.

"Well, I'm practically naked," I say in a tight breath, aware of my braless cleavage spilling over the top of my tank.

"I don't mind." His eyes drip down my body. He walks to my side of the balcony, pressing himself up against the glass border that faces me in a move that's both seductive and vaguely threatening.

We've never been this close to one another before.

I swallow and try to speak, but my eyes are stuck on his chest—a hairless plate of solid ground. "I have to get ready for work," I tell him, which isn't a lie.

"You never answered me. Why were you... rubbing yourself?" he asks.

I don't notice until now but his hand has slipped into the

elastic waistband of his pants. I clench my legs together because Jasper is more than I can handle. Brawny and tall, and way more muscle than I've ever held in my two small hands... but it doesn't matter because Jasper is brawny and tall, and also very married.

"I was... imagining what it might be like to be pregnant," I say, honestly, because my brain is short-circuiting, and a good lie won't arrive.

"Do you want any help with that?" he asks.

Dead silence hangs in the air, but his face is completely serious. *Am I dreaming? He did not just say that to me.*

This should be so creepy, coming from quiet Jasper who barely leaves his home, and hasn't spoken a word to me in years. But it's somehow... not. We know each other intimately, through our strange communication style of voyeurism.

It's not a relationship I can explain to anyone else. Jasper isn't appreciated by Chelsea. Abused, really. And I'm the only one who likely knows it, because I've witnessed it with my own eyes.

"Where's Chelsea, Jasper?" I whisper.

"She took Clementine to her aunt's in the south hills. Said I better have a job when she returns."

I press my own body to the plexiglass wall. My gaze oscillates from Jasper's chest to his hand which has thankfully crested the top of his waistband.

"Why don't you... get one?" I ask him. "A job?" I hate to be blunt, but it seems such a hotspot in their marriage, I can't help but ask.

"I have one. I work from home. I'm a freelance graphic designer, but Chelsea wants me to work in one of those glass boxes." He points at the tall skyscrapers that populate the Pittsburgh skyline. "And I can't bring myself to do that. Apparently, she wants a suit-and-tie guy to display to her friends."

I gape at Jasper wondering how his physical appearance

could possibly be a problem. I also wonder, what friends?—because I've never seen any visitors at the Asads'. "That's too bad."

"Do you want to come over?" he asks.

"What?" I laugh, uncontrollably, and decide this whole thing is a joke. I look at him, expectantly, and realize maybe it's not. "I have to go to work."

"You said that already." He smiles again.

I really need to go, because Jasper is going to get me into trouble.

"I'm leaving for real now." I turn before I can change my mind.

"Fine, I'll just have to sit here and enjoy the view by myself then."

I turn one more time to witness Jasper... watching me walk away.

FOURTEEN

ALLY

ZOOM

I pad the bags beneath my eyes, trying to hide my stress from my fellow colleagues.

I'd die before I shared with my coworkers that I was having marital trouble. We aren't those kind of coworkers; and that's the way I like it.

The zoom screen pops open, my background, a fake bookshelf in yet another home that's not really mine. I quickly adjust the online filter. I don't appear like a woman who's recently moved to a different state and had a mini nervous breakdown, but I am very much her.

If I stayed in Charlotte, Ben would've told people I wasn't with him because I was unwilling to compromise and put his job first for once.

He can be very emotional, the artist side of him, impulsive and passionate. Would it cause him to act out?

He might've even slept with someone else—a younger, fertile woman. His sexual appetite is nearly insatiable. What would he do with himself, being apart from me for months? Until the next school break?

The thought turns my stomach.

Someone mentions statistical numbers on the latest dental care trends since the pandemic that I could weigh in on, but don't. We're running reports for a teeth-whitening company who're capitalizing on the fact that people no longer wear masks. But I can't concentrate on the call.

Or care about such mundane facts.

Especially as the rest of my life is falling apart.

I have a much bigger meeting today to worry about it. And I have to go—all alone.

No man, woman, or child should have to lie half-naked on a table without someone next to them. Ben should be here.

There's a paper gown draped over my body, and a woman in blue scrubs I've never met who is about to stick a lubricated wand inside of me. A screen to my right shows a dark image. I hate the emptiness of it; the absence of everything. I've seen it way too many times.

"A little discomfort here..." she says.

"Okay." It's not the invasiveness of the procedure. I'm an adult. I've been here before and had this very same scan a few months ago.

It's the uneasiness, the unknown of what they might find. Or what they might not find. I've always suspected my medical issues are due to something I lack, inherently. Something that makes me different or undeserving of the miracle of life that seems to come to every other woman around me.

"This is just the baseline scan to confirm you don't have any cysts or other obstructions. We're also checking the thickness of your uterus lining," the tech says. As she moves the wand around, I can't help but think—*This is wrong.*

This is not the natural order of things.

Why haven't I been blessed? Why is my husband not here with me?

"Looks good," the tech says.

She pulls out the wand and wipes it off.

"Great to hear," I say. And I'm annoyed I have to go through this process all over again, but it's the clinic's policy. They don't rely on *old* records.

"You'll be sent for labs next, and all the results will be sent to Dr. Batey."

I scoot up on the table. "Will I meet her today?" It would be great to see the woman responsible for creating my future family. And put a different face to this process than Emily Daugherty.

The tech, who's cheery the way techs are, keeps smiling as she says, "Oh no. Not for today's visit. Just scans and blood-work. Batey will see you at a future appointment to review the results."

I nod, wiping the goo from between my legs. Dr. Batey is begin-ning to feel like the wizard in Emerald City. Will I ever really see her? Will she appear, or is this all an illusion? Dr. Williams was much more interactive. He even sent emails after my appointments to check on me. I've received nothing from this woman but a bill.

The tech leaves, but my blasphemous thoughts continue.

One of the ten commandments—*You shall not make for yourself an idol.*

I've built Dr. Batey up as someone who will create a child for me, but I shouldn't do that. It's still in God's hands.

My bare arms and legs crawl with uncertainty, torn between what's morally right and wrong. I'm so tense, I could scream into the void. But no one would hear me.

Especially, my husband.

I'm most afraid that they'll discover my greatest fear with these tests. That at my core I'm not made for motherhood.

There's something wrong with you.

When Ben said that to my face, I know he meant more than physically.

We're a million miles away from our reverent church on the Sedona mountainside, an enlightened couple taking the world one adventure at a time.

How he's spoken to me, treated me, since we've hit this stumbling block, has been unimaginably painful.

It's also why one of the babies in the unmarked grave beneath the poplar tree belongs to someone other than Ben.

God was punishing me then.

And he still is.

I don't talk to *him* anymore, but it's another reason I want to go back to Charlotte. I crave his closeness like a warm blanket I can retreat beneath whenever the world turns cold. Whenever Ben turns cold.

Like today.

Ben knew I needed him at this appointment. And he's not here.

I scoot off the table, and return to the patient dressing room with the metal lockers, thinking about how I never even told Sebastian that I left. We promised we wouldn't speak to each other again after the pregnancy. It was for the best.

But now it feels like desertion.

One day Sebastian will drive by my old house, and see all the lights in the house are off, no cars in the driveway.

And then another day he'll cruise by and see a For Sale sign in the yard.

The yard where he knows our baby is buried—for sale too.

How that would undo me if I rolled past his place and saw the same thing.

It's a fact I couldn't reveal to Ben.

But to me, Sebastian is safe. Sebastian's always been a safe person to tell my secrets to.

Sebastian is terrible for me, but he saved me from myself years ago in a way that makes him impossible to forget him now. Even though Sebastian is—Sin.

FIFTEEN

ALLY

SIN

2005

Our trailer park is rife with poverty. Right before school let out for summer break, there were three cases of lice. Not unusual in this godforsaken town located just outside of Crowder's Park; a forgotten wasteland.

I fought with my mother again today because she refuses to move out of here, to the apartment complex I found closer to Charlotte.

On this hot Carolina summer day, I'm out here instead of in the slightly cooler trailer.

Someone is screaming at their dog to come back into the chain link fence that surrounds their modular home.

I don't like that dog. It's never bitten me, but with its temperament, it just might.

Sebastian, cutoffs and a long-sleeved shirt and a hat, rolls up in his beater car. "Wanna go to the swimming hole with me? You look hot."

I know he means sweaty, but there's a hint of a double entendre in his voice.

I've known Sebastian since I was a preschooler. We talk to each other in the small, snippy doses that come from an unhappy childhood, more tired and defeated than playful. He's never invited me to hang out before, in seventeen years, and I'm suspicious. "I'm supposed to cook dinner. Promised my ma."

He smirks. "Still manager at the Dollar G?"

"Yeah."

Sebastian laughs, as if he could do better.

"It's a good gig for this town. Keeps a roof over our heads," I say.

Sebastian eyes our piece-of-shit house, and we both know nothing in our neighborhood is a prize to be had. "Come on. Live a little. It's summer. Go for a swim. All you do is work and study. School's out, Ally."

He's hit a nerve, because it was true.

Everyday living in Shelby as a teenager, all I've done is plot and scheme for a way to leave. I've never tried to enjoy myself. Ever since Dad took off, it didn't seem like a place worth making memories in. "Fine. Have it your way."

We reach the swimming hole and swing on vines that could snap at any moment, plunging us into the babbling brook below.

They never do, but I drop into the water willingly anyway.

The cold water massages my skin. I watch as the white foam swirls around my thin arms.

We splash each other. Sebastian doesn't seem to like it, because he dunks me a few times, but not too hard. He lifts me to resurface, and I'm gasping for air. "Jerk."

"Do you need mouth-to-mouth?" he asks.

I splash him again, and smack his muscled shoulder, giggling. "No!"

When we take a break on the creek bed, he reapplies my sunscreen without me asking—works out the knots in my neck.

His strong fingers feel good on my tight muscles. "Aren't you tired of always playing it straight?" he asks.

Stream water trickles off both of us, droplets hanging on the tip of his nose, his lips. We're inches apart from each other now, and I never did notice how pretty his eyes are, his lashes long enough to hold water too. "Yes," I whisper.

He kisses me then, and I let him.

All summer long...

My first major aberration to the church was committed with Sebastian—Fornication. But it wouldn't be the last.

SIXTEEN

EMILY

GOD COMPLEX

I still haven't worked up the courage to tell Batey I've decided to use her fertility services. I was all gung-ho when I left my mother's house, strong and steadfast in my convictions, but Monday rolled around, and Jasper distracted me, leaving me sore—*I wish*—that I always make the practical choice. I wish I could let myself go.

It makes me wonder if I'm making the right decision here.

Batey's the very person who convinced me to freeze my eggs, but sometimes she scoffs at female patients who endure the fertility process by themselves. I can remember her comments after one single woman inquired about going it alone.

She cried during the consult. This one won't even survive the fertility shots. Guaranteed.

Batey prefers to work with partnered couples who have a solid support system, and the occasional single, strong-willed career woman. But I know she doesn't regard me as so.

Someone as meek and mild as you needs a strong plus one, she said, after my egg-extraction procedure.

I've decided on how I'll sway her, though.

I'll tell her the viability of my eggs is a concern, and I don't want to wait a minute longer. I'm a great candidate. No health issues or financial barriers to my treatments. Scientifically, it will make sense to Batey, but socially, she'll view me as a failure. I can't handle the judgment right now.

Not to mention, Batey has slapped another #911 on my desk. My nerves are shot from dancing around my IVF announcement, and I really don't want to do this consult. The last one almost did me in.

Dr. Batey rifles through papers on her desk, jamming them into her briefcase, paying me no mind. *Put your foot down, Emily.*

"Dr. Batey... the last consult didn't go so well. Maybe you should take this one. The patients were really mad you weren't there, and—"

"Is that why you disobeyed my orders? An upset patient has never stopped you before. We're all unhappy when we're delivered disappointing news. What made the last one any different?" She looks up, only briefly.

"She asked... a lot of questions. Questions that made it hard to tell her no."

Batey stops paging through the stack of papers on her desk. "Questions, as in Corini-questions, or something else?"

I squeeze my iced coffee at the mention of Dr. Corini. She's the one patient who almost blew Dr. Batey's cover. Dr. Corini showed up for her appointment with numerous studies on when to implant embryos, at day three following fertilization, and when to implant at day five.

She questioned our procedures and I nearly broke down and told her about Batey's strange rule. Batey only implants embryos at day five—no exceptions. If the embryos aren't of the highest quality at day five, she'll scrap them or pass the case off to someone else so her success rate doesn't drop. Before Corini, not a single patient questioned our practices. There's nothing more dangerous to Batey than an overeducated patient.

My boss knows how to rattle me. "No, no, just generally bad. The couple was testy because you weren't there. I also know them personally... so..." I won't elaborate there. It can't help my case.

"Emily, the only way you're going to conquer your fear of communicating with others is by facing them. This will help you in your personal life as well," she preaches.

I nod. Batey is a self-serving egomaniac with a dire need to mold the world in her image. I think of Batey's pointy, polished face standing at a podium a thousand miles away giving a lecture that makes her sound like the smartest woman in the world, while I suffer in the violet-gray room of tranquility doing the hardest part of her job—counseling the patients.

This is a terrible time to tell her about my decision to use a sperm donor for IVF. She'll blame my inability to find a partner on introversion and insist the only way I'll meet someone is to enhance my communication skills. I can't help but think after my interaction with Jasper that she might be right.

"But..." The office phone rings, interrupting us.

"I told you Anderson's cleats were in the mudroom," Batey yells into the receiver at who I can only assume is her husband, a subservient actuary who works from home. I've overheard Batey scream at him with belittling comments before, but I've never heard him shout back.

"I can't believe you called me at work to bother me about soccer cleats." And—s*lam, slam*—goes the phone as she hangs up.

"The nerve of him calling me. Who does he think I am, the housekeeper?" she snaps.

It's a sad irony that she's dedicated her life to creating families for strangers, only to neglect her own. "You didn't tell me Anderson was playing soccer. Is he in a league that's year-round? Hopefully, you'll be able to catch a few games." Maybe she'll reconsider taking the appointment today if I soften her up, but that's the very statement which makes her stop her paper shuffle and glare at me.

"His father can be the cheerleader. I'm a busy woman. I'm doing more than changing lives. I'm creating them. My sons will understand when they're older. A boy needs his father more anyway," she says.

"Right," I say. But they won't understand when they're older; they'll just hate her instead. Everyone knows boys who don't have good mothers end up being the worst husbands and fathers in the world.

"We don't just have a job to do here. They say doctors have a God complex—well, it doesn't get any closer to God than this." Batey catches my eye again and the gleam in hers is downright scary.

I don't respond. We do help bring life into the world... but working for someone who thinks they have a similar job description to our holy savior can be rather difficult at times.

Batey chirps, "Well, you got what you wanted. That couple. Your friend..." she says this with such spite that I'm sure she doesn't have any real friends herself "... they made the schedule for next week."

"What?" I grab the edge of Batey's desk, and then pick up the schedule right from under her nose. She leans back and stares at me like the space encroacher I am. I don't like that Ally made the schedule before me, but even if she did, I'm weeks ahead. I've already had my eggs extracted.

"Well, that's what you wanted, isn't it?" she asks.

It's not what I wanted. I wanted to be first!

"Yes, fine, but there's something else I want to talk to you about." The words burn on my tongue. Ally doesn't get to have a baby before me.

With Ben. In my own lab.

Batey stands up, papers in her leather messenger bag pushed neatly down now in their dividers. "Better make it fast. I'm flying standby. Trying to make it to New York early."

"I've decided to undergo IVF. With the eggs you encouraged me to freeze years ago."

Batey blinks, only once. "Very well."

"On my own. With a donor."

"I assumed as much," she says.

I place the clinic's weekly itinerary back on her desk. "And I want to be on the schedule... Right now. For next week."

Batey blinks twice. "Well, you work here. Make it happen. I'm not Anderson's cheerleader and I'm certainly not your secretary."

And with that, she's out the door. And I'm stuck with her consult.

It seems an even trade for now. I've negotiated what I want —on the schedule as soon as possible, and she gets what she wants—out of this #911.

And Ally Holiday... gets what she wants too.

Or does she? Is Ben pushing her to try our services because the two of them can't get it done on their own? I sensed so much hesitation from her, and none from him.

My fingers trace the corkboard in Dr. Batey's office that holds the photos of the many babies who were conceived through our clinic. My hand stops momentarily on the faces of twin girls who almost didn't make the board.

They're Dr. Corini's twins.

Dr. Batey pawned Dr. Corini off on Dr. Woo.

I exhale deeply, and walk out of Batey's office with my drink, feeling as though I've conquered a small mountain. This is too much, too early. It's seven thirty on a Monday morning and I haven't even drank all of my Starbucks yet.

According to my latest edition of *OK!*, my favorite actress, Jennifer Garner, likes iced black coffee. So, in her honor, and because today is supposed to be a warm one, I picked up my very first iced coffee this morning. I think the reason I read crappy tabloids is to escape reality. One thing I've learned—there truly are certain things you can't buy—love is one of them.

Dignity is another.

I sit at my clinic table in the lab, a new celeb magazine by my side, and stare straight ahead.

"That bad, huh?" Ralphie asks.

Ralphie is one of the lab techs. He's a quiet kid in his twenties who speaks to me only when he needs something, and I adore him for that. We work great together—in mostly silence.

"Batey pawned another consult off on me," I say.

"Unbelievable. When?"

"In about an hour," I say.

Ralphie's mouth spreads into a slow frown. "Lady's going to bring us all down. You should tell her that. Gotta grow a pair, Em."

"I'm afraid that's impossible. Even in our lab." I laugh, and so does Ralphie.

I don't feel good about following Batey's orders, but I need her on my side to approve my rushed schedule. She's my doctor now. If I piss her off, she'll push me back until Christmas.

"Don't look so down. You got any hot dates planned from one of those websites you were scouring? You need to forget about this place for a while," Ralphie says.

"No. I think I'm done meeting men on the Internet."

Ralphie chuckles.

"I can't even reply to any of the guys who've recently selected me as their preordained match. The whole idea of finding love through a computer-generated system is pretty much the opposite of romantic for me. If people were meant to be catalogued like lab animals they would've been born with better genetic markers and paired up at birth," I say.

"Hmm... Maybe we should work on inventing *that* app,"

Ralphie jokes as he moves around samples beneath his microscope lens.

I settle onto my own laboratory stool. "Seriously, all of the encounters from the dating website start and end the same. Some guy trying to live up to a profile they created that's usually false and grossly bloated. Not to mention pictures that don't match the real person."

"That's just wrong," Ralphie says.

"Pair up early, Ralphie. Dating profiles lie," I advise.

"I'm not trying to lock it down at all, Miss Emily."

I fasten my goggles to my face. Nothing is more real than what we do in this lab. That's why it's hard to connect with people online, I think.

My phone buzzes in my pocket.

"Damn it, Lisette."

Lisette reveres Batey, and since I run the magic show here, I'm her gloved assistant. It's time for my consult...

SEVENTEEN

ALLY

VOICE

"I just needed to hear your voice." I strap my arms across my chest in a hug as I rock in the front seat of my car.

"Ally... we agreed we wouldn't... do this." There's noise in the background, and Sebastian is probably at a construction site. I can visualize him in a hardhat and a neon vest, carrying a clipboard, leading a team to build something like a bridge or a city tower—men's work.

Something more physical and productive than making lesson plans for the next, great... papier-mâché animal.

Even so, I bet he would've dropped everything at his jobsite to come with me today to my doctor's appointment if the situation were different.

If it was his child we were trying to create.

Sebastian helped me bury our baby, whereas Ben never saw our losses as real children. The difference between the two men is blinding to me some days. And at the same time, when Ben is disappointing me, like today, it's all I can see. "I moved, Sebastian."

Ben is the one I vowed before God to love and cherish.

Ben is also the one who asked me to marry him—not Sebastian. Sebastian's love didn't have a staying quality to it in the past. Could it now?

"What do you mean... you moved?" His voice is snarky, and I understand why. He and I may have talked a good game about relocating from the south, but it's where we belong.

"It's temporary, but I moved back to Ben's hometown in Pennsylvania."

There's silence on the other end of the line, except for the faint sound of scraping metal and men's voices. "Why? Are Ben's parents... sick?"

"No, they're fine. We're all okay. But um... he wants me to use the fertility clinic here and he got a job at a local school, so it's just until I get pregnant."

"It doesn't sound temporary. And I thought you were against... clinics."

He makes it sound like I'm doing something sinister. Like I'm going to an abortion clinic, instead of just the opposite, a place to create a life. But it will never feel that way to me, and he knows it.

"I was..." I rake my fingernails over the legs of my jeans. *It is wrong, isn't it?*

"And what changed?" he asks, doubtfully.

I'm not sure how to answer him. The last we spoke I wasn't going to consider IVF. That was before my fight with Ben. But I'm still not convinced IVF is the solution. I can't say that if I get pregnant in this hospital, I'll fully accept the child manufactured there. Something about the way this child is created will always feel tainted to me because it's not the way God intended.

I still want a family more than anything, but what if I'm not able to love him or her because they weren't made in love? What if I can't bond with them because they were formed in a laboratory? "It wasn't my idea, but I decided to give it a try." My fading voice gives me away.

"Right. So, Ben is making you do this. Because the bro's had everything handed to him and he can't stand not having kids like all of his other privileged friends. You're cramping his style."

"That's not it, Seb. He just wants a family. So do I. Today was hard. At the doctor's office."

There's more noise in the background, like someone's operating a saw. "Why wasn't he there?"

"We have a lot of appointments coming up, and he had to miss this one."

"I see. Well, my offer still stands, you know?" he asks.

I stare up at the interior hood of my car, blinking back tears. This is why I called him. This is what I needed to hear. Sebastian is my temptation, the poisonous apple that somehow tastes so sweet to me sometimes, I can't help but take a bite.

Just a nibble. Please God, give me that. "Where will we go?" I whisper, like I used to when we were younger.

I can still see us lazing on a sizzling July day, the sun burning brightly in the sky. We're sprawled out on your mother's patchwork quilt like a jackknife, a book in your hand you're not reading. My head is in your lap and my feet are curled to the right, yours are stretched straight ahead. You always were a long drink of water.

You'd be wearing a long-sleeve shirt to protect your skin, a floppy hat over your eyes.

You'd answer something like, "Mobile, Jacksonville, New Orleans. My cousin runs a Creole kitchen in Baton Rouge. Could get a job there. You'd have to deal with my family, though, and that side is wild."

"No worse than mine," I'd say, dazedly.

I could see us in any one of those places. Stuck together on quiet hot and hazy days. Reading books, making love, and swimming until our legs gave out.

Sebastian is my past, and our time spent together feels much like a fantasy. It's probably just that. Ma said it's easy to find the imperfections in things that aren't new because they haven't had a chance to wrinkle yet. It's one of her little sayings that stuck, but right now it's hard to heed her advice. And Sebastian's far from new.

You say, "How about, Miami, Galveston, Venice Beach?" He always rattles them off so fast, I'm fairly certain Sebastian's brain doubles as a Geography encyclopedia.

"You're traveling way east this time with the last two."

"Farther away from Pennsylvania. I just want you to be happy, Ally. It's all I've ever wanted."

There's yelling in the background. "Hey, I've got to go. Call me if you come back into town, okay?" He hangs up, and I'm left wondering about a lot of things.

Why am I doing this if it's making me so unhappy?

Sebastian's invitation to call him when I get back into town is the one that jumps out the most. It's against the rules. The very strict rules we made the last time I had a rift in my marriage and things got out of hand. Does he see that it's almost over between Ben and me? He's sharp-witted like that, but maybe it doesn't take much to see the obvious deficit in our marriage.

I'm afraid I'll go to Laurel's party and everybody else will notice it too.

That I'm not happy. That Ben's not happy. That we're both utterly miserable with each other. Will a baby make a difference? Or make it worse?

"How was your day?" Ben asks. He drops his bookbag on the floor with a sigh.

"It was rough," I admit.

Ben grabs a glass out of the cabinet, fills it up with water, takes a long swig. "Did you get poor results at the doctor's?"

"No, Ben. But they could've found something today, and you weren't there with me."

"Ally... you've already had this exact same test. If there was something that was going to pull up on a scan, they would've probably found it by now. This was just a preliminary and some bloodwork, they said."

I glare at the obtuse man that doubles as my husband. "This is a new facility for me. New staff. How do you know they weren't using special equipment or tests we haven't had access to before?"

"Well, were they?"

My body temperature is rising at all the questions. The fact that I said I had a bad day without him should be enough for an apology, or at the very least, a hug. "I don't know. I guess not, but that doesn't take away from the fact that I was at a new hospital undergoing tests that were stressful."

"Well, I had to start a new job which was also stressful, and I promise I'll be at the next one. Did you see Emily there?" He places his hands on either side of my shoulders, but I shrug him off.

Is he trying to make me angrier? "No... you're missing the point."

"And you're being very difficult."

I steam in utter disarray, and then wonder if maybe I *am* the one missing the point. Why would Ben bring up Emily? Was his reasoning for not wanting to go to the clinic related to her somehow? I know he talked to her in the hallway before he came back from using the restroom. It was written all over his face when he sat back down. What did they discuss?

"Why don't we go for a hike, blow off some steam? We could both use the exercise," Ben says.

"I don't want to hike with you," I say. *Because I might throw you off a fucking cliff.*

"Suit yourself." He charges off, up the stairs. I can hear the slamming and unjamming of drawers as he searches for his workout gear in our mess of an upstairs.

Ben's solution is to escape from me into nature. He'd like me to come along with him, like the old days, but all I can think about are the times I spent in the weeds long before him.

In the company of a different man, with long, tanned legs that dangled into the water beneath us. I'd like to escape somewhere, that's for sure.

To—Miami or Galveston or Venice Beach...

EIGHTEEN

EMILY

SHUFFLE

Ally is on the schedule today.

I'll steer clear of the procedure floor, but I'd be lying if I said I wasn't overly curious about the results of her initial scan. From the moment she said the words—*research is my life*—everything feels like a competition.

I want to corner Ben and ask him, *What drew you to her? What was it?*

Her personality? Her looks?

Or is it because she reminds you of me?

I'd never have the gall to actually do it, but when I sit alone at night watching Netflix, I imagine I'm one of the brave characters on the screen who does.

I've been working with the practice coordinator to get on the schedule as soon as possible, and right now I'm banking on at least one or two cancellations to expedite the process. I'm already ahead of Ally. My healthy eggs were extracted years ago and frozen.

But I'm behind, because I have no partner and haven't visited the sperm bank yet or started my shots.

I don't want there to be something wrong with Ally—exactly. Maybe a reason to delay, but not anything that would hinder her treatment.

I want Ben to be happy. I really do. A family was always an essential part of his future plans. He deserves a child of his own.

I just want to be first.

I want to make my new baby-on-board announcement before Ally does. Is that so terrible?

My overpriced coffee doesn't go down easy today.

I can feel the competitiveness inch up with my acid reflux. It's more than a bragging-rights contest to me, though. I want to steal back a little piece of what should've been mine.

If I'd made different choices back then, and if Ben had waited for me a little longer, it would be him accompanying me to this clinic—not her.

There's a catty urge to spoil her gleeful moment. To show up at Laurel's and announce—

I'll be about a month or two ahead of you, how cool is that?

Only to have Ally still going through the shots and retrieval process. Maybe it'll shake her. Maybe I want that.

It'll be hard enough being the only one at the party without a plus one.

Gathering with our rowdy bunch of college friends for the first time in years will be overwhelming, and I can't think of a better time to scoop Ally's baby news.

I deserve that, don't I? I may have wished that he'd come back someday—just not with her.

BUGOUT

Ben's been acting funny since he's been home, and at first I thought it was the new job, but now I think that maybe he was steering clear of accompanying me to the clinic for a different reason—Emily. Is she the real reason he moved home?

I hate to think it's possible, but judging by his posture right now, he's withholding something.

"Why won't you tell me what you two discussed in the hallway? Is it something so awkward that you won't join me on my doctor's visits?"

"It was nothing. I just asked her to put a good word in with Batey," he says, hands up, as if he's been caught.

"Why didn't you tell me that?"

"Because I thought you'd get mad."

"I am mad. I don't want someone to take us on as a sympathy case. I want physicians who're dedicated to our case."

"They are. They wouldn't have agreed to treat us otherwise."

I turn away from Ben and march up the stairs. It's normal for couples to have disagreements, but it's probably not natural for wives to have secret bug-out bags they stash in their closets. I hear the front door slam shut moments later.

Corroborating with his ex about my medical care. I wonder what else they talked about in that hallway. They were out there a long time...

When Ben pulls this shit, I pull out mine.

And I begin to fill it with clothes Sebastian might enjoy.

I finger the fringe on a tiny bikini that probably doesn't fit me anymore, but Seb won't mind. It's neon pink and loud and flashy—and it would go perfectly on Miami Beach.

Jean shorts are next. Too short. Definitely not Christian-like.

Because if I'm abandoning this life, I'm quitting my previous one altogether.

I've tried to walk the path, built my life in His image. I've prayed and prayed for help with my marriage—a family. But I haven't received any answers or divine guidance.

And I'm tired.

I'm so fucking tired.

I wipe at the tears as I toss a sundress in the suitcase. One that skims my thighs. I bought it years ago and never wore it, tags still attached. Flip-flops are next. My dress shoes can stay here, because I'll be leaving my job behind too.

That's the escape that Sebastian offers.

Sebastian's not just some ex I can't get over, he's an alternate reality I can jump to at a moment's notice. A true vortex, unlike the ones in Sedona, that I can step through to a different realm; a dangerous option to have in a failing marriage, I realize, because—*The grass isn't always greener*—but it really is outside of Pennsylvania.

It's summer here and the grass is already turning brown,

and it doesn't look like this down south, ever, and I just can't make this place my home.

The sad part is, Ben has no idea how easy it would be for me to leave him and never come back.

When he threatened desertion for his teaching job, it was hard not to just let him go.

And call Sebastian immediately, and tell him I was on my way. Now, I'm beginning to think that might've been what he wanted. While I was thinking about returning to my old love, was he doing the same?

Is this what happens after the novelty of marriage has worn off?

I fantasized about Ben returning home, all my belongings gone—*How dare you leave me?*

Ben knows how my father exited my life, and the extra sting his own departure would mark with it.

But I was still trying to follow the path. I was still attempting to honor my marriage vows.

I have fake passports.

Sebastian made them for me the first time Ben and I hit a rough patch. They're still in the zipper compartment in my suitcase. It's a way to *leave without a trace*, Sebastian said.

It's not that Sebastian is a perfect oasis. I know he's not.

It's that he has imperfections and accepts all of mine, and always will.

I'll never not be enough for him. He doesn't necessarily want, or not want children. He's neutral on the matter.

He doesn't believe in conventional marriage. He doesn't care if I have a high-powered career.

We were happy once without any of that. And we can be happy again.

I could take a break from it all. Leave the rat race and the expectations, jump off the corporate hamster wheel.

Withdraw half of our savings—mine and Ben's—even though, if I'm being honest, it's mostly *my* money. And I could use it for something else instead of paying for the portion of the IVF treatments the insurance won't cover—because it won't cover it all. The money could go toward making a new life on the beach with Sebastian. He could work construction, and I could do something simple, perhaps a gig in the tourism industry.

I love the outdoors and exploring culture.

My current job has me stuck behind a desk.

Instead of dreaming about trips I don't venture on anymore with Ben, I could be leading an airboat into the Everglades or blowing a whistle at patrons on a party peddler excursion around Miami. A job that has me interacting with people at a real level instead of just observing them from behind the scenes.

It might sound ridiculous to anyone else, but the confines of corporate America and a quietly discontented husband make the perfect concoction for a clean breakaway. I never have to worry about the offer expiring with Sebastian. His romantic relationships don't last because he doesn't believe in marriage—but he said with me, he'd do a "life partner" relationship. An offer of monogamy from Sebastian has always been just enough to keep me hanging on.

As I throw a lacy thong on top of the dress, I do the thing I always resort to before turning to a complete life of debauchery and living in sin. I call my mother.

"I miss you, darling." Her voice sounds harried.

"I miss you too, Mama. I'm thinking about coming home already." I push down the clothes in the carryon to make room for more.

"For a visit? When? I'll make sure to clear my schedule."

After almost thirty years, Mother still works at the Dollar General. Her mobile home in Shelby is paid off. I've offered to put her up in a community center closer to Charlotte where she can interact with other adults her own age, but she won't hear of it. And she doesn't want charity. She says the job gives her purpose, although I never understood how living a life of dealing in junk retail could do such a thing.

"No... I don't know if I can stay here, Mama. I don't like Pennsylvania. And... I don't think I can handle the clinic testing. It doesn't feel right. At my core. In my gut."

My mother sighs. "If you leave, your marriage might not survive."

"It may have already run its course, I'm afraid." It's the first time I've said the words out loud, or filled the suitcase to the very top. It has more meaning to me than it should. Every nerve in my body inches me forward to zip it closed and dash out the door.

I could do it. I could leave Ben today and never look back.

"*Fight.* Fight for your marriage, Ally," she rasps. "You'll regret it if you don't."

"You, of all people, expect me to let scientists make a baby and put it in my belly?" I can't believe we're debating a topic she's been adamantly against since the moment I brought it up. It was only when Ben threatened leaving me—moving to another state—that she changed her tune.

"No, of course not, but that's not your only choice... You can talk to Ben about adoption if his way doesn't work out. Marriage is about compromise. If you run out on him now..." She doesn't finish her sentence, but she doesn't have to.

"Ben doesn't want to adopt," I tell her. "And neither do I," I say, because the idea of raising my own child is daunting enough. Raising someone else's in the state of my current marriage seems impossible. This will only work if it's something we created together. I don't know why, but it's something I know as well as the pattern of veins on the back of my hand.

"Try, Ally," her voice runs dry. "If you don't, you'll regret it. If you try all you can, and it still doesn't work, you'll be able to tell yourself in the end that you gave it your best shot."

I close my eyes at her words, because I know she's right.

Ben is a good man, if only a little insensitive and dense at times. He very much still wants a life with me. He moved us here to give us a fresh start.

My husband is the righteous path and turning to Sebastian would be giving into my dark side. Turning toward temptation.

"I'm trying, but it's hard," I tell her.

"Marriage is hard. Life is hard," she says.

Truer words were never spoken, although I realize it's been more difficult on my mother. I can't help but think her advice comes from a different place. A desperate woman still working retail in her sixties in a dead-end town.

I could do better on my own. But she is right.

I should at least try it—his way. Even though it's the last thing I want to do.

"Okay, Mama. I'll try. But don't be surprised if I show up on your doorstep one day."

"You're welcome anytime."

We end the call, but I know it's not her doorstep I'll run to.

Sebastian and I have a no-text policy.

His work phone is issued to him from the Carolinas AGC, a trade association made up of contractors and construction-related firms. When he's called me in the past, the cell phone log just shows—Associated General Contractors of America. I've called the association plenty of times over the years for a variety of home repairs, so it's raised no eyebrows with Ben, who is not a handyman of any sort.

Texts open us up to exposure, but Sebastian must've felt my neediness through the phone. As I'm thinking about him, he sends me a single message, as if he can sense that I need to hear from him. I'll delete it right after I read it.

Sebastian: Maldives sea turtle and Rehabilitation volunteers needed. Click on link.

TWENTY

EMILY

CHOICE

A little girl hangs perilously off the railing of one of Mount Washington's overlooks.

Mount Washington has two large circular lookout spots, prime photo-op locales for prom pictures and special occasions of all varieties. But today, during rush hour, the tourists stand back and point for a different reason.

No one wants to extend a hand, or more likely, become involved with the child in danger of plunging three-hundred-and-sixty-five feet to her death.

I pull my Land Rover over quickly, because I know that little girl.

I dash out of the vehicle. "Clementine!"

She swings her legs back onto the oval cement safely. There's a collective sigh from the crowd that has gathered. If she'd made different choices—if I'd startled her so badly that she'd slipped—people would be staring at me like I was a monster instead. But for now I'm a hero.

These are the decisions we make when it comes to life and death.

I find myself pondering these ideals more and more at work as the #911s stack up, but nothing quite like this.

"Hi, Miss Emily," Clementine says, with no inflection in her voice, indicating she doesn't realize how much danger she was actually in.

"Come here, right now!" My arms shake as she falls into them. I give her a hug and pet her warm head.

She looks stunned as she stares back at me. I can't help but notice she's dressed in a cute summer romper. "You need to be more careful. Never go near the railing again without an adult."

She gapes at me, still unsure. "Oh-kay," she says in a sing-songy voice.

I kneel down beside her, brushing the sticky honey-colored hair she shares with Chelsea off her head, taking one of her hands in mine, red and bruised from where she gripped the black, hot railing. "Where's your mother?"

"She's sleeping on the floor. I asked her if I could go for a walk and she said yes."

None of this sounds right. "What do you mean she's asleep on the floor? Is your daddy home?"

"No, he's trying to get a job." She smiles sweetly. I nod. The second statement tracks.

"Can we get ice cream? I brought my money," she asks. Just then I notice the change purse Clementine has attached to her wrist. What a smart little three-year-old. She was walking to get ice cream, just up the street at the parlor on Shiloh Street.

But she must've gotten distracted by the view.

Tonight the sky looks like someone split open a ruby red grapefruit and spread it overtop the clouds. I open my mouth to tell her yes in regard to the ice cream, but blue and red lights roar down the road, snagging my attention. Someone must've called the cops.

The officers wind up the hill in their vehicles, and then climb out and rush over to where I'm crouched beside Clem.

"Is this your child, ma'am?" a male officer asks. He's gruff and angry, probably because he thinks I'm the negligent parent here, letting my kid dangle over a mountainside and all.

"No, she's my neighbor. But I have real concerns about her mother. Clementine said her mommy was asleep on the floor." I make an urgent expression at the officer and he softens a bit. "Can I let you in the gate that secures our townhouses, and can you please do a wellness check on her?"

The female cop who stands firmly behind her partner says, "Yes, ma'am."

When the officers open the unlocked door to the pristine, well-decorated home, the vile smell hits me before the sight of her.

Chelsea's passed out in her living room, swimming in a pool of her own vomit. Clementine tries to run to her mother, and I swoop her right up, covering her eyes.

The male officer checks Chelsea's pulse. "She's alive." As the female officer calls for a medic, I spy a bottle of vodka at Chelsea's side, and I've seen enough.

"Please tell her father Clementine is with me. I'm taking her to get ice cream."

I'm not sure the officers hear me, but I carry Clementine outside before they can direct me otherwise. I don't even have Jasper's cell phone number. "What's wrong with Mommy?" Clementine asks.

"She's sick. But the officers are going to make her feel better. Let's get some ice cream."

Clementine scrunches her cute little face up, and then immediately perks up. "Okay."

"Earth to Emily." Cat waves a hand in front of my face. "You can't be that out of it from a sip of wine."

The three of us—me, Cat, and Laurel—sit around a mound of papers. Cat was just as much a part of my life as Laurel before she moved away.

I haven't told my oldest, truest friends about what happened with Clementine earlier, though I'm not sure why. I'm distracted, though.

It's hard not to think of Jasper's exhausted face when he returned home to reclaim Clementine, confined in a monkey suit and tie he'd put on to please Chelsea. All buttoned up in his tailored Armani, yet he somehow seemed more exposed than the day he spied on me from his balcony, barely clothed.

The reality of it all is sad. Not only is Jasper a victim of domestic verbal abuse, he's also dealing with a wife who has substance abuse issues. Now I know all their dirty laundry.

Her random rageful outbursts make a lot more sense to me now too.

When he reclaimed Clementine, all Jasper said was, "I finally did as she asked and tried to get an office job and it was more than she could take. I think it bothered her that she had nothing to scream at me about."

It's one of the most dysfunctional statements anyone has ever said to me, but strangely I understood what he meant. I soundlessly handed over his adorable daughter. There are no words for exchanges of that sort.

I tried to go back to normal life after that, but this isn't our average college reunion either.

Years ago, we sat around a table just like this one, at Cat's South Side rowhouse and decided to break up with our boyfriends together. We crossed out every initial we'd carved in her kitchen table—E+B—as if slicing a blade into our palms and sealing it with blood, ritualizing the act—*We shall liberate ourselves from our men.* Back when I tried to be impulsive and convince myself I needed an adventure to fulfill my dull life—a foreign landscape, different partners...

It seemed like such a solid plan at the time. I wonder if these two ladies realize how much I regret it, seeing as how they came back and coupled up with the very men we vowed to separate from.

And I'm still here alone—paging through potential sperm donors.

"You didn't have to drive all the way up here, Cat," I say. Some people have circles of friends, whereas I have a mere triangle. Caterina Morello Marcel makes up one third and she lives in the D.C. Metro area.

"You kidding me? I wasn't going to let the two of you choose your baby's father. You need my mediation." Cat pulls her dark hair back into a ponytail, getting down to business.

Cat is the happy medium between Laurel and me; the diplomatic negotiator to our indecisive deliberation; the gentle soul who soothes my cynicism.

Cat picks up the stack of papers I laid on the counter next to a red pen. "So, they're just in a catalog by number? Like ordering a sweater online or something? Do you get a picture?" she asks.

"No, and I'd actually rather not be able to visualize him. Then, I'll always be looking for him. I don't want to be walking down the street, and think I see him everywhere."

"Like your sperm donor is haunting you," Cat rationalizes. Laurel giggles.

"Ya, something like that," I say.

Cat focuses on one of the donor's profiles. "Well, this one says he looks like Kevin Bacon."

"Cat, can you put a red 'X' beside that one, please," I order, smiling tightly.

"Yes, girl. That one'll haunt ya," Cat says.

"Everybody... cut loose, footloose! Kick off the Sunday

shoes!" Laurel sings. She jumps off her barstool and starts dancing around. I know we're all thinking about the fraternity brother who did his homecoming skit to that movie-inspired dance routine and split his pants, forever ruining the actor and the movie for us.

But I don't want this to be funny.

This is *not* funny. This is my life.

"Come on, guys." I put my head down on the sharp-edged tabletop, a surface not conducive for head resting—or children.

"Come on, Laurel. Regroup. Regroup, please. See, this is why you need me here, Emily," Cat insists.

"Okay, I'm sorry. Although, celebrity look-a-likes are a great way for Emily to picture her baby-daddies without actually seeing them. She loves her movie stars," Laurel says. She strokes my latest edition of *People* magazine sitting on the table.

"Are there any in there, by chance, that say they look like Chris Hemsworth?" I ask.

"Hmm... Not that I see. Let's try to focus," Cat says. "So, Emily, what is it you want from your baby's father? There's education level, ethnicity, height, eye color, extracurricular activities." Cat sets the clinic's donor database back down on the counter. It makes a loud slapping sound.

When I walked to the donor department, they asked me to fill out a candidate profile sheet to narrow down my selection. But I didn't want to rule anybody out, so I had them print the entire database. Now the specs on the paper are jamming my brain with so many descriptions and figures I can't register them all. There's so many profiles and categories, the words all blur together.

"Just think, if you could pick any guy for this baby, what would he be like?" Cat asks.

He'd be just like Ben. But if I can't have Ben, this is who I'll pick...

"Educated. Master's degree or doctorate, if possible.

Ethnicity doesn't matter. The donor doesn't have to be tall, but that doesn't hurt. I don't care about eye color. Athletic isn't bad, but I wouldn't sacrifice brains for brawn."

"Okay..." Cat scans the pages. Laurel is being strange, observing us now from a few feet away, glaring at the papers with uncertainty as if they actually contain some of the male specimen on them.

"How about number three-seven-zero-nine? Blood type A-. Irish-Italian-Welsh. Six feet tall. One hundred and seventy-seven pounds. Hair: brown. Blue eyes. In Architecture graduate school. Occupation: student. Hobbies: reading, running, playing guitar, travel. Pregnancy reported: yes. Religion: Agnostic. Pets: dog."

"What does 'pregnancy reported, yes' mean?" Laurel asks.

"It means he's fathered other children through IVF," I answer.

"How do you feel about that?" Cat asks.

"Not great, but how can I expect to be the only one?" I pull my hoodie tighter around myself, a mixture of excited-happy and nervous-terror streaming through my body. I'm picking a father, for my baby—right now.

"Okay, so pros and cons of this one?" Laurel asks.

"Well, he's probably super-young if he's a student, in his twenties, most likely, so that's great for healthy sperm, but at the same time, how many other kids is this guy going to father? Kind of "scary" my baby could run into one of its siblings and not even know it." I shiver at the possibilities.

"I never thought of that," Laurel says.

"Neither did I." For as much as I've studied the field of fertility, I can't believe I haven't thought of it. My only reservations have been the medical and genetic consequences of the process, but I neglected to examine the social issues. There're so many pitfalls to using a sperm donor.

"What if my baby unknowingly runs into one of its siblings

later on in life and things get weird?" I ask. A word I learned at Cambridge resurges from the recesses of my mind. Consanguinity—the fact of being descended from the same ancestor.

"Can't you keep tabs on him to make sure that doesn't happen?" Cat asks.

"You can, but I don't want to keep tabs. I want to be totally disconnected from this guy."

"Right, the ghost-donor," Laurel says.

"Right," I confirm.

"Well, what did you like about this one?" Cat asks.

"Architect. I love design. I'd love to say, your daddy was an architect... And he's tall, and I like that he can play a musical instrument."

"We'll call him the architect and we'll put him in the 'maybe' pile. Next."

"Number three-seven-one-zero. Lawyer. Blood type O+. African American. Five foot seven. Brown hair. Brown eyes. Christian. Pregnancy reported: no. Hobbies: coaching, cooking, running."

I wrinkle my nose.

"Not liking that one."

"I don't like lawyers. They're arrogant. And he's short, so our child will be too, and life's hard for me as a smaller person, so, they'll definitely be tiny, because if you combine five foot two and five foot seven, you definitely get short. So, I dunno."

"Well, you can be as picky as you like, I guess, but I wouldn't jump to any wild assumptions," Cat argues.

My eyes must have scorched her through the lenses of my glasses, because the next thing Cat says is, "Okay, so let's red-x that one."

Laurel is giving me crazy eyes, and I decide I can be as crazy as I like in this case.

Cat says, "Number three-seven-one-one. Oh, awesome— graduate degree in biology. Medical research assistant. Blood type O+. Latino. Six foot one, and one hundred and seventy-eight pounds. Brown. Blue eyes. Christian. Pregnancy reported: no. Hobbies: hiking, fishing, outdoors, travel. He has a dog."

"Sounds great, Emily. Research assistant," she says, but I'm not that impressed.

"Why the heck is he just an assistant if he has a graduate degree?" I ask.

"We don't know how old he is," Laurel remarks.

"If he has a graduate degree, he should have moved beyond an assistant," I state. "He's either not ambitious enough or not smart enough to move forward."

"And Kevin Bacon keeps looking better and better," Laurel jokes.

"It's okay, there're a few more with advanced degrees here. And if you don't find one in this pile, there're other clinics. Maybe if you don't pick a guy from your local database that'll lessen your worries about the siblings mingling later," Cat offers.

"I really trust our procedures for screening, especially for diseases. I know the sperm in our bank is of the highest quality," I argue.

"High-quality sperm 'ere." Laurel laughs.

"Oh, God Laurel." Cat laughs, swinging her ponytail.

"Do you think Zach has high-quality sperm?" Laurel asks.

"Well, he made your two little beautiful bundles, didn't he?" I ask.

"Seth must have super-quality sperm, because we made three, and didn't even shoot for the last one," Cat admits.

"It must be rough having accidental babies," I chime.

"Oh, Emily, I'm so sorry. That was insensitive of me," Cat apologizes.

"It's okay, I know you didn't mean it. And it's the truth, so..."

Everyone stares at me with the type of pity I loathe.

They don't know how serious I am about the accidental babies. There're a few isolated incidences where I've had a one-night stand and wished something went amiss, praying for missed periods. I used to think I was insane for trying to manifest such a thing, but looking at my present situation, it doesn't seem so wild. At least I'd know the guy and would've gotten pregnant the natural way, and could've given the child some semblance of who their father is.

"Okay, number three-seven-one-two. Blood type: O+. Six foot three. Two hundred and thirty-five pounds. Italian, Irish, German. Eyes: hazel. Hair: brown. Masters in Exercise and Sports Science. Occupation: teacher. Christian. Pregnancy reported: no. He has a dog. He's all about exercise and he plays the violin."

Laurel announces, "Winner."

"Yes!" Cat agrees.

"He sounds like a jock. What is he, a gym teacher?" I ask, not so sure.

"He sounds hot. Your baby can get the brains from you, no worries," Laurel reasons.

"But what if the baby gets his brains and my looks, then it's screwed," I ponder.

Both of the girls just glance at me as if I'm the biggest buzzkill in the world. "It's been proven through clinical research that at least fifty percent of intelligence is inherited and some studies point to figures closer to seventy percent. I can't just let some random jock be the father of my baby," I say.

"He has a master's degree, Emily."

"Yeah, in sports."

"Ah, you're tough, girl. Although, Italian, Irish, could make for a bad temper," Laurel debates.

"Very true," Cat agrees.

"So, that's it. We've got the architect who's fathered the

world, so my baby can marry its sibling. And we have the jock," I summarize.

"Don't forget Kevin Bacon," Laurel jokes.

"Oh, yes, how could I ever? Dear God." I sigh.

"So, we're out of graduate students. Which one of these dudes is going to be the daddy?" Cat asks, impatiently. Cat is a doer, and she obviously thought her job today was to get this assignment done.

"None of them," I cry.

"Come on, Emily, they aren't so bad. These are all smart guys," Laurel rationalizes.

"Well, you said brains over brawn," Cat reminds.

"Yes, but I'm having a hard time with the fact he's fathered other children and I'm wondering if it's like one or twenty other kids, and if he's just doing this to get through school or it's something he plans to do for life."

"Can you place an inquiry about that?" Cat asks.

"I could, but it could take months to get answers. Our clinic limits its donors to no more than twenty-five pregnancies, but now that seems like a lot," I puzzle.

"It doesn't really matter, does it? These guys are all selling their sperm. Eventually, somebody will get impregnated by them, right? And that should be a good thing, because it means they have good sperm," Cat reasons.

"I suppose. I'll have to think on it," I say.

"Okay, well, let's stop thinking on it for the night. We might not have found the guy, but we sure narrowed it down to two candidates for Emily's baby-daddy," Laurel advises. "This is a positive thing."

Cat bites on her lip in displeasure. Her type-A personality is probably dissatisfied with not accomplishing the goal at hand.

"Yes, girls. Thank you," I say.

They push the catalog to the side, but I can't stop thinking about the donors.

There, in that stapled pile of black and white specs, is my baby's future father. I've dreamt of who he would be since I was a little girl, and somehow it seems so bleak that I'd find him in something as rudimentary as a stack of papers. This isn't how the fairy tale was supposed to go.

Laurel removes a bottle of Chardonnay from the wine fridge, uncorks it, and pours us all a glass. We pick at appetizers and try to talk about something else, but everything with this group ultimately circles back to the past. I don't know how we get there, but the breakup pact is brought back—of all nights.

Cat recalls how Seth made it all of two weeks separated from her. After me and Laurel left, Cat said she did nothing but cry the whole time. She said, Seth was gone, and we were gone, and she just caved.

I've applauded their relationship since day one, but Laurel's seems unjustified to me. It's unfair I'm the one sifting through printed pages of sperm donors, and she had the grand European adventure with other guys while her nice husband-to-be sat at home and waited for her to return.

"We promise not to bring any of this up at the party, Emily. Everyone just wants to see you," Cat announces.

Laurel drinks a little faster. "Ben wanted to have a friendly little reunion since he's back in town."

Laurel is lying. She does this thing where she deflects her decisions onto—*something someone else wanted*—because she doesn't want to own her action. Ben didn't want the party.

Laurel did.

Laurel loves parties. I won't debunk her lie just like I've let so many others go in the past, because most of the time she does this so she won't piss anyone off.

"It'll be great to see the guys," I say, shaking my head, sinking further into the comfort of my ratty sweatshirt.

"Zach and Seth and Hooch will all be there... Seth says he forgets what you look like," Cat mentions.

"Did you tell him he's not missing much?" I retort.

"Emily, stop that. Look, Hooch is still single, and—"

"Nooo!" I protest.

"Well, at least you won't be the only single one there is what I'm trying to say," Cat says.

"No way, you were going to try to hook me up with Hooch. I'm not that desperate."

"Well, just come, okay. You'll be with me and Zach. It's not for a couple of weeks," Laurel tries.

"I'll be really emotional with the fertility shots by then. I'll see, but I'm not promising anything," I offer.

"Oh, yes. I can't wait to poke you with needles again," Laurel jokes.

"You don't have to. My mom can—"

"Emily, it's okay. I've got you. I'll stick you wherever you need." Laurel laughs. Then Cat giggles. Then I'm laughing so hard my glasses slide down my nose.

"I'll think about it," I say, still giddy.

"Fine, I'll take that for now. Looks like you've got lots to think about." Cat pats the stack of donor papers, and sips her wine. This choice is going to weigh heavily on all of us, because it's a big decision we're making together. Just like the last one.

TWENTY-ONE

EMILY

PACT

2008

"The pact" occurred at Ben's studio apartment in Regency Square after a party. I still remember how the moonlight bounced off the nickel-pecked hardwood floor, casting shadows off the white, exposed brick and hand-painted canvases on the walls. Ben was going on about me leaving in a week, and how much he was going to miss me.

At this precise moment, I was aware Laurel was having the same talk with Zach, which prompted me forward. I wouldn't let Laurel down. We'd been through everything together, and we were going to break up with our men together too.

In my mind, I'd always have a second chance with Ben if we were meant to be. We shared a lot of history. We were forever bound by our experiences—including the one tied to Professor Cook that came with a prison sentence if we were ever caught.

"What's wrong, Em?" Ben asked. "You should be excited about your trip."

"About going to Europe..." That was how I started the conversation that would change everything.

"The longest six months of my life, you mean?" Ben asked. His brown eyes exuded warmth and kindness. I wanted to wrap myself in him forever and forget this silly arrangement I made with my friends.

I avoided the question, pointing instead to one of my favorites of his paintings on the wall in front of us. "I love that one. We've had some great memories."

We visited El Capitan at Yosemite in the beginning of March when the snow was just starting to let up, but that's not how Ben painted it. This view of the mountain was in the dead of winter with purple-grays storming across the apex of the mountain, furling into white tumbleweeds that escaped through the top, resembling icy teeth and the angry mouths of a thousand Nordic gods.

"We *had* some great memories. No need for all of the drama, Em. I've got lots in store for us when you return. It's just the wait that's going to kill me." He gaped at me like an expectant child, and I almost chickened out.

But just like El Capitan, the world was big and we were small. How were we to know what role we were supposed to play and who we were destined to be if we didn't explore every option? At least that's what the logic sounded like when Laurel, Cat, and me hatched the plan over some cocktails.

"Well, then maybe we should branch out, so there's, no, um expectations," I suggested.

Branch out? Those weren't the words I used in my head when I planned this speech. I wanted to take them back and edit my words, but they were already out there, and I couldn't retract them.

"Branch out?" Ben stood up and backed away. "What exactly does that mean?" His smile crumpled, and he plunged his hands deep into his green vintage flak jacket, legs spread apart in a hardened *What the fuck* look.

I panicked. "The stress of it all, Ben. Us trying to be a couple when we're thousands of miles apart. This is the time when we're supposed to be figuring out who we are and where our place is in the world."

It was 2008, the housing crisis on the fringe, the financial bubble already popping, the world tinged with uncertainty.

And I was killing the one sure thing I had—Ben.

"I don't understand. Em, are you breaking up with me?" He wouldn't look at me, wiping at his eyes with the sleeve of his jacket. The patch on his arm—Stowe—stared back at me in all of its snow-capped glory. It was Ben's favorite snowboarding mountain from our Vermont ski trip.

"There's more to this world than just you and me. Maybe we should explore that." Even as I said the words I didn't believe them.

This whole idea was a huge mistake. I knew it that very moment as Ben's eyes filled with tears. I hurt him so badly he could barely speak.

"You want to see other people? Is that what this is about? Branching out? *Exploring?*"

"Ben, isn't there anything you've ever wanted to do without me attached? You've talked about going to Alaska and living off the land and moving to Utah so you could snowboard until you're practically blind," I said.

"Em, none of those things matter without you beside me. I can't believe you don't want to be with me anymore. What did I do? What happened?" He cried then; a thick, strangled howl like an animal caught in a snare. The memory of that sound still grates at my heart.

"You didn't do anything..." I tried to grab for his sleeve, but he moved farther away from me.

"Is this about Cook? I *protected* you." Cook had died just

four months prior, our conflict over the matter still in a state of healing.

"Of course not. You know I'll be forever grateful." I choke on my tongue. Is he going to give me up now? Is he threatening me? "I thought, I thought... given the circumstances, it wouldn't be a bad idea to give us a break, just to see where things should go," I continued.

"You did, did you? Well, I think you're heartless and should probably leave now." Ben was having a hard time catching his breath. All I wanted to do was hold him in my arms and tell him I was sorry, and that I freaked out and screwed up, but I didn't. Instead, I did just as he asked. I gathered my purse, walked out the door, and drove home. It was only then that I burst into tears.

They say everything happens for a reason, and when one door closes another one opens. But I believe sometimes you just mess up, and you shut a door you should've kept open, and you never find another one as good. Some mistakes have no silver lining.

<hr/>

It has to be the architect. Definitely, the architect.

After Laurel and Cat left, I cried myself to sleep and had a horrible dream about a young guy fist-pumping on the Jersey Shore, asking me if I wanted to check out his situation. The young man was the Masters in Sports guy, and the nightmare was my subconscious telling me he was the wrong choice.

Then I got out of bed and stayed up until three in the morning going through the entire stack of non-graduate students until my eyes were nearly bleeding with exhaustion. It was useless because none of the donor profiles seemed good enough for my future baby.

When I visited my mother on Sunday I received approval

on the architect. Well, as much as any mother could approve of a sperm donor for her daughter.

And now it's Monday, and finally time to get on the schedule for the next FET (Frozen Embryo Transfer) evaluation. I'll need to have saline injected into my uterus to make sure my uterine cavity is free of abnormalities before I start the process. I'm hoping one of the ultrasound techs will do it for me today to speed things along. But Batey's absence is messing with my plans.

She's supposed to be here today.

After the scan, I'll begin the painstaking shots—the Lupron, which will prevent ovulation, and then the estrogen, and then the progesterone—stuck like a human pincushion full of hormones. If all goes well, after a month, Batey will check my uterine lining to confirm it's the correct thickness to sustain pregnancy, and then it will be embryo transfer time.

My baby fantasies are broken by a neurotic Lisette swinging around the corner in her pencil skirt, chomping on her gum, thwacking her pen at a chart in her hands. "You have to take it. She's not going to make it here on time, and the couple is irate."

"Then I really don't want it," I say.

Lisette shoves the files into my hands anyway. Batey unsettles Lisette more than she unnerves me. The rest of us know Batey isn't a real celebrity, she just plays one at work, but she has Lisette fooled.

"Whoa, I don't do the genetic stuff. Way beyond my scope," I refuse. "Reschedule them." I toss the files back into Lisette's hands.

Lisette is shaking her blonde head at me. She has a high bun in with pouffy, pulled-back bangs that seem to raise her forehead enough to make her look like a retro alien. I'm so distracted by her over-doneness I can hardly concentrate on her words.

"They drove all the way from Philly. You have to at least tell them they need to reschedule. Give them *some* information."

This is ridiculous. I've had it with Batey.

"What about Dr. Woo or Dr. Antonsic?"

"In surgery, off today," Lisette hurries.

Of course Dr. Antonsic was off. He's always off. He needs to retire already.

"Can the nurses explain it?" I ask.

"They haven't been trained. Dr. Batey said you studied this and should know something about it."

"So, you spoke to her? Where the hell is she?" I ask.

Ralphie walks by the lab corridor at that precise moment. "Thatta girl," he mutters.

"Anderson fell down the stairs this morning, hurt his arm pretty badly. Dr. Batey had to take him to the hospital while her husband ran the other one to school. She tried to pawn him off on her husband, but Anderson wanted mommy."

Of course he did. Poor kid probably threw himself down the stairs on purpose to get her attention.

"Ahh," I sigh. Now I feel guilty because she actually has a good reason for not being here, but it's unprofessional for me to handle this case. More unprofessional than the others, because I haven't really been properly trained on the procedure. I deliberate over my options as Lisette sticks the files back in my hands. Her butt wiggles away with an extra measure of defiance as she clomps out of the room in her high heels.

Ralphie is giggling now. "Em, she's got you all worked up today. Wow." I am an extra shade of pissed off than usual, my own stresses lessening my confrontational threshold.

"Just wait until I start taking my hormones." My face is red and hot, and I need to find a new job.

"What do you mean?" Ralphie asks, concerned.

"I've decided to do IVF through FET."

"No way. That's aweee-some!" Ralphie jumps toward me like he's going to hug me, and then plants me with a safe high-five instead. Lab people aren't huggers.

"Thanks. Big decision, but I'm ready. I was going to tell Batey today to put me on the schedule, but I'm doing this instead." I tap the folder in my hands.

"There's nothing like it. Being a parent is the best." Ralphie smiles, proudly. He fathered a little girl in his teens. He didn't stay with the mother, but has done his part to support his daughter. And from what I can tell, he's doing an excellent job.

"Hopefully, I'll know soon, but I've got to deal with this first." I point to the file, flustered.

Ralphie salutes me as I head to the gray consultation room. There's nothing out of the ordinary about the patient file, until I notice the patient's reason for being seen. I try not to place moral judgment on anyone who comes through our doors, because I'm an advocate for everything science can do for fertility, but this one leaves me with a question mark.

Kelly and Marx
Profile: Kelly Amstead
Kelly: 32
Occupation: n/a
Marital Status: M
Previous Children/Miscarriages: 2 children
Surgeries in the last year: n/a
Allergies: n/a
Please list any medical conditions including (diabetes,
high blood pressure, high cholesterol, heart disease, etc.):
_____n/a_____
Reason being seen: After birthing two healthy girls natu-
rally, patient would like a guaranteed boy.

There is no genetic reason listed. If there was one, it would be on the form. There's no further explanation other than the fact that these people *want* a boy.

The couple is at ease when I walk into the room, and why

shouldn't they be? They aren't like the hundreds of childless couples who've come before them, fraught with worry over the possibility of never becoming parents. They're two people in their early thirties who just want to conceive a boy by Christmas.

Marx has a shiny dome and brightly inked tattoos that pop against his skin, chunky metal rings on his fingers, and a grim expression like he means business. Kelly seems the opposite, prim and proper, sitting with her legs and arms crossed in a trendy black jumpsuit.

"Firstly, let me apologize that Dr. Batey couldn't make it. She unfortunately had a family emergency," I start.

Marx cracks the knuckles on his left hand. "My wife scheduled this appointment months ago, and we really wanted to start this process sooner rather than later. I'll be going out of town for work soon."

"You know we drove all the way from Philadelphia?" Kelly asks me.

Marx scoots forward in his chair, a look of extreme annoyance stretched across his face.

"I know, and hopefully I can answer some questions for you about gender selection and PGD," I say.

They nod in restrained agreement.

After I explain my knowledge of PGD, and the process of implanting only the male embryos, I discuss the shots and the precautions. Also, the fact that even though PGD is nearly one hundred percent effective in gender selection, there's always the chance it can produce the other gender, multiples, or that the implantation might not take at all.

Marx cracks his knuckles on his other hand now.

"So, there would be a chance for twin boys?" Marx perks up. Kelly frowns, clearly not interested in this prospect.

"Certainly, if we implant two embryos and they both take. There's always a higher chance for multiples with IVF."

"Then we'd be even," Marx says. He's smiling when he says this, making it sound like a logical sentiment of family balance. I'm not sure about that.

"Kelly, do you have any questions?" I'm becoming concerned this pregnancy is all about Marx's wants and needs. Does this woman even want a son? Or another baby for that matter?

"Well, Marx is gone a lot fighting, so the thought of chasing around two twin boys and two older girls is quite exhausting," she admits.

Marx pats his wife's hand. "If you'd let me get you a nanny, it would help, and you could go to your exercise class." Even though he looks a little rough with his tatted-up arms, I can tell he really loves his wife, and that he wants her to want this too. But does she?

"Fighting?" I don't want to ask, but I have to report signs of violence regarding prospective couples.

"You don't recognize him? Marx Amstead? He's a UFC fighter. Wants a boy to carry on his legacy," Kelly says, admirably.

And it all makes sense. There just isn't enough testosterone in the house for this guy.

"Oh, no, sorry. I don't really watch a lot of sports," I admit.

"Bet you love them Steelers, though? We're Iggles fans if you didn't figure that out already," Marx says.

"Right." The only thing I loathe worse than an overzealous Pittsburgh Steelers' fan is a diehard Philadelphia Eagles' fan.

"Not so much any kind of sports fan," I say.

Marx is smiling at me, and nodding, trying to connect, even though we don't have a wire between us that's compatible. I can see it, though. That look. The one a lot of future parents express, where they'll do anything to have *that* baby. This procedure is about more than making Marx a future wrestling buddy. This man wants a son. I just hope Kelly wants one too.

"Well, if we're all done here, I'll refer you to the nurses to discuss next steps."

They nod, and I'm out of there quicker than Lisette can scuttle away in her tight skirt.

I sigh in relief after I make it back to the lab.

When will it be my turn?

All I could think about from the moment I made the decision to have a baby is having that baby. I'm totally one of those women who've contracted baby fever, and by the end of the day, I've convinced my favorite ultrasound tech, Marjorie, to shoot up my uterus with saline and take some pictures. It turns out my uterine cavity is in perfect shape, open and willing to receive an embryo.

Come to Momma.

After putting my clothes back on, Batey is waiting for me in my office. She appears worked up with puffy circles under her eyes and none of her usual flashy jewelry to complement her suit.

"Hello, Dr. Batey," I say.

"I wanted to apologize to you, Emily."

I almost fall off my chair. "Huh?"

"Anderson hurt himself, and insisted on having me with him. He's nine fucking years old, and I don't understand why he's still such a baby. Hopefully, these kids can grow up a little faster so they're not still whining for mom over every cut and scrape."

"So, it wasn't serious?" I ask.

"No, he did break his arm."

"Oh, please don't worry about it. That's okay," I say.

"It's not okay. I shouldn't have personal blips come between me and breakthrough medical procedures."

Dr. Batey is unreal. She's not apologized to me one time for missing a consult when she was late due to work arrangements, but here she is pleading for my forgiveness over her son's broken arm. In what world does she not realize it should be the other way around?

"I'm sure you'll miss them needing you when they're older," I insist.

"I'm sure I won't."

And she wouldn't. And it's sad. She'll never be the mother to reminisce about her children's toddler days being the best of her life. When they're older, self-sufficient, and out of her hair is when they'll be at their best for her. I can't wait another minute to tell her my news, and I figure, coming off her apology, it will go smoother.

"I had my scan today. All good."

"Splendid," she says, clasping her hands together. "Have you selected the lucky father from our plentiful bank yet?"

"I did, but I have to tell you it wasn't as plentiful with donors with graduate degrees as I would have liked. And no doctorates," I complain.

"Well, what type of men do you think ejaculate in a cup for money, dear?" she asks.

I shrug. "There must be some do-gooders with a family and a doctorate—"

"Who are well-paid upstanding citizens who probably have families of their own and enough wealth that they don't have to ejaculate in a cup for some extra cash," she says.

I hate the way she says "ejaculate", stressing the JACK, like it's a person.

"I get it. I got one I'm satisfied with. A student going for his Master's in Architecture."

"Young. Good. How did the PGD consult go with the folks who wanted a boy?"

And just like that, we're back to business. "It went okay.

They were upset. And the guy's a UFC fighter, kind of rageful, but a good candidate... physically. Ask Lisette for a follow-up."

"Lisette? Is that the strange blonde woman behind the mountain of hair who keeps leaving me urgent voicemails?" Batey asks.

I laugh, and remember why I went to work for this ruthless woman. Efficient and extremely sarcastic—just like me.

"Okay, well, duty calls. Let me know once you're all set to be implanted and we'll see if we can make a little Emily. Or a little architect. Husbands are overrated, really. They're good for the heavy lifting and the extra income, but you don't need the income, and you can always hire a handyman," she says, matter-of-factly. What a perfect answer. I guess she does lump me into the strong career woman category after all.

Strangely, her logic makes perfect sense to me this time. "I better get back to it," she states, edging her body toward the doorway. I let her go, feeling a rush of relief that I've made my announcement and everyone is officially onboard with my decision—even Batey.

TWENTY-TWO

ALLY

LABOR

I've made it almost three whole weeks with my bag zipped and
stuffed in the closet. It looks like an old carryon. Why would
Ben go snooping in my luggage anyway? He'll never borrow my
bag—it's pastel pink, and he has his own.

Today is the Labor Day soiree at Laurel Quinn's house.

I was hesitant, but Laurel's charming stone and Tudor
home feels safe to me at first glance.

As I exit the car, Ben rubs my shoulder. He's been extra
sensitive lately, asking me how I'm feeling, double checking his
calendar to make sure he doesn't miss any important appointments. Ben rings the doorbell.

Laurel greets me with a tight hug, dressed in a long, flowing
sundress.

The bangles on her wrists dangle along with her earrings.
She's got an easy flow to her that pairs nicely with her dimly lit,
ornately decorated house—vases and bright colors and professional family photos on the wall—candids too. She likes
photography.

"So nice to see you, Ben!" Laurel cheek-kisses him. "Ally! It's been ages." She leads us through the house that smells of vanilla and cinnamon, then gestures for us to walk through to an expansive walkway with its rustic exposed wooden beams, and past the professional outdoor kitchen gleaming with top-of-the-line appliances. The lighted wonderland she's created outside is waiting for us, and Laurel stands by poised for compliments.

"It's lovely," I say.

"Thank you," she gushes. And I suppose I can try to like it here. And her.

"It's the first time we'll all be back together again since our weddings!" Laurel exclaims.

We're the first couple here, and I hate to tell Laurel I don't remember much about my own wedding day, and certainly not hers. Ben and I started dating after "Laurel and friends" were married.

"How're you doing with the fertility shots?" Laurel asks as she straightens a napkin I just nudged out of place.

I startle at her comment. Ben promised our treatment wouldn't be the topic of conversation tonight. He's disappeared into the house with Zach and I can hear them laughing inside somewhere. "I'm on my third week..." I say lightly.

"Oh good. How're you feeling?" she asks. *Is she always like this?*

"How's *who* feeling? Is someone sick? Tell me you have to go pick up the kids at your mother's?" I hear an unidentified female voice, and turn around to find who I vaguely remember as Caterina, "Cat". She's the female friend from Ben's old photos with dark hair. Her husband, Seth, is likely the extra voice in the house with the guys.

"Oh, I was just asking Ally how she was feeling..." Laurel makes an annoying "O" expression with her mouth like she doesn't want to say anything in regard to what she's referring to, even though it's obvious everyone here already knows.

"Ally, hello!" Cat yelps and hugs. *These women.* "Oh, yes, the shots and hormones... whatnot. That must be trying. How're you doing?" Cat places her hand on my shoulder, and it's too much too fast.

"It's a process." Are they trying to bond with me? I like to go in slow—start with a subject of interest not so close to my enlarged ovaries, and then ease into the heavy stuff from there.

"Shots? Shots! I wish I could do shots!" There're men infringing on our conversation now and I glare at Ben like I'm ready to leave already. *You promised*—my expression says. He has a stupid grin on his face, and I doubt he even knows why I'm upset.

And then, *she* appears, and everyone whoops and hollers. "Emily!" Zach yells.

Emily waves back and waltzes through the glass patio doors holding a covered dish. She wears a peasant blouse and a jean skirt, juvenile-looking, but cute, the way tiny women are.

Zach greets Emily first with a quick embrace, and then she makes her rounds with the warm hugs until she reaches me, where she stops dead in her tracks and awkwardly stares at me like the outlier that I am. I actually had my arms outstretched to accept her too, and she's the one who pulls back. "Oh, hello, Allyson."

She had to have known I'd be here. Ben mentioned this party the first time we met in the hallway at the clinic. Why's she acting so odd? My arms drop at my sides. Maybe that's her "normal," the strange little scientist that she is. "Hi, there."

"What were we all talking about? I don't want to break up the party," Emily says.

"Doing shots, apparently," Seth says, a brainy type, thick glasses, tall and scrawny. He has that mildly exhausted look that screams—*I work my ass off at my smart job so I can provide for my family of five.*

"Oh, I can't do shots," Emily says.

"Not those kinds of shots." Laurel nods in Ally's direction. "Seems you two have a lot in common."

Emily bites her lip at this information, and I couldn't be more curious as to what Laurel is referring to.

A loudness roars around through the gate. "I need help with the keg!" a man yells.

The men run toward a guy I don't recognize with a voice that could shred a mountain. I actually place my hand over my ear at the sound.

"That's Hooch," Cat informs.

"Hooch?" I ask.

"Jaden Hooch," Laurel clarifies.

Emily's lips twist in a way that leads me to believe she doesn't like him much.

The four guys haul a keg of beer and drag a plastic tub filled with ice to the outdoor kitchen area.

"I have spritzers too," Laurel tells me.

"Not drinking right now, but thank you," I say.

Laurel offers me a tight grin and I wonder if I've insulted her. She's the type of woman who would never let you know if you did.

The men are making cavemen sounds like they're struggling over there. "Ben, you tap it. You were always best at that," Zach says.

"Oh, he'll tap it! Ben, *you're so good* at it!" Hooch says, while bending over.

The men bust up laughing and so do the women. I don't find the crude humor funny, and even less so when Ben climbs behind Hooch pretending to mount him.

"Oh, they're just messing around!" Laurel tells me.

"Right." *Animals.*

TWENTY-THREE

EMILY

FRIENDS

Ally seems rather tight. And stuck up, like she doesn't care for Ben's friends one bit. Or Ben, for that matter.

Maybe it's the hormones. The Lupron shots have made my ovaries feel like hardened golf balls taking refuge in my abdomen, and I've already gained weight.

Enlarged ovaries are a side effect of the medication, but I didn't remember it happening the first time I took the shots for my egg extraction. My ovaries are literally weighing me down, and they're so sore and angry, I fear they might bowl right through my pelvis.

I'm sitting beside Seth and Cat at one of the tables, and Cat's rattling on about how they almost had to cancel because their youngest contracted poison ivy, and the babysitter didn't want to catch it, but that it cleared pretty quickly.

Laurel returns with a wine chiller and a bottle of Chablis.

"Hi, ladies... Ben's wife," Hooch says, nonchalantly, as he walks over to greet us. Hooch was the only other person here beside me who missed Ally and Ben's wedding, his absence due to a family funeral.

"Ally," she corrects him.

He nods. Laurel shoots me a sideways glance. And I've just noticed that while Hooch's voice is still large, the rest of him has downsized. He's Hooch—minus about one hundred pounds. "Looking slim there, Hooch," I say. He smiles, awfully proud of himself.

"Oh, are you two not friends on the Gram? Emily probably missed your big transformation a few years ago," Cat deducts.

"Yeah, so I did intermittent fasting and Keto and it changed my fucking life, and now I'm a total babe," Hooch explains.

"Wow. Well, you look great," I blurt out. It sounds like I'm flirting, but I'm really not, and he totally takes it as a come-on, because he hugs me. "Thanks, Emily." And then leaves a sloppy kiss on my cheek. Yuck.

Hooch still isn't anything close to a babe. He has a square jaw that juts out into a strong bulldog resemblance. I'm not sure if it's an underbite, but it does cause him to spit sometimes when he speaks.

Hooch moves around the table to accost Ally next.

"Nice to meet you," she says, extending her hand instead to avoid a hug. Ally doesn't stutter, and she has politely and smartly avoided a Hooch-smooch.

There's an empty seat next to me, so Hooch sits there, and smiles at me, strangely. *Great.*

The appetizers are served next. Laurel has gone all out: fruit salad, chicken kabobs, meat and pepperonis tray, a veggie tray, and some sort of smoked meat on a cracker. Nothing is store bought, my go-to for dinner parties.

Laurel hand prepped it all. I don't know when she finds the time to be so domestic with a full-time job as a senior purchaser for a major clothing company.

Hooch piles some meat and cheese onto his plate and the

only thing I can think about is that he doesn't need any more pepperoni because his breath already reeks like beef jerky.

"So, I hear you two are trying to have a baby," Hooch says to Ben and Ally with absolutely no couth. It's IVF. Something has obviously not gone right with conceiving their child the natural way, and if they wanted to talk about it, they would. Ally's face clouds with disapproval.

"We're trying," Ben says. Ally's arm pulls closer to his, and I just know he's squeezing her hand under the table; the same way he used to squeeze mine. He *really* does love her, and this baby could make or break them.

"You're in good hands," I say to break up the tension.

Hooch makes a stupefied face. "Wait a second... Emily is making your baby?" he asks, exasperated.

Ally is now visibly uncomfortable, shrinking her tall body down into the chair and scouring a piece of celery with her teeth. She doesn't have anything substantial on her plate; a couple pieces of vegetables and fruit, no meat or cheese.

"No, no, I just work with the doctor who will be doing the procedure," I clarify. Damn it, why did I say anything at all? Why do I ever open my mouth?

"Well, that's some crazy shit," Hooch says as he swallows his beer and then goes back to the keg to fill up another cup.

Ally is fanning herself. Even though I want to hate her, she looks so sweet with her medieval braids trailing back behind her black glasses. She's quiet and serious like me too, and I can totally empathize with her right now, because this process is so very stressful.

"There'll be plenty to celebrate next year. We're going to have two baby mommas at the table," Laurel announces.

What the fuck, Laurel?

She probably doesn't want to leave me out of this pre-baby conversation, but she really should.

"Yeah, Em, we heard you're going to have one on your own. You always were a liberated one," Seth remarks.

Seth's comment hangs in the night air like sticky residue while Ben and Ally's internal gears turn to catch up. Ben's appear slightly slower than his wife's.

"Wait... you're doing IVF?" Ally asks. Her face has drained of all its color.

"Yes," I reply meekly. *This has nothing to do with you!*

Yet this has everything to do with your husband.

"Maybe we can have joint birthday parties," Laurel goes on, clapping her hands together.

Please, please stop.

"Thanks, but I don't think that will be possible. I'm using frozen eggs, so I'm most likely way ahead of Ally's schedule. My eggs have already been extracted so—"

"Maybe not. Ally started her shots a while ago in North Carolina," Ben says.

What?

"They're looking at the first week in October for my transfer," Ally adds, a slight smile sneaking up on her face.

And why didn't I know about this? It wasn't in the chart, but I only looked at the quick view, and I was in such shock I didn't do a deep dive. My stomach sinks to the goddamn floor. Laurel might just get her wish.

"That's the same week as my transfer," I announce. Laurel bounces up and down in her chair—she loves drama. Does she want me not to be okay? Would that be entertainment for her? Are Ben and I and our weird IVF-trio-ring like some sick soap opera to her?

These paranoid emotional swings—goddamn hormones!

"You should totally call Lifetime and sell them the movie script. You can't make this shit up," Cat says.

"Well, we need to see how the movie ends before I sell the rights to it," I joke.

All I've done since I've counseled the Holidays is picture our futures. All three of us. It's refreshing, because up until this point, my focus was on the past. It's ironic that the very person who's left me stuck in the Stone Ages for so long is the very same one to bring me back to the present.

"What's to question? The ending will be two beautiful babies with similar birthdays. That's how the credits can close with the two families and the babies with their little party hats on. Oh my God, joint birthday party with you and your ex and your test-tube babies," Laurel muses.

"No one calls them that anymore," I correct her.

But that was one of the Hollywood scenarios I created. Another one was that Ben would have a boy and I would have a girl and they'd fall in love, and we'd finally have the connection that had always been meant for us. Or they'd both be the same gender, star athletes, rivals even, and we'd sneak glances at one another as we cheered for our children to kick each other's asses.

"Whatever. It's just so bizarre and cool. You guys actually have a lot in common after all these years and tonight should be fun." Laurel's so positive all of the time, and I want to believe her.

"Is that a problem? That we're scheduled for the same week as you?" Ben has finally caught on to the conversation, but he probably could tell I wasn't happy about the clinic scheduling.

"No, no, I was just thinking how odd to start your fertility treatment at one clinic and then switch," I lie. It's not what I was thinking at all, but it works as a suitable excuse.

"Well, I loved Dr. Williams, my specialist, but there's actually a very good reason for it. Ben didn't know if he was getting his job until the last minute. I started the treatments, and I was going to stay down there and finish the shots out with my old doctor. I really liked him. But I just couldn't do it. I didn't want to be away from Ben that long, and you know how the treatments are... I certainly didn't want to make that drive or fly in for every doctor's appointment. Being separated from Ben for months just didn't seem reasonable, you know?" she asks.

Silence falls over the group. Laurel gulps loudly as I sit there in pure pain. Ally couldn't have known what she's said is daggers to my heart.

But it is. Ally isn't able to leave Ben for a couple of months.

I left him for six months, and then two or so more years.

And that's the big difference between us, and it's the very reason he belongs with her and not me.

"Totally, he's your husband," I agree. Ease spreads over the group.

It's an omission that if I was married to Ben I would never want to be apart from him either. But the sad part is, I would probably be fine with the separation if it was to elevate my career. Maybe I don't deserve to be with anyone at all. I excuse myself to use the bathroom—where I cry for five seconds—and then stop.

TWENTY-FOUR

EMILY

BREAKDOWN

After my mini-breakdown, there's a lot more drinking. How else am I supposed to make it through the rest of the evening? Hooch has made the announcement he's also found a teaching job in the area and is moving back to the burgh.

At the good news, Ben and Hooch have "*Ohh Arred*" and chest-pumped. Oh joy, the gang is back together again.

As the party moves on and the night grows darker, Hooch's chair has moved closer to mine. The intention here is clear. Nothing would cement our circle more than me coupling with Hooch.

That is *not* happening. Even though Hooch teaches fifth grade science, and is a self-proclaimed "science guy," I can't imagine having a single thing to discuss with him. It's not like my science background makes me even remotely interested in his lessons on the current state of plant life photosynthesis and respiration.

His hand brushes my knee a couple of times, but I've

managed to inch away. Under the enchantment of the Chinese lanterns, Hooch's underbite has gotten smaller, and he hasn't spit on me for a good fifteen minutes, but he's still Hooch.

These hormones are terrible.

There's a scientific scent to human mating called pheromones. I'm sure Hooch has taught a lesson on it. Animals actually have a physical smell they emit into the air to let their potential mates know they're willing and ready. Human beings have pheromones too, and are often unknowingly attracted to an individual's scent.

I cringe at the thought that I can't control mine, and that I'm pumping unnatural substances into my body that're potentially turning him on. *Ack.* It's pitch black out here now except for the glow of the lights, and no one can possibly notice me clenching my legs together beneath the table as if a *Do not enter sign* is strung between them.

We're actually all mingling quite well, and to my disfavor I begin to like Ally the more I get to know her. They've changed the subject of their own children's misbehaviors to future baby names, which is good because I can bring myself back into the conversation.

"I like older names, like Audra and Stella for a girl and Jonah and Caleb for a boy," Ally announces. I approve of her names for Ben's future children, not that she needs my consent, but it pleases me his kids will have traditional names.

"So, what're your names, Em?" Ben asks me.

And I think, how odd of Ben to ask me what I'm planning on naming my children. A long time ago, we decided on Grayson and Liam, but those names were killed and buried the day Ben married another woman.

I fan myself briefly, as if to alleviate the sex smell from my being. "I like Seraphina for a girl and Maddox for a boy," I reveal.

Ben looks slightly disappointed. Not that anyone else would notice, but his smile twitches for just a moment, and I wonder if he expected me to say Grayson and Liam.

"You celebrity whore!" Laurel yells, throwing a piece of cheese at me.

"What?" I ask, swatting the cheese away just in time, flinging it back at her.

"Um, hello, Jennifer Garner's daughter and Angelina Jolie's son," Cat mocks me.

"They're great names," I defend.

"Emily is a complete celebrity gossip addict," Laurel explains to Ally.

Thanks for making me sound like a superficial airhead.

"Those are great names," Ally agrees.

"Don't steal them," I spat.

The words are out of my mouth before I can stop myself, and Ally's eyes pop open like I just said she was a bitch.

"You called them, Em. You've got total dibs," Ben says, rescuing me.

And I can't believe Ben and I are sitting around a table fighting over baby names. If everything goes as planned, and we're both implanted the first week of October, it will be on a Friday. It's just how our schedules run. If both pregnancies take, Ally and I will become pregnant on the exact same day.

Then it will just be a matter of who delivers first.

I sigh at the thought of her birthing her baby an hour before me, and the big name announcement being made, and it will just slaughter me if it's one of *my* baby names. Petty, petty thoughts. "I'm sorry. I think the wine's getting to me." I offer my lame-ass excuse, but Ally doesn't say, "That's okay." No one says a word, and the only one not frowning at me is Hooch, who is drooling instead. It's clearly time for me to leave.

"Well, I think whatever name you guys pick," Hooch says,

"it will make a wonderful addition to Ballyson. Huh, how about it, Ballyson?"

Bad joke. Hurtful joke. Slam to my heart.

There was Kimye (Kim Kardashian and Kayne West) and TomKat (Tom Cruise and Katie Holmes), and much like them, despite the fact they seemed like a good fit at the start, Bemily had parted ways too.

Bemily was what Hooch had playfully named my and Ben's relationship after he'd drunk one too many at a college party we'd all attended, but the name had stuck until graduation. And he now transposed his brief moment of creativity onto Ben and Allyson, and inadvertently brought up our old nickname.

"Yeah, no buddy," Ben comments, lowering his eyes to his empty plate.

Everyone laughs, but it's a low rumble; a quiet punch in the gut to Emily. Again, Ally couldn't have known this might be hurtful to me, so she just kind of side-eyes Hooch.

Hooch has made me feel like garbage, and used celebrity humor to do it, and it hits me at all the wrong angles.

I scoot my chair away from him.

I whisper something unintelligible in Laurel's ear just to get away from the leering bulldog. "Beef jerky."

"What?" she asks.

"Nothing," I whisper back, and she looks at me with a screwed-up face.

"I'm cutting you off soon, but you have to eat a steak first," Laurel demands. "You're my date tonight and I'm treating you to a filet."

Laurel's next course is filets and skewered vegetables that Zach fired up for us on the grill. Ally doesn't eat any of the meat, and I wonder if she's a vegetarian or just super vigilant about her diet. There—she does have a fault. Ben likes a good eater. She's setting her future Audra or Stella up to be anorexic.

"Emily doesn't need you, Laurel. She can get a date any night of the week," Cat says, giving me a wink.

"Uh huh. False. Pittsburgh's ranked one of the worst cities for dating in the entire country." My comment dampens the mood, but it's a fact I know all too well.

"Oh, come on, I doubt you have a hard time getting a date, Emily. Smart, pretty, successful girl like yourself," Hooch flirts, nudging my side.

Don't touch me.

"Do you think I'd be having a kid all by myself if dating didn't suck here," I say a little too bitterly. I notice Ben stop chewing his steak. And Ben *loves* steak.

"If you'll excuse me, I have to use the ladies' room," I say, even though I just went.

Up until now, I've managed to make my choice about being a single mother appear dignified. I am the woman who doesn't need a man. I can do this all on my own. But I just admitted the real reason I'm having a baby all alone is because I'm inept at finding a proper partner.

I take a deep breath as I exit Laurel's powder room, and I'm preparing to return to the party when another pair of black-rimmed, red-tinged eyes meet mine outside the bathroom door.

"Emily, do you have a minute to talk to me in the kitchen?" Ally asks.

Oh, dear God, please don't make me.

"Sure," I sniffle. There's no hiding my swollen eyes under Laurel's incandescent hanging lights. We sit on opposing stools —the granite, galley kitchen island the only thing between us. That, and one last piece of chocolate mousse pie. My mouth salivates.

"What's up?" I ask. I settle into the micro-suede stool.

Ally is visibly upset now, and her extra estrogen is making my extra estrogen weepy, and I don't want to cry. Not in front of her. But I can almost internalize what she's feeling, drink in her desperation for our unfortunate situations. I try to concentrate on the hand-shaved chocolate on top of the pie instead. How does Laurel get the shavings sliced so thin?

"I just want to start off by saying thank you for being so gracious with Ben and me at the hospital. Dr. Batey was our first choice, and we knew you worked at her clinic, but I didn't realize the great extent you would have on our case. And I honestly don't think Ben did either." She pauses, mouth hanging open like she wants to say more.

I'm not sure what she wants from me here. My brief outburst has quelled at the surface as I try to process her intention for this little speech. Every display of human emotion is a moment of inspection for me so I can understand it better.

"You're welcome. It's my job," I comment.

"I know it is, and I realize you're very good at your job. I get that, I do. I've read so much about the importance of the lab and how what goes on in there can really affect the ou–

outcomes." And she begins to cry. And then my chest burns and my eyes prick with tears and I try to focus on those little flecks of chocolate on the cake like they're magic pieces of courage that can see me through this, but it doesn't work and the tears spill over onto my cheeks too.

"But I just want to make sure you're okay with this whole situation, and you've made your peace with Ben, because I need to know my babies will receive the best care," she manages to get out through hiccupping sobs.

The little pieces of chocolate are a blurry, fudgy mess now, and my cheeks are wet with sadness. I hate this more than when I used to sit on my living room floor and stare at old college photos of Ben and imagine what she might look like.

It's hard to hate someone you can't see, but now I see her, and I don't hate her at all. Ally has done her research. She knows how important my role is to the conception of her child, and out of all the women who've come through my clinic who

I've wished gave me that kind of recognition, I don't want it to be her.

"Ally, I'm happy for Ben, and I've only ever wanted the best for him. He should be a dad." I choke on the words.

"I know. I know you do. It's just, out there you sounded mad you hadn't found anyone yet, and I need to make sure you're okay with this," she admits.

This is all my damn fault. Nothing that comes out of my mouth can ever be right. Ally just clued me into the fact that everyone at the table probably thinks the same thing—I'm still hung up on Ben.

"It's got nothing to do with Ben, I promise." *But it does.* "I will take care of your embryos, your future babies, like they're my own. You have my word." *And I will.*

Ally smiles, and I know I've somehow made my blunder outside better.

"Is everything okay in here?" I hear Ben bellow from the screen door that has just slid open. "What in the world?" he asks, taking a step toward the hormonal duo of crying women hovering over the chocolate pie.

"Get out, Ben, we're on estrogen!" Ally yells. And I laugh. He backpedals with the most confused expression on his face, and it's fun for a single moment that Ally and I have an inside joke Ben can't share.

"I can't take it anymore," Ally says. She plunges a fork into the pie.

"You better be sharing that," I demand.

She throws a plastic fork across the table and we devour the last piece of pie as a very confused Ben makes his way back outside.

"Do not. Go. In. There," I hear him say from outside as we finish up the whipped cream.

Allyson Holiday and I are laughing and crying and devouring pie together, and I could've never imagined in a million years I would befriend Ben's wife. Then again, he's married another version of me; how could I refuse her?

Instead I made a promise to create her a child, and a very special second promise to Ben to do the same.

A promise I will keep.

TWENTY-FIVE

ALLY

SAME

Laurel didn't have monogrammed gifts for us, but she did let the cat out of the bag, and I can't help but think she did it on purpose. Ben doesn't bother to ask the question—*So what did you think of my friends?*

He sits quietly in the driver's seat, fiddling with the satellite radio, as if any song could appropriately be fitting for *my ex-girlfriend and wife are getting pregnant in the same week.* He should at least switch to a country music channel if that's the mood he's trying to set.

Finally, he dares to look at me. "What?" he asks. "I didn't know, Ally."

"That seems to be your defense for everything lately. *I didn't know I'd get the job, and realize that meant uprooting our lives. I didn't know Emily would be handling our case. I didn't know Emily would be going through IVF the very same week we are!*"

He sighs. "It's crazy. I'm sorry, but it seemed like you two were getting along in the kitchen. Emily could probably use someone to commiserate with. She's going through this process all alone."

"That's her choice. Which brings me to my next question. Why did she decide to do this now? Right now. Those eggs have been frozen for... what..."

"Eight years," he says.

I snap my mouth shut. "How do you—"

"She got sick eight years ago. That's when she froze them. Before her treatment."

"Why do you know that?" Have they been keeping in touch? Like Sebastian and me have been... keeping in touch?

Ben sighs. "It was hard learning she'd gotten sick when she moved home. I remember..."

There was an undercurrent between Ben and Emily tonight that I didn't like. It would make me feel one hundred and fifty percent better if Ben had broken up with Emily way back when, but that's not how it happened. It's hard to picture Emily dumping Ben to gallivant around Europe, but then again, I didn't know her then. Perhaps she was more lively than the subdued semi-robot who spits out clinical factoids like she's reciting poetry to herself.

"I might be traveling home to visit my mother after the next checkup," I declare.

Ben doesn't flinch. "I can't come with you. School's just started. I can't take a day yet."

"That's okay." Because then I can catch up with Sebastian and you'll be miles away. "I just need to see her."

And human beings who make sense and don't act like they're stuck in a fifteen-year time warp.

"I think you'll feel differently about everything after the transfer," Ben says. "Emily is going to make this happen for us." I don't understand how he's so sure.

It's interesting—Ben telling me how I'll feel.

This man has no idea how much worse it will be for me

after the transfer. "Ben, what makes you think this pregnancy will be any different to the others? I never had trouble getting pregnant. I had trouble staying pregnant."

Ben opens his mouth to speak and then shuts it. Did he really think IVF was the cure-all here? "Well, they're going to analyze your eggs and the embryos before they're implanted. That's gotta help our chances."

He does think this process is a silver bullet. And our lab-created baby is the secret weapon. "What if that's not the issue?" I ask.

He sighs again. "I just wish you'd be more positive."

"And I wish you'd understand how hard it is to be positive under the circumstances. I miss home. I'll feel better after I see my mother."

"This is your home now," Ben says. "Those people tonight welcomed you in like you were one of them. We didn't have that type of circle of friends in Charlotte. We never went out with friends." Ben says this as if he's been at a loss for years, yet it's the first I'm hearing about it. I'm guessing tonight just reminded him of what he's been missing out on.

"They don't seem like my kind of people," I say. "Laurel is a bit catty. Why would she blast her best friend's baby news? Cat just watches everyone like she's better than them. Hooch has no manners. Seth and Zach are okay, but immature. And you're immature when you're with them." It's like I can't help myself. I swear these shots they're giving me at the clinic have truth serum in them.

"That's about the most judgmental thing I've ever heard you say. *Wow*. So, you really hate them?"

"I don't hate them. I just don't understand them. Or you when you're with them. You're like a different person." One I don't like...

Ben shakes his head. "Laurel asked me to share her number with you, and for you to reach out. She means well. She just gets overexcited about things. She really worked hard on her party. To welcome you. Can't you try a little harder instead of giving up after one night?"

I look away and think—*yes, she did.* Perhaps I am being unreasonable. "And what if I try harder and I'm still not happy here?" I ask.

"Then we move back to Charlotte," he says. "I'm not going to make you stay here if you're truly miserable."

"Really?" I ask, feeling a million times lighter already.

"Yes. But you have to at least try."

"Deal."

I find myself at a local Target with Laurel Quinn. She's playing the role of my personal shopper, but the things she's picking out are giving me absolute anxiety. "Oh, these bottles are the best, but you'll want to register for a bunch of different kinds because you won't know what the baby likes, and neither will he or she!" Laurel laughs as if this is hysterical.

I make a cringe-smile, because we're putting the carriage way before the baby here. But I have a prescription for what I have to do to get back to North Carolina, and humoring Laurel is one of those things, so here we are... in the baby aisle at Target, preemptively placing items on a registry for a child who doesn't exist yet.

Laurel seems jazzed, though. "Ooh, how about a rock and glide? They didn't have those when my kids were little." She points at an infant seat on a pedestal that vibrates when you push a button.

"Sure," I say, imagining a real swing set beneath my poplar tree at home instead of this prefabricated one.

Laurel's phone rings, and she lifts her finger up at me to *hold on.* "Hey, Emily..." Laurel sounds hesitant to speak to her friend, and I know it's because she's with me. So... Laurel didn't tell her we were going shopping together. The jury is still out on this girl. Is she trying to foster true friendships or cause trouble? There's something about her that makes me not sure.

"What's not right?" Laurel asks.

Emily said, *That's not right.*

I heard her.

What's she referring to—me and Laurel, her bestie, shopping together, or making a registry for an event that isn't happening yet? I can't say I'd disagree with her on either front.

"Yes, she's aware of the chances..." Laurel says with a scoff.

My fingers wrap tightly around the shopping basket. Emily thinks I'm an idiot, and that I don't understand the very real possibility that this might not happen for me. Like I'm some kind of fluffy, head-in-the-clouds woman who believes everything will be just fine. I'm not that girl.

"We should go for yours next week—"

And she's cut off by her friend. As she should be.

This is ridiculous.

I see a pair of long, drapey pants and think about how nicely they'll go over my swimsuit when I'm in Miami Beach—with Sebastian. Ben has no idea how much these forced friendships in this stressful environment make me want to flee south, way farther than North Carolina.

I'll run. Just watch. I'll run so fast your head will spin.

TWENTY-SIX

EMILY

CONTROL

I am officially no longer in control of my body or my emotions, and I feel like someone needs to restrain me for the next couple of weeks. It concerns me, what kind of monster I might evolve into once the transfer is complete. Hopefully some of the stress of IVF will be alleviated once I become pregnant, and I can focus primarily on the baby.

With any luck, my body will recuperate with its natural hormones, versus the synthetic ones I've been juicing up with. And then, perhaps, I can reach some sort of steady state with this emotional roller coaster I've been on since I graduated from Lupron to Lupron plus estrogen and progesterone.

There's the nagging thought of Ally Holiday, and knowing she's going through the same thing, and that she has Ben beside her to weather the storm. She has someone to tell her it's all right when there's no certainty that everything will be okay.

Chocolate mousse and tears only go so far.

Ally and I had a moment that evening, but every day since I've been riddled with guilt and uneasiness. I lied to her, but how could I tell her I want nothing more than to be in her infertile shoes, standing next to Ben, preparing for his first child—our first child.

I think my friends know it too. And to make matters worse, ever since Ben has moved back, it's like Zach has grown a new attachment called "Ben." It's a rare occasion when I speak to Laurel on the weekend, and they don't have the Holidays with them—like today at Target.

How can Laurel be targeting with Ally?!

Why did he have to move back and mess up my life?

At first I thought it was a good thing, but not anymore. There are some days I still wonder if I'm doing the right thing, having this child on my own.

While safely in the confines of the laboratory, Ralphie asks me, "So, when's your transfer?"

I'm peering through a microscope. "I'm going to thaw four of my eight eggs, and see how many made the freeze." Batey wanted me to have two extractions—*the more you reap, the greater the potential harvest*—but that would have meant prolonging chemotherapy even more, so I opted for one, which yielded a total of eight eggs.

"Good idea. You have to bank that at least two will make it," Ralphie says.

Once I found that lump in my breast, I just wanted it out. It was hard to think about the future when I didn't know if I'd survive the present. My mother was wary to even let me do one extraction. She was worried the cancer might metastasize to other areas in the time I had to wait to have my fertility procedure, and so was I. Now, looking back, I kind of wish I'd taken Batey's advice and done two rounds.

I've got eight of my own eggs—and then it's Game Over.

"Probably three," I say, optimistically.

"You're right, probably three. I'm excited for you." Ralphie beams.

"Thanks, Ralphie, that makes two of us."

"We have to go to Target and get you registered," Laurel chimes into my cell on the way home from work.

The leaves are starting to change, and even though I'm trapped in rush hour traffic on the Boulevard of the Allies, I can see the autumn-colored treetops of Mount Washington inviting me home, winking at me as the foliage comes into view.

"Laurel, you really need to calm down. I'm not even pregnant yet." I grip my leather steering wheel tighter. Doesn't she realize what these questions can do to someone in my position? It's like picking out your wedding china before he pops the question.

The exit for the Liberty Bridge is coming into view, but some asshole who hasn't properly waited her turn to merge is trying to cut me off from the right. I'm so angry, I want to side-swipe her with my SUV, and knock her right into the guardrail. She's still coming with her incessant flashing red turn signal.

And I am still not letting her in.

Screech. And she almost bites the guardrail.

Violent honking follows, accompanied by a nice hand gesture I can clearly see in my rearview mirror.

Wait your turn like everyone else! I've had to wait forever.

"Is everything okay, Em?" Laurel asks.

Clearly, these hormones should come with a warning label.

"Oh, just a little scuffle between me and an aggressive motorist on the Liberty Bridge," I say, although I'm pretty certain there's now an accident behind me.

I don't dare look, because even though the other driver was in the wrong, I could've prevented that accident if I just let the female motorist in my lane. *Not today, Karen.*

My aggression came down to more than road rage and

hormones. I've had my fill of doing people favors, and making allowances and promises to the ones who don't deserve them.

Why am I making promises to your wonderful wife, Ben? I left you, but you didn't wait for me either. Excuse me for wanting a fulfilling career.

"Oh, don't you love it? I hate merging onto that bridge. Well, looksey, even if this round doesn't take, you've got other frozen chickies in the freezer, right?"

True—my best friend does pay attention to me when I speak.

"You can allow yourself to get excited, Em."

"Excitement can lead to profound disappointment. And since when do you call me, Em?" *That's Ben's name for me. And Ralphie's name for me. Only they have rights to it.*

"So, this *is* about Ben?"

"No, it's just that you never called me that before he moved back."

"It's catchy," she explains.

Not true. The name "Em" isn't catchy, it's the way Ben says it that's catchy. Ben's exuberance is contagious, and when he and Laurel are in the same room their personalities play off each other. She's feeding off of him the way she used to in college, and there's no way for me to explain this to her without it sounding accusatory, because it's totally innocent.

"Right, well, if you could just call me by the name you've used for the last ten years, that would be preferable."

"Sorry... Geez. Just before you get more mad at me, the poor girl had no idea what to buy for a baby and she has no friends here," Laurel concedes.

Now I am the one cutting people off as I veer into the far right lane of the bridge.

And... more violent honking.

"Emily, should you be driving?"

"So, are you two like BFFs now?" I ask.

"No, no. Ben asked me for help. She didn't ask, and I honestly think she felt a little awkward. It's not like we sat around and painted each other's toenails afterward or anything." Laurel laughs.

"Was Ben there?" I don't know why it matters, but it does.

"No, he was busy doing things at their new townhome. She picked out this cute jungle theme. I already bought it a monkey! I'm all done having babies, so I'm sorry if I got excited about the monkey, but he's yellow, and he winds up and he sings a song, and—"

Ugh, Jungle theme? How unoriginal.

"And what?" I ask.

"I sort of bought you one too."

"You bought me a monkey?"

"I bought your baby a monkey."

"A baby that's not in my uterus yet?" I ask, annoyed.

"Yes, I'm sorry. You don't have to accept my gift," Laurel says.

I don't answer her. She's going crazy too. Someone should lock us all up—the whole lot of us. My emotions are so uncontrollable it frightens me. That woman could have died in the car crash back there and the only thing I could think was, *Good for her, she tried to cut me off.*

"Why don't you hold onto the monkey until the baby's born." I sound glib, because I am. My best friend is cheating on me with my ex-boyfriend's wife. This sucks. My hands are sweating and the ribbed steering wheel cover of my Land Rover is imprinting into my palms.

McArdle Roadway shoots straight up the side of the inclined hill to Mount Washington, and I shouldn't be going so fast, but Laurel has me all revved up. I reach the top of the hill and the light turns red. I slam on my brakes and my whole body jerks forward, making my phone hit the dash and tumble to the ground.

"*Emily. Emily,*" my Bluetooth shouts.

Scientists are structured people. Our protocols have specified controls, validations. This thing with Ally and me suddenly feels like some sort of competition—or an experiment—and I've lost all control.

"I have to go!" I shout. I end the call. The traffic light changes to green and I turn right.

Her excuse about Ally having no one else is crap. Ben has two sisters who live in the area and could've taken the time to bond with their sister-in-law. Ben doesn't have to ask my best friend for help. And my so-called best friend could've told him "no," made up an excuse—any excuse.

The truth is that Laurel is enjoying playing expert-baby-shower-shopper. She loves babies, and she relishes schooling people on how to do things they don't know how to do. She's complicit in all of this.

It's possible Ally isn't as much like me as I thought. Baby décor is the last thing on my mind. The only matter of importance should be a successful transfer, followed by a positive pregnancy test, and then the detection of a heartbeat.

After that, let's celebrate.

But until then this all seems preemptive and supercilious. Ally has to have done the research, so this doesn't make sense. Has she lost it, even worse than me?

I've seen IVF not work for no apparent reason on a weekly basis for the last nine years of my life. How can she be so sure hers is going to take?

These questions are goading at me as I drive my car too roughly into my tiny garage spot.

I text Laurel.

Made it home okay. Just curious. Is Ally fully aware of the possibility of failure with IVF?

Laurel texts me right back.

Oh thank God. I was in my car, getting ready to come over there and make sure you were still alive. 🩶🩶🩶😌. *Ally just said she's been praying on it and has faith God will bless them with a baby*

Ah... the God card.

I've seen religious people like Ally use IVF as a last measure when everything else failed, and those were the ones most crushed when God still wouldn't bless them with a child. It's like they took it personally, as if God didn't answer their prayers because he didn't think they deserved a baby.

Marybeth, Ben's mother, is probably over the moon about Ally and her beliefs. All of her children have biblical names, and even though she never quibbled at my lack of devotion, I think it deeply bothered her.

It isn't that I don't believe in God entirely. I do believe there's something spiritual going on up there. It's just that I have a stronger belief in science and evolution. Factual evidence I can see, touch, and smell—control. Although, right about now, nothing seems in my control, and I decide I could use a little prayer too.

If Ally can pray this baby into existence, maybe I can pray her and Ben out of mine.

TWENTY-SEVEN

EMILY

MIX

Monday

October greets Pittsburgh with what the weatherman calls a wintry mix. My extra hormones don't like being cold, and they're cursing especially hard at his forecast.

There's a lot more on my mind today than the weather. I couldn't sleep last night, because the week ahead will be a tough one. Ally is having her eggs extracted today. The number and quality of eggs retrieved will be a huge determining factor in the outcome and success of her in vitro fertilization.

Incubation tray number three has been waiting patiently for future baby Holiday's arrival. This week feels so different than the others.

Every day I appraise the stainless steel, refrigerator-like incubator as just another device at work. It looks like nothing more than a stand-up freezer with ten pock-marked rows inside. Except, unlike a refrigerator, it's far from cold. The temperature is set at 36.5 degrees Celsius, 100% humidity, 5% CO_2 concentration—nice and toasty for the chicks to thrive. Most other clinics kept their baby brewers at 37 degrees Celsius, but given my grad school education, I'm insistent on the slightly lower temperature.

If I'm ill or on vacation, Dr. Batey cancels appointments.

She doesn't trust anyone else to work with her patients' samples.

Ralphie isn't in the lab yet. I've gotten there extra early despite the poor weather. I pat the fertility incubator lovingly. This week it will house the lives of Ben's future baby, and mine, and it's so very important that it does its job.

The lab is spotless, but I take the time to wipe it down again. There cannot be any contaminates—not a speck or germ to muck up the process. The future life of Ben and Ally's baby depends on it. And so does mine.

Ally is probably awakening from sedation now. Dr. Batey's team have retrieved six oocytes from Ally's aging follicles, which isn't so great a yield. Eight to twelve is considered a good harvest in the world of egg extraction.

With more care than usual, I place the oocytes in their own individual laboratory petri dishes. A nutrient mixture awaits them and mimics the environment of Ally's fallopian tubes.

These little guys aren't just cells, they're potential babies. If I think about each specimen that way, it makes me a better embryologist. Not only does it give my job a real sense of purpose, but it also makes me constructively paranoid, as if I'm potentially committing murder if I make a misstep.

Ally's eggs will need four to six hours before I can add Ben's sperm to them, taking one of my ex-boyfriend's little swimmers and injecting it directly into Ally's egg. There are other procedures, but Dr. Batey has decided on this one after Ally's history of repeated miscarriages, and it's a great option now that her retrieval has yielded so few eggs.

"How're your eggs?" Ralphie asks, as he slinks around the corner.

"Oh!" I yell.

"Yo, Em, it's just me," Ralphie says.

"Don't sneak up on me, especially not this week," I scold.

Ralphie puts his hands up and smirks. "Sorry. I'll sure be a helluva lot happier to work with you once this is over."

"I don't know about that. You haven't met pregnant Emily yet," I advise.

"Neither have you. Don't go setting yourself up to be one of those bat-shit crazy pregnant women already," he says.

I grin back at my comical assistant. "Well, judging from my wayward moods at this juncture, I'd be worried if I were you."

"I can handle it. You've never met my ex. You make her look like Snow White."

"That's comforting." Sarcasm rings from my voice.

"So, did you get here early to take out your stash or what?" Ralphie presses.

"My hatchlings are defrosting as we speak in the nice little warm bath I've prepared for them. I came in last night to take them out so I could make the Friday schedule. Batey wouldn't come in on Saturday," I explain.

I didn't want to be one day behind *her*; always the girl one step behind Allyson Holiday.

"I can't believe your highness wouldn't make an exception for you," Ralphie quips.

"Yeah, she kind of owes me one, don't ya' think?" I ask.

"Ha. Far more than a single Saturday." He's so right. I need Ralphie's young humor in my life.

"Well, she wants to make sure it's her who's handling the implantation, and she's going out of town Saturday. She doesn't want to let anyone else be responsible for the insertion of my little darlings." I know the way we talk about the samples sounds creepy. Ralphie and I are the only ones who speak about our clinical procedures in such terms of endearment. But today, they really are mine. And Ally's. And Ben's.

I take a deep breath. It's time to inject Ben's sperm into Ally's eggs.

Fresh sperm samples are collected on the same day as the egg retrieval, a timely process. Except, when I reach for Ben's specimen, there's nothing there. There's a slot for the container on the tray labeled "Holiday," but the little plastic cup with his sperm is nowhere to be found.

"Ralphie?"

"Yes, ma'am," Ralphie answers.

"Where's the Holiday sperm sample? It should've been delivered sometime this morning after Ally's retrieval."

Ralphie looks at me confusedly. It has been a busy day. There're ten embryo transfers scheduled for Friday, and I've spent the morning using the Microsort machine for the Amstead case. The dye in the Microsort machine lights up the X (female) sperm brighter than the Y (male) sperm, because X chromosomes have about 2.3% more DNA.

I joked with Ralphie that it wasn't shocking that females had more DNA from the jump.

The machine successfully sorted enough male sperm for his sample, but it's a new, and therefore time-consuming process, and I haven't really taken a look at my afternoon work. A welcome distraction from my own thawing eggs sitting only a few feet away from me in their warming bath.

"I–I don't know where it is." Ralphie blanches. I must have turned an extra shade of white myself, because Ralphie never makes mistakes, and I especially can't afford him to make one today.

I *promised* Ben I wouldn't screw this up. He broke a window for me, risked getting arrested, because I wasn't tall enough to bust into Professor Cook's house myself. The trajectory of my life might be totally different if he'd never found that pill bottle.

I would've never made it to Europe. The incident happened my senior year. Certainly, I'd be held up with a trial or at least mandated to remain in the U.S.

I would've never studied at Cambridge. I... would've never broken up with Ben. I wonder if he thinks about it. The consequences of the "favor" he did for me. And if he will hold it against me now if I don't come through for him.

Ralphie is on the phone in an instant. His look of panic turns to stark amusement, and I can't believe there could be a bit of humor in this situation.

"Uh, um, okay." He snort-laughs. "And what do you want me to tell Emily?"

"Uh huh. Whew, we thought I'd misplaced it." Ralphie sighs.

He hangs up and turns around to face me with a look I can only describe as tortured amusement.

"So, that, um missing sample, that was from your ex-man, right?" Ralphie asks, puffing his cheeks out, trying to conceal a laugh that's threatening to bust at the seams.

"Yes, what the hell is going on? Where's the sample?" I ask, frantically. There's a very specific way I do my procedures. In this instance, I don't like the eggs to wait more than six hours in the petri dish before they're injected with the sperm and it's now nearing the six-hour mark.

"Your boy wasn't able to give a sample," Ralphie reveals. Then, he lets out a rip of a laugh. "Bawaha!"

I chew on my cheek, trying not to join him. This is preposterous. Ben is the most hypersexual man I've ever met. He once bent me over in the coatroom at the theater where he worked because libraries are too cliché and he wanted to do it in a public place. Was the small porn room they provided for the men too much for him? I couldn't believe it.

"Well, he needs to produce, these eggs can't just sit here like this," I panic.

"Maybe you should, uh, go help him along," Ralphie jokes.

"*Ralphie.*"

"Emily, this is hysterical."

"It's not," I say. It wasn't the first time I've seen this happen, but it's been a while.

The other two patients who've failed to produce a sample had decent excuses. The one guy was a recent prostate cancer survivor trying to use IVF because his sperm was compromised from the chemo and he only had one of his testicles.

The other was a nervous dude who used too much of his anti-anxiety medication beforehand and couldn't get aroused. Both of the women were livid with their husbands and Dr. Batey refused them implantation on the day she promised.

If I was particular about my procedural process, Dr. Batey was maniacal, and she made exceptions for no one.

The phone rings in the lab as I stand with my hands pressed to my sides. Ralphie laughs silently, jumping up and down mouthing, *Oh my God.* I pick up the phone, but it's just to make it stop ringing. I really don't want to talk to anyone.

"This is Emily," I say.

"Emily, it's Tessa."

Tessa is the nurse who would be on the hospital floor with Dr. Batey today, assisting with extractions.

"Yes," I answer.

"There's a patient here you counseled who's requesting your presence," Tessa says in a hushed tone.

"Who?" I ask.

"Allyson Holiday, do you know her?" she asks.

"Yes, she's... a friend of mine," I explain. What is going on? Why does Ally want to see me?

"She's asking for you. She wants to see you. She said she has some questions. Do you think you can break away for a minute?"

Ally can't possibly want to talk to me about Ben's inability to get off in a plastic cup. It's probable she doesn't even know he couldn't produce a sample. He would be wise not to share that information with her on the day she's been placed under anesthesia and had her ovaries probed for viable eggs. Any woman who's been pumped full of hormones for weeks, and put through that invasive procedure, would be unsympathetic to Ben's hardship right now.

"I guess... I'll be down shortly." I hang up the phone and stare at it.

"What is it, Em?" Ralphie asks, concerned. I delicately place the phone on the receiver.

"Mrs. Holiday would like to see me."

Ralphie busts up laughing again.

"Ralphie, this is not funny." I'm practically crying now. This isn't going well at all.

"I'm so sorry. I'm sorry, Emily, but it is kind of funny. I'm going to stop laughing now. I don't want to upset you. But hey, Em, your guy, um, Mr. Holiday? Did he have, uh, issues getting his soldier to stand to attention, if you know what I—"

"No, Ralphie. He's an artist. He was spontaneous, even."

"Then, maybe you should go downstairs and paint him a mural or something so he can get it done." Ralphie is full-on snorting now. I can just envision him drinking with his buddies later in his apartment, telling this story.

"I have to go to the procedure floor," I say.

"Does she know?" Ralphie ask.

"I don't know."

"Well, are you going to tell her?"

"I don't know."

"Emily, you don't have to go. This is not your job. Let Batey deal with it."

"I don't want Batey to know. Don't tell Batey," I plead.

"Why?" Ralphie asked.

"Because Ben's going to deliver this sample today. He has to," I say.

"Gentle Ben, eh?" Ralphie pops off again.

"Call the nursing station for his sample, Ralphie. Do you hear me? Tell them the implantation depends on it and that it's timely!"

"Okay, will do," he says.

"Oh shit, I have to go." I'm sweating as I leave the lab. I take off my gloves and use the bathroom to wash my hands and clean my glasses before I visit Ally.

I punch the button on the elevator, and am almost hit in the face with a new baby balloon. I'm reminded that I work in an actual women's hospital where surgeries are performed and children are born. This idea escapes me some days and weeks when I'm really sucked into my lab work, totally behind the scenes.

When I arrive, Ally is propped up in her hospital bed, her dark hair pulled up in a bun on top of her head. Her black glasses are fastened on her face and her eyes look groggy and half-closed behind them.

"I told her not to call you," says an older brunette I can only assume is Ally's mother.

"It's okay," I say. "Ally, what is it?"

"It's Ben. He came here and stayed with me until they put me under, and he promised me he'd be here when I woke up, and Ben never breaks promises—" she starts.

No, he doesn't.

"I haven't seen him," I say.

"I thought maybe there was a chance he went to see you, or you'd at least heard from him or had seen him in the hospital.

His phone is going straight to voicemail, and he never turns it off. I'm a little worried," she admits, dazedly.

Ally is coming off heavy sedatives, but she seems really nervous beneath her shrouded sleepiness.

"No, I have no idea where he is," I say.

Although, I have a slight idea.

Our other gray room is loaded with porn, hand lotion, and really bad art hanging on the walls. Maybe that's the turnoff. Those awful displays on the wall.

We were given a brief tour of the sperm bank when I came to work here, and one photograph of a black and white half-opened rose in a flimsy black frame came to mind. It left me wondering about the color of the rose. It was a poor photograph to begin with, but who takes a picture of that type of beautiful flower in black and white?

"I told her he probably lost track of time," her mother began and then seemed to lose her words. "But it's been a while now." She sighs.

"I'm not sure what to tell you. He hasn't contacted me."

I realize I'm doing very little to comfort Ally, but I really need to get out of that hospital room and back to my lab. Hopefully, Ben will have produced something by then, and this can all be resolved quickly. But if not, someone needs to give the guy some encouragement, because if he blows this, his wife will never forgive him. We need a fresh sample. Like now.

"So, everything looks okay, though?" Ally asks, fear laced in her jumbled words. Tears pool in her eyes like an oasis of hope waiting to be realized, and for every bit of nervousness her body language can't convey, her facial expression is doing it for her now.

"What do you mean?" I ask, clueless.

"My eggs. Did I get enough? Do they look good?"

I haven't realized until now that Ally has a stack of papers on the tray table next to her. More research, it appears.

"Oh..." I stall.

"I just read about the conditions in the lab and the techs and the embryologists playing the biggest role in the success of the procedure. The doctor is basically just the courier. The one who delivers the embryo that you produce in your lab," she says. She is my favorite person in the whole world in that moment for saying that. I wish more people saw my job that way.

"Yes, it all looks good so far," I lie, because she's stroked my ego in just the right way. It's also necessary to hide the truth because her husband and his sperm are missing. And I lie because I hadn't taken even the slightest peak at her eggs because there's no point until they've sat for a while.

And most of all, I don't reveal all the tiny details, because if I told her she yielded a less than average number she might have a complete mental collapse.

"Oh, good." She sighs.

My stomach clenches at the ticking clock on the wall. It's past the six-hour mark. I need to get back to my lab. I have to get ahold of Ben's sample.

"Okay, well, I really need to go back to work. I'll let Ben know to come see you right away if I bump into him. You rest up." I advise.

"I'm sorry I called you down here, Emily. I just wanted to let you know I trust you with our babies. I trust you, Emily," she says in a low voice, laying her head back down on the pillow and closing her eyes. Her mouth seems to run dry, raspy. She's asleep in an instant.

Her mother shoos me gently with her hand, letting me know it's okay for me to leave the room. One hand flap, and I'm out of there.

TWENTY-EIGHT

EMILY

Monday Afternoon

"Well?" I ask Ralphie as I throw my white lab coat back over my body. Ally's words, *I trust you, Emily*, are haunting me into action.

Why can't she just hate me for being her husband's ex-girl-friend like every other hot-blooded woman in the world? My feelings of obligation to Ally are way stronger than they should be. But I do not like to disappoint people who are counting on me, and especially at work.

"It just arrived. Your man pulled through," Ralphie says, pointing to a plastic cup of sperm labeled—*Holiday*. Ralphie leans back in his chair, hands entwined behind his head, grin spread across his face. He and I will have a good laugh about this someday, but today is not the day.

"Thank God. There's still hope. You didn't tell Batey, right?"

"Nope." Ralphie is still cheesing.

"Stop that."

"What?" he asks.

"That," I say, pointing to his smug face. "Okay, I have to get to work."

It's well past two o'clock now.

"Even though today has been very entertaining, do you mind if I bail? I went through all of the charts and labeled the samples. My daughter has a basketball game tonight, and it's out of town," Ralphie says.

"Do your thing. I'm going to be a sperm-injecting queen for the rest of the day." I wipe the sweat off my brow, wash and glove my hands, and then begin to prep my station. Temporary relief floods my body.

"That would sound so fucked-up if we didn't do what we did. I mean, because a lot of ladies in town could tell you, that I am, in fact, a sperm-injecting king." Ralphie chuckles.

I crack a smile. "Yeah, yeah. Get out of here," I yell.

I'm all alone in the lab now, and anxious to transform these eggs into beautiful embryos. Beautiful Holiday embryos. All brown hair, and brown eyes, and wide smiles, and some Garner-like dimples if they're really lucky.

But I decide to check on my eggs first.

Placing them under the microscope makes me extremely nervous.

How many have survived the freeze? The statistics for survival is around seventy-five percent, so I'm hoping I have at least three good eggs from my thaw of four.

The first egg calms my nerves. It's absolutely perfect—gorgeously round with no dark imperfections. The zona, or outside barrier of the egg, is of ideal thickness. It looks like a lovely little, clearly colored circle with a rubber band skimming its outside perimeter. When I discuss my work with nonclinical people, I describe the zona as the shell of the egg. It holds all of the cells in their place until it's time for them to multiply and grow.

The rest of my eggs look identical to the first one under the microscope. I couldn't be more pleased. They've all survived!

Survivor. It's a constant whisper in my ear. I am a survivor, and my eggs are survivors too.

Their cell division isn't quite where I want it to be for sperm injection yet, so I place them back in their lab dish. A couple more hours and they'll be ready for the architect's fine seed. Future baby Daugherty might be a builder, or a scientist, and will most likely have blue eyes. Hopefully, the architect's eyes are a prettier shade than my gray-blues.

Emotion sweeps over me, making me take hold of the laboratory table. My chest tightens at the thought of what's going to occur in the next couple of hours. I've been so overwhelmed with other people's baby drama I haven't gotten to enjoy any of my own.

I am creating my baby today. With my own hands. *Oh my God.*

Tawny volunteered to handle my sample, but I won't dare let anyone else touch it.

The inspection of Ally's eggs is next.

I'm more petrified to look at her eggs than my own. There's been so much pressure on me to get this right, and Ben's little missing sample scare has me unhinged. He's a man who literally crawled over broken glass for me. I have to do the same, whatever it takes.

My hands sweat beneath their latex as I place them under the microscope. They're warm and sticking to the gloves in an unnatural way. It's like my body can sense danger, or maybe it's just my nerves.

I see the first of Ally's eggs and I'm immobilized. I shut my eyes, hoping I'm imagining it. I hold my breath at the nightmare beneath the scope, and silently wail—at Ally's rotten egg. *Shit*.

I quickly pull myself together, right myself on the stool, and mentally prepare myself to take a look at the others. *It's only one. Come on.*

My breath is unsteady as I erratically examine the rest of her sample. And I cry out loud.

Thankfully nobody else is there to hear me. I freeze again, but my body shakes in place like a leaf caught in an ice storm. "No, no, no! Why, why, why?" I say to myself, and to the God Ally has prayed so hard to; the same one who's just let her down.

None of Ally's eggs are viable.

The majority of them have broken zonas, their insides spilling out the sides like insufficient chromosomal floodgates. The cells in the oocytes will never grow or multiply, because they've arrested before they had the chance. The other two are marred with dark spots which indicate severe abnormalities. Forget day three or five. They haven't made it through day one.

I have never seen such poor-quality eggs in a woman who's under the age of forty. It's an absolute tragedy, and something no amount of science can ever fix.

I check her file feverishly for something to make sense of all of this. It's amazing Ally was able to get pregnant at all.

Perhaps, at one time, Ally had somewhat viable eggs, but once they became embryos they weren't strong enough to sustain a full pregnancy, or even make it through the first trimester. Now, she doesn't have any viable eggs, and no chance of forming a healthy embryo.

My heart rips in half for her thinking about what this couple must've gone through with her other pregnancies. How much loss they've experienced already. This is supposed to be their solution. My renowned clinic, my skills, my lab, are supposed to be their saving grace. And I've failed them.

Tears run down my face and collect in my open mouth. Of all the people to have this happen to, in all the labs in the world, it has to be Ben and Ally, and it had to be mine.

My feelings of pity and injustice quickly turn black and angry. I promised Ben I would make this happen for them. He supported me in my worst hours. I was so desperate to get that pill bottle out of Cook's house, I'd looked online for criminal hired hands.

Not to mention, I lied to Ally and her mother.

There's a witness to my lies. Ally was sedated and I could've told her she heard me wrong when I said her eggs were all right or that I misunderstood her question, but there was a very conscious party there beside her who heard every false promise I made—Ally's mother.

I made Ally promises I can't keep. She'll blame me even though it isn't my fault. I told Ally her eggs looked great. She'll research the hell out of this failed procedure and discover I lied to her, and then she'll assume I did something to sabotage her pregnancy.

Perhaps there will even be a lawsuit or criminal investigation into why I said her eggs looked fine when the majority of them are in fact dead, probably two hours after they made it into the petri dish, and the others malformed. Ben could pile on and say it isn't the first time I performed an assisted death and told no one—and good Lord, what if they interviewed my mother on the topic?

My intentions were good. They're always good. But how can I ever explain myself, and who will believe me? I certainly have motive to make things go south. She's the wife of my ex. It will make it appear as though I had malicious intent if I'm found out.

It's almost time to inject my eggs with the architect's sperm, but it seems selfish to be thinking of myself when Ally lies in a hospital room a few floors away.

It isn't fair. They're good people, a great couple. And she's been dealt the worst fertility hand in the deck.

And here I am, a single woman with no prospect of finding a father for my child, and my eggs are perfect. I almost wish we could trade places.

It will be no loss to this world if I don't reproduce—but Ben?

Ben should have children. I've never met a man who wanted children as badly as Ben. Some little person should know the kind, soothing sound of Ben Holiday's voice. Ben should be able to pass down his creative talent, and show his offspring how to use a paintbrush, because he's a wonderful artist, and probably a fantastic teacher.

What's worse than loving children so much that you make it your vocation to serve them, only to be denied the ability to have them yourself? It seems a cruel way to spend a lifetime.

There should be a highchair at the Holiday family table for Ben's baby.

And that child should grow up surrounded by the army of other loud Holidays, fighting for space around the long dining room table that was always crowded with so much love.

My baby will have me and my mom, and that's really it. I have only a couple of aunts, an uncle, and a few cousins who live out of town.

I fight to steady my breath as to not draw attention to myself from outside the lab. My vision blurs with tears, and I hate tears. Scientists abhor this defunct in the emotional spectrum. *Why can't we control it?*

There's no way I can face the Holidays with this news.

I can't. I simply cannot do it.

The responsibility could be shifted to Dr. Batey, but she'll be attacked with a battery of questions regarding my false responses to Ally's questions for which I have no good defense.

My job is basically on the line. I royally screwed up, and out of everything I've done wrong, my career is the one thing I've always gotten right. It's my shiny star in the otherwise dark pit that is my life, and this situation I created for myself could compromise it all.

In spite of what's happened with Ben and me, and all of the obsessive hours I've spent thinking about him, there's never been a part of me that didn't wish him the very best. The mental images of Ben as a father are jarring my brain, searing across my temples.

Ally is more sensitive than me, and she wasn't able to leave Ben for a couple of months even though it would've made her treatments easier. She deserves this more than I do. So does Ben.

Ben should be a parent.

Ben can still be a parent.

Adoption is a possibility, but I don't know Ben and Ally's stance on that. If it was an agreeable option, it would've happened by now, right? Using a donor egg might not be an option for Ally given her religious beliefs. It's unlikely she'll go any further using someone else's reproductive specimen when she shied away from using her own for so long.

Their marriage will fall apart because of what I've done.

They'll fight for months over me, and Ally will blame Ben for using my services in the first place. He'll feel like it's his fault, and it'll throw him into a depression. He always felt things deeply—high highs and low lows.

Ally will say things like, "*I told you it was a mistake to trust her!*"

And then Ben will hate me too. He might even give me up to the police regarding Cook. I can't stand Ben hating me.

And then he'll involve Laurel and Zach, Cat and Seth. They'll all turn against me. I'll be made the immoral villain with an ax to grind with my ex. Then, I'll be suspended from work pending a criminal investigation.

I'll lose everything I ever had because I made one fucking mistake and opened my mouth when I shouldn't have—because I have no verbal tact.

I trust you, Emily, I really do.

Those were Ally's last words to me. I can practically hear her saying them to me over and over again, her mother waving me out of the room to leave.

Go on, Ally's mother told me with her soft brown eyes, *Get back to making my daughter a baby.*

My head pops up for air, and I'm shaking so hard, my glasses are rattling around on the tear-stained bridge of my nose.

I survey my surroundings, searching for an answer. My new goal is to stop the erratic breathy-gulps and calm the fuck down.

A picture of Melissa Gilbert stares back at me from the cover of one of my *People* magazines. She looks dignified doing an expose on *Little House on the Prairie.* She likely didn't have to work after the show aired with all of her *prairie* money, but she probably still performs anyway because she loves it. It's her passion and maybe she'll be lost without it. Just like I can never be happy without my job. If I don't have children, my career is my only legacy.

I cannot lose this job.

I will do anything to protect it. Ben and Ally will still have each other if they can weather this storm, but I will have nothing. I risked it all for this job. I lost Ben because of my career. I can't be left with neither.

Melissa Gilbert seemingly winks at me, and it's then I remember the most recent Lifetime movie I've seen with her in it called, *Switched at Birth.* It's based on a real story. The movie is a heart-wrenching tale of two baby boys accidentally switched at birth in the hospital nursery. Years later, a medical test for a rare medical disorder for one of the boys proves the mother and father are not the biological parents. The worst part of the entire movie is watching the parents realize they might have to give the baby they raised to somebody else.

My tears are now caked on my cheeks as my thoughts become blacker and clearer at the same time, like an opaque mask made especially for me. The fact is, it makes no difference what embryo Ally has implanted in her uterus. All that matters is that Ben and Ally have a child to raise together. A healthy baby with Ben's wonderful genes.

They'll never know the difference...

"No, no, no, Emily," I whisper to myself.

I imagine Melissa Gilbert whispering back from the magazine cover, "Yes, yes, yes, Emily." Her innocent face is coaxing me into a bad place.

"Laura Ingalls Wilder would so disapprove of your behavior," I say out loud as I rise to greet my eggs. My mini breakdown has left me not right.

"Hi, little ones." I sniff.

I can only see through my darkened mask now. Sometimes my mind does this—goes into viewer mode. It's like I'm watching life through a television screen. Removed and present at the same time.

What would one of the character's in my favorite shows do in this instance?

The idea has been formed, and if it's going to happen, I have to do it now while Ralphie isn't here. And while all the samples are still fresh. It will be easy to implant Ben's sperm into one of my embryos and pass it off as Ally's.

All I have to do is denote that one of my eggs has died during the freeze. According to statistics, that should be the case anyway. Then, I'll scrap one of Ally's bad eggs and place it in the biohazard bin and say it's mine.

No one ever went into the biohazard bin looking for anything.

Things went into the red bin and never came out until

they're emptied into an I-didn't-want-to-know-where wasteland, so I'm good there.

Then, I'll tell the Holidays tomorrow when I go to check on Ally's sample that the other eggs arrested overnight, and that only one viable embryo remains. I'll pray that one makes it to the blastocyst stage, day five. If the God Ally had prayed to wanted this baby to happen, maybe he put me in this position for a reason.

A chill runs over my hot flushed skin. It's like Dr. Batey said, "*People say I have a God complex. Well, it doesn't get any closer to God than this.*"

And it doesn't. And now it's my turn to play God.

My face is numb and stings with tears. Even if everything does take, implanting only one embryo still leaves Ally with a chance the implantation won't take. There may be something else wrong with her besides the eggs, but sacrificing one of my own will solve all of my problems for the time being.

There's no way anyone will find out.

I'm the clinical supervisor.

No one double-checks my work. I double-check theirs.

There isn't another person who reviews my specimens.

My subordinates don't question me on processes and procedures. If I deliver one viable embryo, the Holidays will be disappointed, but if Ally does her research she'll have to understand this can happen, and her rational analyst brain will be okay with this less-than-ample result. And if she's okay with it, Ben will be good with it too. And if he's fine with his wife's reaction, then he won't hate me. There'll be no investigation, and I'll be out of the woods.

The rest of the logic can work itself out later. If this is going to happen, it's gotta be now.

With my black mask of denial on—that doubles as lab glasses—I walk over to my specimen, and then the syringe.

The syringe is now in my hand.

The hero of my fictitious show decides it's best to use the syringe to extract Ben's sperm. My hands are moving over to my eggs instead of Ally's rotten ones. Without another thought, I inject Holiday sperm into my single egg, and I place that egg in a petri dish under tray number three marked—Holiday.

In the next breath, I take one of Ally's bad eggs, photograph it for evidence as my own, and then dispose of it in the red biohazard bin. If the techs check the sample in the morning they will assume the rest of Ally's sample went bad overnight if I didn't denote otherwise.

All of the numbers add up. Ally had had six eggs in her incubation tray, just as I indicated from her retrieval.

And in my tray I've recorded that one of my eggs has unfortunately perished in the freeze. There are three of my healthy eggs left. I hesitate for a moment before I inject the architect's sperm into my own eggs.

Ben's sperm is right at my fingertips. There are enough strands left. Ben produced about fifteen strands of sperm, and I only need to use one.

There's plenty of sample left to inject more eggs. The black mask is making me lose my judgment and I have to pull away from the table for a moment and think.

"Don't, Emily," I whisper to myself through my brain cloud.

Melissa Gilbert attempts to talk back, so I throw her onto the ground, face down, and stomp on the magazine. She's trying to turn my life into a movie so she can play me in the lead role later.

But it would be nice if they were siblings, I hear Melissa say from the floor.

Damn her. She's right. I'm likely not going through this process again. Not after today. And Ally will not have any opportunity to give this child a sibling. It seems the right thing to do.

They'll never know. You control the lab here, Melissa whispers in her prairie voice. *Just like you controlled the meds to help your father.*

She's not wrong there. Sometimes we're placed in positions to play God for divinely guided reasons we can't explain.

It only makes sense when I take Ben's sample—and inject it into my own eggs.

TWENTY-NINE

ALLY

LEAVER

I dozed off between the time Emily left and Ben arrived.

Ben—*There he is.*

"Where were you?" I ask him.

He opens his mouth to respond, then says nothing.

The subtle movement in the corner of the hospital room reminds me that my mother is there. She rises from her chair. "I'm going to grab a coffee so you two can catch up."

"I... was in the wing where they collect samples. Giving... my sample," he says. "It has to be done right after your eggs are extracted."

"It's been hours, Ben."

He shrugs. "I'm sorry I wasn't back yet when you woke up. It's a big hospital."

Ben is not a liar. He's not smart enough for that, but for some reason I feel like he's lying to me right now, and I can't figure out why that would be. The same way he withheld from me during our first consultation with Emily. Until I grilled him about it.

"Did you get lost?" I ask him. He doesn't have the best sense of direction.

"Sort of. It just took me a while to get back to this wing, is all."

Sort of? Sort of took you awhile to get back to your wife after a major procedure?

"Emily was here," I tell him. I blink and take a sip of water, but he's still standing a good distance away from me. Shifty-looking, like he just held up a convenience store and is trying to decide whether he should stay or run.

"Oh yeah." He sways from one foot to another. "What did she have to say?"

"Come here, Ben."

He takes a step forward. "What?"

"What's wrong with you? I could use a hug. You haven't even asked how I am?"

"Oh, I'm sorry." He leans in, but barely touches my slouchy shoulders in my paper gown as he gives me a quick grab.

"Did something not go right?" I ask.

"No. Nothing on my end." He rocks on his heels and looks away.

"What about on my end?" I croak. What is he not telling me?

"I don't know anything about that. What did Emily say?" he asks.

He's sitting at my side now, a little more focused. Perhaps it's time to suggest adult ADHD medication. I've held my tongue on the matter, but he certainly isn't getting any better as time goes on. And living with him isn't becoming any easier either.

"She said she looked at my eggs and everything was fine, but you never know... the next few weeks are the real test."

"Well, if Emily said they looked good, then they are." Ben

brightens. His complexion warms, the blood returning to places that seemed vacant of circulation when he first arrived.

But something feels really off here.

First Ben's disappearance act, then him lying about where he was.

Then Emily's over-assurance that everything was fine. It's almost as if she was overcompensating for something.

Ben too.

"Okay." I close my eyes, hoping it's the drugs making me sketched out. But behind my lids I hear my husband walking away from me again. He hasn't been present for most of this process. Maybe it makes him queasy, the science of it, the specimen and fluids, and he can't tell me because the whole thing was his idea.

Or maybe it's because he's reached the end of his rope too, and if this all doesn't pan out, he's the one ready to leave me for not being able to give him the life he always wanted, a move right out of my father's playbook.

THIRTY

EMILY

Ben… is right in front of me.

I'm still in shock from what I've done, but I'd know the back of his head from anywhere; the tiny cowlick that sticks up when his hair's too short, but falls perfectly to the side after a couple of weeks of growth.

He's starting school soon. He probably just got cleaned up by the barber.

I needed another caffeinated beverage. Or perhaps I just had a strong desire to flee the lab after the crime I just committed—to make our babies, mine and Ben's.

They're ruminating right now, their growing cells. Will they get my light hair or his dark hue? Will they be on the taller side like him or short like me. Quiet and observative, or outgoing and creative.

I gulp down my Frappuccino at the dangerous, dangerous thoughts.

Oh my God… what have I done?

If I tell him what I did—what would Ben's reaction be? Should I come clean now so there's no weirdness between us?

Would he maybe even understand? Since he put so much pressure on me to get this right.

I can't stand here behind him as we both wait for the elevator and just pretend not to see him like the awkward watcher that I am.

"Hey, Ben."

He jumps a bit, turns around to discover me, and slides his phone into his pocket as if I've caught him doing something he shouldn't be doing.

"Emily! Hey."

I haven't been alone with Ben since our uncomfortable negotiation in the hallway during his consultation. I fear I'll lose my chance to say anymore when the elevator dings and the doors slide open. The people who're waiting for a ride climb inside.

"I'm waiting for the up elevator," I tell him. I'm sure he's waiting for the down to go to the lobby. I stopped on this floor to grab a drink. I wonder what he's doing here. Where he's going? Who was he texting?

"Ooh…" He hesitates and then watches the doors for the down elevator shut. I squeeze my afternoon treat because it must mean he wants to talk to me. Why? Does he know something?

"Ally was looking for you earlier," I say.

"Yeah, she's sleeping now," he says. "I need some fresh air. This morning was a lot."

I try to hide my smile. "She doesn't know… about your delay."

He blushes. Gosh, he's cute, even if he was a bit of an ass the last time we spoke in private. "Thanks for that. I had to take a walk afterward. I just couldn't help but think, you know, about how hard all of this has been, and if it's the right move. Do you ever wonder about decisions you've made and if you had a do-over, if you'd make different choices? Because I don't know... If this doesn't take, I don't think we'll make a round two."

You're right, Ben. You won't make a round two, because there won't be enough specimen left for you to try

And by decisions, are you wishing you wouldn't have crawled through Cook's window for me? Because I kind of wish that too. Even though I might've been incarcerated, I might still have you.

I fight for words. What a loaded question. Do I have regrets about my decisions?

Would I do it again, break up with Ben—*no*. Choose to do IVF alone—*yes*. Create Ben's baby with my DNA—*maybe*? "Um, sure. We all have doubts. But I tend to lean into the idea that we're all on a path, and the obstacles laid out there are meant to teach us something."

The obstacles. And the opportunities.

"Right..." He's staring at me, and I'm wondering what he's referring to exactly. He and Ally's fertility, or our past together. Does this bump in the road make him wonder if life would be better with me? This is perilous water we're treading here. He and Ally's relationship is obviously strained from this procedure, and I already have too many connections to the Holidays.

My elevator door to go upstairs dings and slides open. I'm the only one waiting. "It's okay if you don't want to try again. Lots of couples choose to do just one round. Well, I better get back to it. But if you have questions, Ben, call me."

He rocks on his heels and smiles. "Okay, thanks." I lock eyes with him until the doors shut, and I sink into the walls.

He's having doubts about Ally. He's insecure about their relationship. But the question I'm really wondering—is he still thinking about me?

THIRTY-ONE

EMILY

BUZZ

Tuesday

Light hits my eyes at odd angles, electronics buzzing in tripli-
cate, and I'm suddenly aware it isn't the first time the alarms
have gone off. I grab my phone. It's Ralphie. I have like a
hundred missed calls.

"Hello," I answer.

"Em, where the hell are you?"

I look at the clock. It's after 9 a.m. *Fuck.*

"Not feeling well this morning," I say. It isn't a lie. My head
is pounding. I hardly remember opening the wine last night, but
there's the bottle on my bedside table. No glass. Just the bottle.

"So, are you calling off, because there's some shit going
down in the lab? Kind of need you here. If you aren't coming in,
I would have assigned your work to Tawny or Ellen," Ralphie
says, obviously upset. It's a wild week, and we don't exactly
have the kind of job where you can pull a no-show.

"I'm coming," I announce.

"I can't believe you didn't call in late. Everything okay?" Ralphie asks.

"Yeah," I sigh. "What did you mean about shit going down in the lab?" I wipe the sleep from my eyes.

"The Holiday sample went to shit. I took a peek and had to label five of the six as goners, and then there was one that was perfect. It's bizarre. The reason I examined them is because the patient has called here three times to check on her sample, and Lisette keeps having to tell her that neither Dr. Batey or you are here."

"Oh my God."

"Not like you're supposed to tell her anything anyway, but I sure as hell can't. I've emailed Batey about it with the results, and asked her to kindly call the poor woman. No response from Batey, though. No surprise," he huffs.

The Holiday sample!

Ben Holiday.

Ben Holiday's sperm with my embryo.

Labeled as Allyson Holiday's sample.

"Em?"

I breathe into the receiver. The gravity of it all didn't settle in until I was home alone, away from the lab, but when it did, I medicated myself with alcohol until I passed out. It's all too real now. "I'm on my way."

I hang up the phone. It all comes back in flashes and waves, my stomach lurching—then me dry heaving over my toilet, because I haven't eaten anything since noon yesterday.

What have I done?

There didn't seem like any other option yesterday. All alone in that lab. Just me and Melissa Gilbert and the samples. The good ones and the bad ones. Ally's and Ben's and mine. Then, mine and Ben's. Somehow it doesn't have a damn thing to do with my feelings for Ben, but no one will ever believe that.

At least it isn't me who discovered the anomaly of Ally's

one good embryo this morning. But apparently I am the one who's going to have to explain it to her. It's not customary for patients to call the lab. It isn't protocol, and I am under no obligation to return her messages. But this isn't just any patient, it's Ally. I see that she's called my personal cell too.

She knows from her research that by today I should have a better idea of the health of her embryos, and she wants to know how they are.

It's almost ten o'clock by the time I actually arrive at work. The inside of my mouth tastes like a nail file and my head hurts every time light touches my eyes.

It's definitely been a rough night.

"Holy shit, you look like hell. If you're really that sick, maybe you shouldn't be in here," Ralphie comments.

The lab is crowded and noisy. Tawny is barking and Dr. Woo is squawking, and Ellen is moving too slowly.

When I don't respond to Ralphie, he hands me my lab coat.

"Your sample looks great, by the way, sorry for not mentioning that. I didn't mean to snoop, but that wife of your ex had me all up in her trays, and I couldn't help but look at yours. I gave Dr. Batey my best assessment of the Holiday sample, but we're waiting for you to officially scrap her five bad embryos," Ralphie rambles.

It physically hurts to speak to him, so I place Ally's specimen on the microscope and proclaim, "Wow, you're right. They are bad." I sigh, trying to sound surprised, but I am so mentally and physically exhausted I can hardly fake my distress.

"As if you doubted me." Ralphie is beaming. As cocky as he is, he loves my validation. "You don't have to call that woman back. Actually, I wouldn't if I were you. She sounds nuts. Let Batey earn her salary," Ralphie advises.

"Why was she so upset?" I ask, worried.

There's no way Ally could possibly know what happened, but paranoia is already settling in. The moment Ralphie said the words, "*it was bizarre*," in regard to Ally's solo good embryo, my stomach knotted in two.

No one else was supposed to look at those embryos but me. Sure, I could've said five had died, but Ralphie saw the disparity under the microscope between the quality of the good embryo and the bad ones, and it's glaringly different. If I wasn't so careless and had actually arrived at work on time this wouldn't be an issue.

"She said she needed to talk to you about her sample. She said the same damn thing about three times just like that. 'I need to talk to Emily about my sample,' in this quiet, disturbing voice. And she wouldn't say why."

How can she possibly know something is wrong?

This already is not going as planned. Some people have the ability to lie and live dangerously. Hell, some people even thrive on it. I am not one of those people.

"I just sent Dr. Batey a text message to contact her," I tell Ralphie. My time with Ally needs to be limited now until I figure this out. The decision has to be made whether I am going to keep that embryo or make it mysteriously perish like the others somehow.

Can I really let this continue?

But can I really live with myself if I destroy what I created?

What I produced is a potential life. It has legal rights. So, destroying it is like committing murder. Not only is it morally wrong, it could definitely get me fired, a civil suit on top of that.

"That's right. Defer responsibility. Is your ex's woman a headcase or somethin'?" Ralphie asks.

"She's, you know, just very emotional. It must be so tempting for her to have a friend in the lab," I defend.

"A friend? Why you friends with your ex's girl?"

"Ben and I dated a long time ago," I explain. I'm getting hot with nerves and my head is pounding.

"Uh huh," Ralphie says, skeptically.

"I have to work now," I say, putting him off.

For two hours straight, I don't speak another syllable to a single person, and I work, tuning out Tawny's throaty banter and ignoring Ralphie's bad jokes. But in between working, I think about the magnitude of what I've done.

I've abused my power in the worst possible way and I've created a potential nightmare scenario for the Holidays.

An error in the lab.

Samples mislabeled.

A baby is created.

But only one of the parents is the biological one.

It sounds like something off the Sci-Fi channel.

"Em?"

I hear Ralphie, but I don't feel the need to answer him. Didn't he understand me when I told him I wasn't feeling well? Can't he see I'm drowning in my own thoughts? Suffocating in my bad decisions?

"Em," he repeats.

"What?" I ask, sighing and then relinquishing myself from my microscope.

"What is up with you?" he asks.

"I don't feel good, but there's too much work to call off," I lie.

"Do you want me to tell your visitor you're too sick to go out to lunch with her? Although, she might lose it if she knows you're in here, all ill, with her sample and shit. This momma's claws are coming out way before the cub."

"What're you talking about?" I hear my heart throb in my ears.

"She's here. Guess she didn't want to take no for an answer." Ralphie is smiling. He's enjoying the show.

"You're talking about Allyson Holiday, aren't you?"

"I sure am." Ralphie smiles again.

"What the hell is she doing here?"

"She wants to grab lunch for just a half hour of your time, she says."

"Tell her I'm a bit under the weather, and I'll touch base with her soon. Play it off like it's nothing too serious on the health front," I say. Ralphie needs to make her go away until the sword between my temple disappears. Everyone has to fade into the background for a few more hours. Ralphie is like a pesky little kid hanging on my pant leg today, and I feel the sudden need to kick him off.

"Yes, ma'am," Ralphie says as he walks away.

It's especially odd for Ally to be here. She should be resting and preparing for her implantation on Friday, not loitering in the clinic, looking for answers. The whole thing is kind of insane.

"Okay, think I got rid of her. Lisette is pissed. Said she's calling security if she comes back."

I'm actually okay with that. I need to buy myself some time. It all feels like a dirty gamble anyway. The single embryo may or may not take.

Let it ride or kill the secret before it gets out? Horrible decisions.

The Amstead sample is now in my possession and I am placing ten viable, potential UFC fighters in the incubation tray, right under Ally's single embryo. It's as if all the embryos have faces this week. Our whole future could be in this machine. Artists and scientists and fighters. The future babies in this containment unit right now could rule the world.

And in that moment I know there's no way I can eradicate the Holiday–Daugherty embryos. The only ones of the lot that're the perfect mix of art and science.

Picasso and Einstein.

Paint and precision.

Ben and I are like lost soulmates in time, brought back together in the ultimate act of selfless love. I am giving a part of myself to him so he can live out his dreams with Ally forever, and he's giving a part of himself to me, so I can live out mine. It's a beautiful act of sacrifice, and it has to be the right choice.

THIRTY-TWO

EMILY

PEACE

Wednesday

In the span of the next twenty-four hours I make peace with the Holiday–Daugherty samples I procured, especially the one for Ally that I've mentally named—Bemily. Peace doesn't mean I am not racked with guilt and regret, it just means I've made an acceptable space for my decision for now. Bemily's creation was not out of spite or lust or revenge, it was an act of love, on both fronts.

I did it so Ben could have a baby.

So he would not end up with a wife who was depressed and bitter and terminally unfulfilled. I did it so he can have the life he was meant to live, with the child he was supposed to raise.

There might be some self-serving reasons behind my decisions, like covering up my lies, and protecting my job and friends, and preferring my own child share Ben's genetics to a complete stranger's, but they aren't the primary reasons.

The motivation for this genetic manipulation is to give

someone I truly care about something he deserves. It's about creating a life that will mean something to the world someday, and bestowing it to parents who will raise it right. And as long I keep reminding myself of that fact, I'll be okay.

There's a good chance the single embryo won't implant anyway. It will be as much my loss as hers, but only one of us will be able to grieve. My silent selflessness will help me through this; the anonymous donor.

Ben might not see it that way.

He'll look at it as another way I've failed him. Just like in college when he thought he could count on me until the very end after all he'd done for me.

He's looking for me to come through for him now, and I must.

I see what I've done as a gift. I gave a piece of myself, my own flesh and blood, so that Ally may have her own.

Although Ally might see it as an abomination. Her Christian background would reject my theory. Ben's too. He'll tell the authorities all—that he should've had me locked up when he had the chance.

Cold prickles march down my spine like ice chiseling my vertebrae. There's something so right and so wrong about all of this, but in my heart of hearts I know it's more good than bad.

The lab smells like static energy today. People move so fast in small quarters, I feel an internal burning, like overused radio frequencies, but everyone seems to be on their own wavelength today.

My workday is progressing nicely.

The cells in my sample continue to grow and flourish fabulously, and I have every confidence Dr. Batey will have three amazing blastocysts to choose from in my sample, two of which she'll implant on Friday, one of which she'll freeze.

A brief vision of raising triples on my own flashes before my microscope-indented eyes. It won't happen, because I'll only allow them to implant two embryos, but that means twins are a real possibility. *Ben's twins.* I swallow hard at the thought.

The lab phone rings and Ralphie answers it. Dr. Batey hasn't bothered me with a single consult since I started my own IVF process. Probably because she's afraid I'll scare them off with my beastly behavior.

"Where're you going?" I ask Ralphie.

"Lisette wants me," he says, irked.

"Why?" I ask, my stomach tightening.

"Maybe she lost her pen she keeps tapping at everyone and needs my help finding it," he jokes.

"Right," I say.

Ralphie returns promptly, making me jump. He's staring at me with that blanched, yet not look and I instinctively take my latex gloves off. My hands are sweating. I'm nervous and this is bad.

"What is it?" I ask. But I know the answer already.

"That whack woman is back again. She asked if you're feeling better, and if she could please take you to lunch."

Did she ever hear of email?

My confrontation threshold is at about a one on a ten-point scale right now. I've half-convinced myself I did all of this just so I wouldn't have to explain myself to her later. Confrontation is *that* painful for me.

"I don't think that's a good idea," I reply.

"Em, you can't hide in here forever. If she wants to talk to you, she's going to find a way. Why don't you just answer her questions, and then politely ask her not to visit you at your place of work again?"

I shake my head at the words of wisdom from my twenty-six-year-old assistant. "Well, isn't that mature advice," I tease.

"I have a daughter, remember? How do you think I teach her how to face her fears?"

I sigh. He's right. And the longer I put Ally off, the more suspicious she'll become.

"Okay. Phone Lisette and tell her to have Ally meet me in the lobby in a half hour."

"What am I, your bitch?" Ralphie asks, holding the phone up for me to call.

"Please, Ralphie," I plead.

"Em, you sure are lucky you have me," he says, giving me a playful grin.

"I've never doubted that for a moment," I assure.

THIRTY-THREE

ALLY

TRUTH

"Emily, I'm so sorry. I don't mean to bother you." I tower over her in my wedge sandals, which makes my affront feel more aggressive than it already is. It's bad enough I lied to Ben and told him I've been shopping with my mother the last two days, when really, I've been coming down here. Meanwhile, my mother thinks I've had checkups every day, and it's only a matter of time before she figures it out.

"It's okay, Ally. I've just been ill, and I didn't want to get you sick before your transfer." She holds out her palm rejecting my attempted hug, reminding me of Ben's pathetic embrace in the exam room.

Why have these two gone cold since the procedure?

My gut tells me Emily and Ben are up to something, and for the first time I wonder if they're doing something behind my back. Are they sleeping together? Ben hasn't touched me in weeks, but I assumed it was because of my treatment.

"I heard. Are you feeling better? Are you going to be okay for your transfer on Friday?" I ask, concerned.

Emily tilts her head sideways as if she hasn't considered this. "I'll be okay," she confirms. "And if not, I have connections to get me on the schedule as soon as possible."

"Right..." I look around at the bustling office. "Where shall we go for lunch?" I ask. If I treat her to a meal, maybe we can return to that place in Laurel's kitchen where we cried over chocolate pie. Emily was really on my side that day. Since then, it feels like nobody is, and I can't figure out why.

"What did you have in mind?" she asks, fully aware I am out of my element in this new city.

"If you just want to grab a coffee and chat, we can. Or if you're hungry..." I trail off.

"I could eat," she proclaims.

"How about that Primanti Brothers place. Ben raves about it," I say.

"Sure, it's a sandwich shop staple. Nice and quick." Emily gestures me toward the elevators.

We walk down busy Forbes Avenue and I have to struggle in my wedges as Emily progresses nicely in her nude-colored flats. I'm not sure why I dressed up for her. Perhaps I just needed to make myself bigger in a situation where I'm feeling very small.

It's stuffy and crowded in the restaurant, and I have to shoulder-wrestle three men to make my way up to the ordering line. My face falls as I read the menu.

"Oh, no. I forgot you don't eat meat," Emily says.

Two men in ill-fitting polo shirts glare at me like I'm from another planet.

"I can always find something," I promise, loud enough for them to hear.

"They put coleslaw and fries on all their sandwiches and they have salads, so that's a plus," Emily says, and I can't tell if she's being sarcastic.

"I'll take the turkey and cheese," Emily orders.

"I'll just have some chips," I say, suddenly not hungry at all. The meat smells mixed with fermented cabbage are making me nauseous.

I pluck a chip out of the bag and fiddle with it before placing it in my mouth, wondering if Emily really forgot I was vegetarian—or if she's trying to poison me—with more lies.

THIRTY-FOUR

EMILY

I sink my teeth into my turkey and cheese sandwich, and Ally sucks in her cheeks in a way that tells me I've revolted her with my carnivorous order.

Wait until she finds out about what I did with her baby!

Shit.

This wasn't the plan.

Distance from Ally until the transfers were over was.

But she can't malnourish my child. As the thought passes through my mind, I clamp down on a piece of slaw. *This* will always be the problem with the scenario I've created.

Not being able to assert myself to protect the child that's mine, if only biologically.

"You know, you're going to need to eat some protein when you're pregnant," I say.

"You can get protein from other things besides meat," Ally quips back, obviously offended.

"You're right, sorry. What's up, Ally? I know you wouldn't normally just pop in and ask me to lunch."

Ally sighs and stares at me longingly through her glasses that're almost identical to mine. "It's my sample. I ultimately only ended up with one good embryo, and I know that happens sometimes, and we can always try again, but I'm just sick about it."

"Single embryo transfer is a popular standard of care around the globe. People who yield ten will often opt to only use one at a time to prevent multiples. I'm implanting two of mine, and freezing the other one for a later date," I admit.

"But you have another one. I don't. I only have this one." Her eyes are watery beneath the rims of her glasses and she's stopped picking at her chips. She is every bit the woman I pinned her to be. If this doesn't work out it will destroy her. And Ben.

"Well, you just have to pray this one will take, just like I'll be praying one of my two will implant," I say, using a religious coaxing method I think might resonate with her. The goal of this interaction is for it to be speedy.

How quickly can I make her go away?

"What if you have twins?" she asks.

"Ahh," I sigh. I get all jittery again at the thought of *Ben's twins.*

"I'm sorry. Oh, how we have such similar and different problems," she commiserates, but her tears are freefalling now.

"It's stressful, I know," I comfort, patting her hand. I shouldn't have taken her here. I should've brought her to a nice quaint little diner, but I'm so self-absorbed and fearful she's going to batter me into a confession I took her to the loudest place around—at her suggestion, I remind myself.

"I just don't know what I'll do if this one doesn't take. Tell me what happened to the others?"

"What?" It's the question I've been dreading. I shove a piece of sandwich far into my mouth and hold up my hand motioning that I need a minute to chew. What can I say here?

I swallow. "It just happens sometimes. The embryos stall

and arrest. They stop growing and multiplying, and they just... die," I whisper.

"So, that's what happened, they just died? They weren't abnormal?" she asks, anxiously, rubbing at her wet cheeks. I am sure she's scoured the Internet, searching for reasons as to why her embryos didn't make it, like a grieving mother forming her own forensic report to give herself closure.

"Some were slightly abnormal," I admit.

Ally pales, and I know I've said too much. She was looking for hope that this round of IVF isn't her only chance of having a child. But it is. Maybe it's better she understands that now before the doctors tell her later.

"I see," she responds, quietly.

There're more questions brewing, but I can't take it anymore. I rub my sweaty hands on my pant legs, looking through the steamy windows for a way out.

"I've really got to get back to work," I say.

"Yeah, I know. I'm sorry," she apologizes.

It's like the night at Laurel's party where her apologies feel like steely knives in my back, only this time it's so much worse, because the only one who should be begging for mercy is me.

"It's all right. I'm glad you feel better about everything," I say, even though I'm pretty sure I've only made her feel worse.

"I–I have a feeling this is my only shot. I'll just die if it doesn't take," she squeaks. And now she's full on crying again, and Primanti's is definitely not the place for intimate conversations.

"I hope it all works out," I say, softly, beginning to get up, and then...

"Emily, I had a dream."

Oh Christ. And I sit back down.

"Ben and I were standing on our favorite mountaintop in Aspen. The one we said we would've gotten married on if it was physically possible, but of course, it wasn't. We joked we'd ski down the slope, and I'd toss my bouquet behind us to whatever bridesmaid could ski the fastest to catch it. But in my dream there were four children at our sides. Four girls. They were in black and white, like an old TV picture, but I could see them clear as day. I was angry they weren't in color like Ben and I. And then in my arms was a new swaddled baby, and it was in color, like us."

I nearly lose my lunch at Ally's recollection of her dream. Both of us are taking off our glasses to wipe at our eyes now.

Ally dreamt about all of her lost children.

"Maybe it means this will be the one," I say.

"Maybe... but there was something wrong in the dream. It wasn't a happy one. The other children in black and white were pointing at the baby, trying to tell me something, shaking their heads in defiance, but I couldn't hear what they were saying. They were out of color and out of sound."

They were trying to tell you it isn't really your baby.

My stomach sinks to the floor. If a bunch of unborn fetuses are the reason my cover is blown, I'm going to lose it.

I can't do this anymore.

If she asks me one more question, I'm going to crack.

"Th–that's awful, but maybe it's just the stress," I manage. My skin is so hot right now I think my button-down is probably stained through.

"I hope you're right." Ally gazes at me then with her big brown eyes, and we're caught there for a moment. She appears to be looking into my eyes for something important.

The truth, maybe?

Well, if she's looking for truth there, she won't find it.

THIRTY-FIVE

ALLY

LIES

Thursday

My mother has her bags packed and is waiting by the door. "It's the most vacation time I could take from the store," she says, guiltily, but her departure brings me relief.

It's hard sneaking around and investigating behind her back.

I kiss her on the cheek. "It's okay, you get back safe." Mother despises flying, and I hate that she's driven so far, but she insisted on being here for my egg retrieval.

"You let me know the minute the results are in," she says.

"Absolutely," I tell her.

When the door closes behind her, relief floods my body.

It was sort of nice having her here, but after the retrieval, her words—*at least you got one*—did little to comfort me. Her bar is perpetually set low. Whereas my expectations are much higher, and I know Ben's were too. He lies, though, and says he's thankful we got a single embryo from the procedure.

I don't buy it.

My senses weren't firing at one hundred percent when I came out of anesthesia, but when I got home I mapped the route online from where the men's donation center is to my recovery room, and it was only about a fifteen minute walk—tops.

It took Ben three hours to make that trip.

What happened in between?

Even if the clinic was running a half hour behind—which is unlikely, because our sample was time sensitive, and the clinic is supposed to be the best—Ben's extended absence makes no sense. If he stopped to use the restroom or grab a coffee afterward, it still took him two hours longer than it should have.

And I want to know why.

My analytical brain can only come up with three plausible options—Ben was with Emily discussing the disappointing news of our retrieval, and didn't want to tell me, so he avoided me instead.

Or he was with Emily somewhere—naked.

Or Ben is having trouble enduring this entire IVF process, and he's not comfortable discussing it with me because it was his idea.

I'm leaning toward one of the Emily options, because she was awfully squirrely in that sandwich shop as well. It's like the two of them are hiding something, and I want to know what it is. All Emily's "God" talk made me suspicious. Ben informed me long ago that she's not religious.

She was just trying to shut me up. Why?

I hear the garage door, and try to decide how to broach the subject with Ben. My implantation is scheduled for tomorrow, and I don't want to stress either of us out. Tomorrow will be trying enough. But I do want to know what the hell is going on.

"Hey! In the mood for a hike or a walk before your procedure tomorrow? You won't be able to exercise for a bit afterwards."

This time I take him up on it. Ben's easier to talk to when he's doing something else. I wish his communication style was different, but we've had some of our best talks on the hiking trail.

I lace up my sneakers, feeling the familiar pump in my calves that used to give me a rush. Ben and I settle on a walk around the neighborhood so we can talk to one another. "Did your mom get on the road okay?" he asks.

"Yeah, long drive... she's supposed to call me when she gets there."

"She said the strangest thing to me..." Ben says, an edge to his voice.

"What's that?" I ask. With my mother it could be anything from the mating pattern of bees to the crystallization process of sugar in homemade fudge. You never know what's going to come out of her mouth.

"I asked her last night if she found anything good on your shopping trips, and she said she hasn't been shopping with you. That you were at doctors' appointments all week."

Ben doesn't look at me when he makes the comment. I was planning on confronting him about his lies, and here he's caught me in a snare. "I needed some space from her."

Ben turns toward me, but now I'm the one not looking at him. "She drove eight hours to see you. You've been saying for months how much you miss her."

"I can't explain it. I miss her, but then having her here this week wasn't that helpful. She lives life at a lower threshold. I always feel like she's threatening to pull me down with her."

"Ally, you didn't have a doctor's appointment, did you?"

"No," she says.

"So, you lied to your mom about doctor's visits, and you lied to me about shopping trips. Where were you?"

His scrutiny is smothering me. "I told you, I just needed some space."

"Is that why you lied to me too?"

"Maybe we're lying to each other." I feel the words burn on my tongue. Part of me has always wanted to tell him about what happened with Sebastian. Maybe if he admits to me that something is going on with Emily, I can reveal my secret, and we'll be even—grounds for a do-over. Even if it's not physical, those two are conspiring about something together behind my back.

They have their own secrets, I'm sure. And whatever it is will piss me off. They have history. They cannot keep things from me.

"What're you talking about?" he asks.

"Something was off with you the day of my procedure." I place my hands on my hips. This neighborhood is so highly suburban that people stare as they walk by at the couple having a little quibble.

"I'm sorry I wasn't there when you woke up, but now you're blowing this a little out of proportion. At least you know I was in the hospital. Where were you the last couple of days while your poor mom sat at home by herself?"

The way he grills me, after all I've been through—being forced to move here, and meet these people, and undergo medical procedures—it's too much. "She's negative. And I just can't let her get in my head right now with her minimalist, Dollar-General-mindset."

Ben's eyes blow back. *"Wow."* He continues to walk, and I quickly catch up.

"This place isn't good for me, Ben."

"Don't blame the place."

We don't speak the rest of the walk, and neither one of us has given up our secrets either. I remain quiet so he won't press me more, and he doesn't say a word either, and I know it's so I'll stop questioning him too.

If this IVF process is supposed to bring us together, it's only worked in reverse.

I've got my running shoes on, and I've never been more ready to take flight. If the implantation doesn't take, my time with Ben must come to an end. He might not understand that it's our undoing, but I sure do.

Then maybe he can stay in this godforsaken town, rekindle his relationship with Emily, and help raise her child. I'm convinced it's what he really wants anyway.

THIRTY-SIX

EMILY

TRANSFER

Friday

The longest week of my life will end with the transfer of two of three perfectly developed, gorgeously cultivated, blastocysts into my womb. The other fertilized one will be placed in the freezer to create a possible future sibling, although something tells me, one baby will be all I can handle by myself.

I can always sell or donate the unused blastocyst. The fertility team playfully calls donor embryos—snowflakes. They're individual and beautiful with their own unique DNA code inputted in a database for someone else to acquire.

This option gives patients like Ally, who aren't capable of producing viable eggs, or men who aren't able to produce healthy sperm, an option to conceive a child. As long as the donor doesn't mind having a little mini-me floating around in the form of a snowflake baby.

I could do it.

I could donate my embryo to an infertile couple. I could

donate it to Ally and Ben, even. Ben wouldn't have to know it's actually his biological offspring.

It's just a fertilized egg and nothing more.

It might be suspicious if the baby actually favors Ben's genes, but in my mind, I'd just be donating my DNA; they'll be the parents. At least that's what I keep telling myself as they wheel me in for anesthesia.

My *other* developed blastocyst, the one we don't speak of, will be transferred into Ally's uterus today. She's probably somewhere close to being taken to a procedure room herself. It isn't too late.

I can come clean.

Tell everyone what I've done. Let them make the decision of whether they'll accept my donor embryo or not.

But my gesture won't come off as sincere. What I did was unethical and wrong. It's also generous and right. I've given them what they wanted, and if they never find out about it, it will be the loveliest little secret of all.

Even if they do discover the truth, somehow, years after the fact, it's still Ben's biological child. By that point, they'll have grown to love the little boy or girl and it won't matter, will it?

I don't know why I'm stressing myself out. It's common for the IVF process to take a couple of rounds before it's successful. That's why I've been reluctant to go baby shopping or even accept the little yellow bootie from Laurel that's stuck to the inside of my palm. *Not as big as a monkey*—she says. At least this isn't my last shot. I have four more frozen eggs in storage. It's just my best chance given my age and that of my eggs.

"Emily, you seem so distracted. I'll be right here, sweetheart. Think of nothing else but positive thoughts for this baby," my mother comforts. She grasps my hand until they won't let her hold it anymore. She kisses my forehead as they take me through the swinging doors.

"Okay," I whisper back to her, but I don't know if she hears me.

Before I can say another word, Tessa has placed a mask over my face, and I'm counting backward from ten to one, but I only make it to three...

———

When I awake, Dr. Batey is beaming at me with her perfect white teeth, the overlapping rows of her gold, shiny necklace gleaming me awake.

"All done, Ms. Daugherty," she says, triumphantly. "You did fabulously."

"Good," I say hoarsely. My throat feels dry and my vision is hazy.

"Do you have any questions for me, dear?" she asks.

"No." In a few more hours I'll be able to walk out of the facility.

I also know I'll experience mild pain, possibly some cramping, and at the very worst some spotting. Then, in ten days or so, I can take a pregnancy test that will be backed up by a blood test to detect for elevated hCG levels. Dr. Batey also realizes I'm aware of all these things, but I guess it's her job to ask anyway.

"Well, I can't wait to see the results," she says. Then, she pushes something soft into my hand with a crinkled brow of sentiment. It's the little yellow bootie I was clenching when I went in for my procedure. It must've fallen out of my hand when my body went limp.

"Thanks," I say.

My mother drives me back to my house and leaves at my request.

Before I go to bed I notice Jasper through the window on the balcony. His expression off the glass reflects terrible conflict.

I haven't seen Chelsea in a while. I know she's been away at rehab, but I don't believe any amount of treatment can transform someone from such a wretched being to a loving soul.

Maybe Jasper's thinking that right now.

I've wondered about them since that night I found Clementine dangling over the edge of the mountainside.

Jasper opened up to me that day when he returned his daughter, but he's retreated back into the safe shell of his home.

Is he waiting for her to return?

Is he hoping she doesn't?

People can be terrible to each other, but they can still love one another, and that is the hard part about relationships. The ones who know you best have the capability to cause most harm. I think of my own involvement in Ben's life. I made a decision on his behalf because I know what's best for him.

There's nothing that can be done now to undo my virtuous act.

Whether Ally's embryo makes it or not will tell me all I need to know.

I hate to be philosophical about something purely science-based, but if Ally really prayed all those months, and if she does believe God played a hand in all of this, her successful conception will prove that to me. It won't make me sway my religious devotion one way or another, but I will have a little more faith in knowing I am a mere instrument in a much bigger plan.

I sit on the balcony with a hot cup of tea. The city lights glisten below me, and I don't notice he's there until he speaks.

"Beautiful night," Jasper shouts.

I jostle a little, spilling my drink. "Oh. You startled me. You need to stop doing that."

He walks over to the glass on my side. His face his gaunt, his cheeks stubbled. He's been through it too, I'm sure.

"Again... I live here," he jokes. "Have I disturbed your privacy?"

I rise from my chair and walk over to the side of my balcony closest to him. He really is a beautiful man—sculpted shoulders, thick eyebrows, lovely dark eyes that are boring right through me right now.

"No, I could actually use the company. I had a medical procedure today." I rub my belly.

"Are you okay?" he asks, concerned.

"Yes, I'm fine. And I'm independent as they come, but I get tired of doing things all by myself sometimes."

"Me too," he says. And his comment is more of a downer than mine. He's married, but his partner is absent—emotionally. Right now, physically. To be married and feel alone most of the time is a sad state of being.

"How's Chelsea?" I ask.

"She's still in the hospital. She's gone away before. It never helps."

"Maybe this time will be different. Perhaps what happened will be the event that causes her to change," I say.

"I hope so. But past experience has taught me otherwise. Sometimes, I just wish I would've made different decisions from the start. Took the warning signs. Then I look at Clementine..." He glances away, into the night air at his confession. We let it breathe because he's just admitted he wishes he would've never married his wife. Their union was a mistake. He's sticking around for their daughter.

It makes me think of my conversation with Ben today on a similar topic. We're all faced with difficult choices, and have to live with the bad decisions we make. One bad move can derail our whole existence.

"Speaking of Clementine, she's been asking about you.

Would you like to get ice cream with us tomorrow? If you're still recovering and can't walk there, we can bring it to you."

"I would love to go for a walk with you and Clementine to the ice cream parlor," I say.

One trip to the ice cream parlor.

A decision to spend time with another woman's husband and child—*a built-in sibling for the one nesting in my belly.*

One artist replacing another.

I hate to think this way, but broaching a situation without dissection is an impossibility for me.

My only hope is that Ally isn't half as good at analytical thinking as I am and that I'm not found out.

THIRTY-SEVEN

ALLY

ALIEN

"Ally... calling again so soon. Ready to come home?" Sebastian asks. "And stop living a lie?"

His voice alone makes me want to cry. "Seb, I had the procedure and something is wrong." I'm holed up in my bedroom, white duvet cover pulled up to my face. Everything in this room is blinding with builder paint.

I can't help but imagine it drenched in red.

"What's wrong, Baby Girl?" Sebastian asks.

My heart crunches in my chest. I didn't want to contact Sebastian, but I didn't know who else to call. "It feels... something is off." I haven't taken off my sweatpants in two days, the looming fear of what lies ahead too much, but it's more than that.

The transfer has left me feeling like... "Like I'm an alien in my own body."

Or like I have an alien in my body...

"Well, go to the doctor, then. Maybe they messed something

up," Sebastian says. "Left an instrument in there or something. I've seen shows on that."

"I don't think that's it. I think they might've gotten it right, and that's the problem."

There's dead silence on the other end of the line. Last time I called Sebastian, the construction cranks and saws in the background provided a buffer. I have nothing to protect me from the truth now but our labored breaths. "So, you don't want the baby?"

I close my eyes and dig my fingers into my palm, clenching the covers. Maybe if I grip tight enough, I'll disappear inside the fibers. That can't be right, can it? A baby is all we've wanted for so long. "No, of course not."

"It's okay if you don't want the baby, you know? Society used to tell women that motherhood was a rite of passage, but the Gen Z population have it right. One out of four Gen Z women have decided they don't want children at all. And that's one hundred percent okay."

I smile into the phone. "I love it when you talk stats to me. So sexy."

"There's more where that came from. Today I learned copper piping is still installed in roughly eighty percent of homes."

I giggle. "Wow. Endless vat of knowledge. Turn on."

"Seriously, though, Ally... if you feel like this whole thing was a mistake. The move. The medical procedures... the baby. It's okay."

I cry. Hard. Because I needed someone to tell me that. Those exact words. "I'm not sure what I want, but *this* doesn't feel right."

"What does Ben say?" Sebastian asks, genuinely concerned, and it's weird every time I hear Ben's name roll off Sebastian's tongue.

"That's the other thing. He was acting strange the day of

the procedure, and so was his ex. I think they're up to something. I have to ask you a question, Seb..."

"Go on..."

"If... I become pregnant. And I decide I can't take it here anymore. Can we still go..." I choke on my words.

"To Costa Rica, Buenos Aires, Rio de Janeiro?"

I smile at how fast he rattles off the locations. "You keep getting farther away."

"If we have a little one with us, we'll need to go international."

Relief and terror flood my body. Relief that he still wants me if I have a child in tow—one that's not even his.

That's love.

It's also terrifying, because I'll have to kidnap the baby if I ever want to be with Seb. Ben would never let me take off with his child.

"I wasn't sure you'd still want me to join you."

"You can always come. When will you know if it... worked?"

"I should be able to tell in a couple of weeks. Could take longer."

"Well, let me know when you find out. You got your passport. I may need to send one for the little person. I'll need their name."

I sigh at the lunacy of his request, but it brings me such peace. "Okay. I better go. I'll be in touch."

"I actually don't doubt it."

Seb hangs up the phone and I'm left wondering why I'm like this.

All I've wanted for the last five years is a baby with Ben, and now that the possibility is real, I'm having second thoughts.

It could be the way the baby was made—the foreignness of being placed under fluorescent lighting, stuck with synthetic hormones, laid on a cold, metal table, forcibly implanted with a fertilized pre-packaged human.

It's so far from what my idea of how I thought I'd create my family, I'm having trouble accepting it.

But more so, my hesitancy comes from Ben.

The lies.

What went into this situation has left me so raw. It's the things I don't have answers to. The unknowns. It's Emily Daugherty, and why she has an integral part in my life now, a common goal of—family.

It's a shared want, like love or sunlight. I could probably live without it, but the thought leaves me cold and dead inside.

Motherhood is a gift, they say.

And she's my cross to bear, grasping at the same rays of light. It makes me wonder if she's my greatest blessing or my biggest curse.

Why do I get the feeling that what leaves me empty, brings her joy?

And that whatever secret she keeps with him will end us both?

THIRTY-EIGHT

EMILY

TEST

Two Weeks Later

The last two weeks, my mind has become a danger zone. I've warned mothers-to-be before me to be cautiously optimistic about their outcomes. But when placed on the opposite side of the consultation desk, I now realize it's impossible to take that advice.

No amount of counseling is going to negate the fact that there may or may not be a child growing inside my womb at this very moment; a little person who would forever become the most important and permanent fixture in my entire life.

So how can I not be excited about that possibility?

I've joined the desperate hopefuls. The last two weeks have been filled with preemptive baby brain. The entire Pottery Barn website has been scoured, items placed in online wish lists. Strollers and car seat browsing for safety features has kept me up late at night.

But this weekend I will put the daydreaming to an infinite rest.

Laurel, Cat, and I have planned a gathering for the big reveal. Originally, I didn't want them there, but Laurel convinced me—*Someone else should be there...*

As in—*you don't have a husband, but you have us.*

Thirteen days from the day of the transfer is technically Monday, but I know results should show up on the pregnancy stick by Saturday. I wonder how many boxes Ally has gone through already. Although I would think I'd be one of the first to know if she received a positive result, and so far I've heard nothing.

Cat arrives first with the food. They've sprung for catered pasta from my favorite Italian restaurant on Mount Washington, *La Tavola*. Joe and Carmella are the owners, straight off the boat from Italy, and their food is out of this world.

I can smell my signature dish, *Pasta terra sole*, through the lid, and my mouth begins to water at the aroma of pasta and ground sausage drenched in a spicy pasta vodka sauce. The garlic scent also tells me they've purchased my favorite appetizer too—greens and beans—a nice touch. I have good friends. At least I have that.

As Cat piles the Styrofoam take-out containers on my kitchen table, I hear Laurel barrel through the door with clashing glass sounds. She's wearing a winter coat with a fur-lined collar, bottles of alcohol in her hands, reminding me of a musician on a *Rolling Stone* magazine cover.

"What is that?" I ask.

Laurel walks closer and I see she's carrying three bottles.

"This one is your favorite. Merlot," she says, pointing to the red-tinged bottle. "This one is sparkling cider," she announces pointing to the yellowish one. "And this one is Tennessee whiskey." She nods to the square bottle of Jack Daniels.

I'm so nervous, I don't want to laugh, but one slips out anyway.

"May I ask about the whiskey?" Cat prompts.

Laurel has a goofy look on her face, and I know a joke is on its way.

"Well, if all goes well, it's sparkling apple cider for Emily and wine for us. And if it doesn't, I figured the three of us could drink the wine together, and then after we leave Emily might want to hit the whiskey."

"*Laurel*," Cat protests, shaking her head of freshly ironed black-brown hair.

"Nice," I say.

"Alcohol is always a good gift," Laurel defers, plopping the bottles on the table as we all stare at each other awkwardly. "Well, why don't we eat first? Cold noodles are gross," she says.

"Definitely." Cat arranges my plain white dishes around my equally plain white kitchen counter. I slurp down the *terra sole*, barely tasting it, just trying to get to the next step in our evening.

Laurel and Cat chatter on about their children and their husbands. It's as if I'm not about to find out one of the most important things in my entire life, and suddenly I'm annoyed I consented to their pee stick party idea. It isn't fair that they've been handed life's most precious gifts so easily, and here I am struggling to get to a fundamental level of the family model.

I've given up on the male component. I just want a single-unit prototype at this point.

Finally, they've finished their dishes and notice I haven't said much and have long finished mine. I didn't even offer to share my appetizer and am now burping up garlic, my stomach an unruly mess.

Maybe it's heartburn? They say pregnancy causes that...

"So, I guess you're ready?" Laurel asks.

"You could say that," I squeak.

"Okay, well, is your bladder full?" Cat asks.

I nod.

Laurel smiles. "Do your thing, we'll be right out here."

Cat has an exaggerated grin plastered on her face too.

"Okay," I say and excuse myself to the downstairs powder room just a few feet away, which is stockpiled with pregnancy tests. You only need one. I know this. But if it's positive, I'll want to take at least two more to make sure. This rationale negates science, and I'm okay with that. Today I'm allowed to be unreasonably hopeful.

I sit on the toilet seat and undo the cardboard box. One line —not pregnant. Two lines—pregnant.

Oh boy, this stress is horrible. And wonderful. How do people do this? All of those couples who've passed through my clinic... I'll never look at them the same again. Having a child shouldn't be so hard.

Everyone deserves the right to a family.

I place the stick drenched with urine on the paper towel lying on the toilet lid.

There's whispering when I exit the bathroom and Laurel is staring at her phone with worry. The girls have already cracked open the wine.

"You've got two minutes before you can't have a drink for nine months. Do you think you can down this glass in two minutes?" Laurel dares me, nervously handing me a poured glass. Cat's wide smile has floated away into the world of whatever they were secretly discussing before I came out of the bathroom, and I suddenly feel sick. This isn't a good time for jokes.

Clenching my belly, I wave the wine off and take a seat on the barstool at my wraparound countertop. This is something I should've done alone. It was a mistake inviting them. It's too much trying to be entertaining and personable while realizing my entire future at the same time.

"Emily, you don't know if you're pregnant yet, so this could be your last glass of alcohol for a long time," Laurel taunts. "You'll regret the pass on this decision ten short months from now, trust me!"

"I have a bad feeling," I confess.

"Oh, honey, you can always try again if this one doesn't work out," Cat comforts.

Laurel is quiet for a moment, which I find unusual, and she suddenly looks ashen as she fingers her phone.

"Maybe not. I have one frozen embryo and only four more eggs that basically expire in another few years. And I don't want to try again. I can't do this again," I decide. And in that moment it's true. I don't think I can go through the emotional ups and downs of this process another time. At least not alone.

"That mini-architect's probably dreaming of building playgrounds in there already," Laurel reassures.

Oh God.

He's not building playgrounds... he's painting them.

"Has it been two minutes yet?" I ask.

"One more," Cat says, watching the clock.

Longest minute of my life.

The clock flashes 6:32 and Cat screams, "Go!"

I'm off the stool like it's caught fire. I wave the stick in front of my face with my eyes half-closed, but I can still see the ominous single line.

It's clear and it's certain—it's negative.

I'm not pregnant. Neither of my embryos have implanted. My transfer has failed.

I open the door with the stick in my hand and step out. The girls are both watching me carefully.

"Well?" Laurel asks, shifting impatiently.

"It's negative." My voice is shaky, and my palms are sweaty, but I'm not going to cry. My shock overcomes my grief and I toss the test in the pullout garbage can in my island instead.

"Oh shit, I'm sorry, honey," Laurel says.

Cat runs over and gives me a big hug and whispers that I can try again and not to worry. Her words are soft and comforting, and I imagine she's a wonderful mother.

A reality I'll never know.

"It's okay," I say, even though it's not.

Holding my breath and all my emotions in, I wiggle my way out of Cat's embrace and run straight for the Jack Daniels on the counter.

"Thatta girl," Laurel chimes from the other side.

As I stride to the refrigerator to grab a Coke, I notice Laurel somehow looks worse than me. She's pasty and squeezing her phone so hard I think it might break. She sees me eyeing her device, and quickly drops it into her purse. It's then that I remember their whispering. Maybe it wasn't about me. The weirdness in the room still hasn't left since I caught them talking behind my back.

"Does one of you want to tell me what the hell is going on?" I pop the top to my soda and pour it into a glass with ice. It fizzes as I pour the whiskey on top, the carbonation heavy in the air like the stench of whatever these two are trying to cover up.

Laurel and Cat exchange a look of horror.

Something is definitely afoot. They think I haven't noticed. It has to be something bad, and I wonder if someone's died by their expressions.

"Nothing. We just feel bad is all," Laurel says, abruptly. Cat just stares at her socked feet.

I stride hotly over to the kitchen table where Laurel is sitting and pluck her phone right out of her purse. Laurel's eyes fling open, and she stumbles to try to chase me as I retreat back to my stool. Cat remains completely still, watching the whole scene take place.

"Emily, don't!" Laurel yells.

But it's too late. Laurel's security code is her birthday—0403. I know that, because I know everything about Laurel, and she knows everything about me. Our friendship has been a completely transparent, beautiful thing, until this moment—when she has lied to me—in a most egregious manner.

There it is on the screen. A text from her husband.

Zach: Don't tell anyone, but Ally is pregnant! Ben is so excited. I hope Emily's test is positive too. We can have a big non-alcoholic party to celebrate.

THIRTY-NINE

EMILY

CRACK

There will be a day when I can forgive Laurel and Cat, but there will never be a day when I can forgive myself. I crack the eggs in the frying pan and watch them sizzle. The yellow-orange yolk plumps up on the skillet, perfectly round and vital, the white outside clinging to the pan for dear life.

The concept that Ally might conceive, and I might not, was always a possibility, just not one I'd thought all that much about.

I had two embryos implanted.

Ally only had one.

I'm slightly younger than Ally. My uterus is healthy and has never rejected a pregnancy. Ally had four previous miscarriages. All of the embryos implanted were made with *my* DNA, and my DNA should've accepted them.

When using my own law of illogical rules of probability I deducted that either Ally and I would both conceive, or that I would conceive and Ally wouldn't, or neither of us would. The current outcome seemed highly unlikely to me. Even though IVF is one big gamble, the odds were in my favor.

But I bet, and I lost—big time.

I lost my baby to Ben and Ally.

The fried eggs hiss angrily at me. I don't want to consume anything, but I haven't eaten since I threw up my pasta the previous evening, following my outburst that occurred approximately twenty seconds after I read Laurel's text from Zach.

Laurel and Cat left after several failed attempts at weak apologies. I understand that some people keep secrets to protect feelings, but Laurel and I aren't that type of friends.

We share everything.

The sulfuric smell of the eggs combined with the leftover whiskey in my belly makes me want to gag again, but the carton of eggs is the only thing I have left to eat in my fridge. The eggs stink, just like my life, and they're sitting there mocking me in all of their round perfection, jumping and spitting at me all the while.

I reach for my spatula to flip them over, and then opt for a fork instead, and I stab those perfect little eggs. Their insides pour out in bright, vivid gushes.

Stab, stab, stab.

Gush, gush, gush.

Then, I throw the whole damn frying pan at the wall and scream. The skillet smacks the kitchen wall and falls to the floor with a clatter. My greasy breakfast sprays yellow-orange all over the cream-colored walls. They'll be a bitch to scrape off later, but I don't care at the moment, because the black mask of denial has finally come off, and there's a mad scientist hiding behind it.

"Fuck!" I yell and sink to the floor. The gas is still burning on the stovetop above me, and the eggs are hanging on the wall like clumpy syrup that's already begun to harden.

It was okay for Ally and Ben to have a successful transfer with my embryo, but only if I had one too. I bang my head off the stove as my practicality tries to catch up with my emotions, but nothing is jiving these days.

It's time to return to the lab, but I can hardly think of going back to the place where I started this mess. What I did was a crime, but until now it didn't feel like one.

Then, there's my own personal failure to face. Of all work-places, mine will be the most understanding. It will be just another failed transfer to them, but for me it's much more than that, and I know I won't be able to hide the devastation from my colleagues.

I cultivated my sample perfectly.

There was absolutely nothing wrong with those embryos and nothing wrong with the sperm and nothing wrong with me. I don't understand why it didn't take, other than the fact that it wasn't supposed to.

Maybe I was placed in that precarious position to give Ally and Ben what they wanted, so I could live in total purgatory for making the decision to turn my back on Ben so long ago.

Ralphie is blowing up my phone. I am way late again, and this whole IVF business has made me a total wreck at work. I'm losing it. My career is in jeopardy. My coworkers will tell me to give IVF another go, like I'm shooting fish in a barrel, but it's not that easy, and I can't take another round of shots.

Besides, I have a perfectly good baby growing in someone else's uterus!

What?

The thought is preposterous now.

It seemed scientifically sound before, when I was simply an egg donor.

In the flash of Zach's text, that egg somehow turned into my future baby, and my role as an egg donor transformed into that of a hijacked mother-to-be.

The toaster pops, making me jump. My phone rings again, and it's now almost nine o'clock. I grab the dry piece of toast, leave the sticky eggs on the wall, and run out of the door.

"Emily, you missed your blood test. Tessa stalled as long as she could, but you're going to have to wait now. I thought this was an appointment you wouldn't want to miss," Ralphie lectures as I walk through the door.

It's day thirteen. This is the official day I'm supposed to have my hCG tested, and even though the store-bought test isn't one hundred percent effective, I don't need a blood test to tell me I'm not pregnant.

"I'll page her," I say.

"You could do that, but you know she has other patients." Ralphie is obviously pissed at me for being late again. Since I've been in hormonal hell, he's been shouldering a lot more of my work, and I assume he's just reached his limit.

"So, did she want me to reschedule?" I ask.

"Same time tomorrow," he says.

"Okay."

"The Holiday and Amstead blood results are already back," he snips, rubbing in the fact I could've had mine already. What a little shit. He has no idea I've taken a home pregnancy test, and that my hopes have already been dashed.

"And?" I ask, already knowing the answer to family number one.

"Holiday positive, Amstead's hCG levels was a positive and also very, very high."

"That's good. Twin fighters," I muse.

"Fighters?"

"Amstead's a UFC fighter. That's why he wanted boys."

Ralphie shoots me an ugly look. "Well, looks like it was a successful day; hopefully yours will be a positive too."

My *People* magazines are stacked face-down, still in their plastic. It's sad how much I've disregarded my old, simple life. I was so much happier when I was barren and boring. It was much less stressful obsessing about the problems of celebrities instead of my own.

I flip over one of the mags with Jennifer Lawrence featured on the front. This issue is a throwback to the *Hunger Games* movies. I stare at the cover with great sadness.

In a world of survival of the fittest, my children didn't make it. Well, one did, but I can never claim him or her as my own.

"You're awfully quiet today," Ralphie comments.

"Rough weekend," I admit.

He shifts his weight back and forth, and opens his mouth several times to say something, then closes it. Tawny walks in next. We work in tight quarters and several of us have complained about her obnoxious odor. It's the scent of stale cigarette smoke combined with a drugstore fragrance that smells more like Febreze. Like any good addict, she lets up until people stop complaining and then starts up again as soon as everyone is too busy to notice.

This morning's waft catches me in a bad way. The toast hasn't soaked up a quarter of the acid in my puked-raw stomach. I try to put my hand over my mouth to block her cross-breeze as she zips past me, but it doesn't help.

The Jack Daniels gurgles in the back of my throat, and before I know it I'm flying down the hall of the wing to the bathroom where I retch up my breakfast. It comes up in large pieces as if my stomach hadn't even bothered digesting the bread, and I suddenly fear choking.

Just like Bridget Jones in *Bridget Jones's Diary*, I fear choking to death in the bathroom, like she feared choking to death alone in her apartment. I totally get that sentiment now. I've never felt so isolated in all my life.

When I return to the lab, I shield my eyes from all of the

onlookers. My career has always been a welcome distraction from life's stressors, but my job has suddenly become part of the problem, and I'm not the only one who notices.

"Emily, you're an absolute mess," Ralphie scolds. "You're my boss and all, and I should probably keep my mouth shut, but you need to pull your shit together."

Tawny's eyes are ablaze and Ellen pretends not to hear anything.

"Maybe she's already having ze' morning sickness," Tawny clucks with a smile.

"No, no—" I begin and then stop.

"Too soon for all of that," Ralphie argues.

"That's not what it is, because I'm not pregnant. I took a home pregnancy test this weekend, and it's negative."

"You risked a false positive with a store-bought test?" Ralphie asks, incredulously, as if it goes against everything we stand for. But Ralphie doesn't understand the interworking of a woman on the verge of finding out her maternal fate.

"I couldn't wait, and it was negative," I say, deflated.

Ralphie's face still holds that ugly look. Tawny appears sad, and Ellen just stares at her orthotic sneakers.

"Next transfer. Yours will come," Tawny assures.

"I'm done, I'm not trying again," I proclaim.

"You're gonna give up, just like that? One failed transfer, and you're done?" Ralphie asks.

"Yes. It's too much on me, and it's too much on all of you. It's more emotionally taxing than I thought, and that's with doing this job every day. I can't imagine being someone coming in blind and having no idea about the process."

I think of Ally's despair then. *I'll just die if it doesn't take.*

I know that desperation now. And I never want to feel it again. In the last twenty-four hours, I did want to die.

"Why don't you think about it? You've come this far with the shots and all," Ellen adds, quietly.

"I've made up my mind. It's not for me. Maybe I'll find a nice man someday who will go through the process with me, but I can't do this to you guys anymore." No one argues with me there.

If I had a partner, it would be different. If I was making a baby for someone other than myself, the pain would be shared, and not so all-consuming, but I just don't have the strength to try again right now by myself.

The day is calm and Batey hasn't checked in with me even once to see how I'm feeling since my transfer. Our numbers have gone down since I started my treatments, and I can only imagine she's withholding her own private lashing for a less sensitive time.

I try to focus on my specimens, but the only thing I can see is a little blue-eyed infant screaming back—*Momma*.

What the hell am I going to do about Bemily hanging out in Ally's belly?

For a brief moment, I consider revealing the identity of Bemily, but that could get me fired, and possibly put in jail. I could try to pass it off as a laboratory error, and place the clinic under a gigantic malpractice lawsuit, but the Holidays will likely file a civil case against me too, because I'm Ben's ex-girl-friend. It wouldn't be a buyable story that the only mistake I ever made in my entire career was on their case.

I wiggle on my padded stool, and I don't know how long I can keep this a secret. Melissa Gilbert's wrinkled pages are gazing back at me, and if I had my fork from this morning, I'd stab her too. She's the one who told me to do this.

Tessa pops her bronzed, curly-q head through the door, and asks me if I want to have my blood drawn real quickly.

"She already did an at home test, and it said negative," Ralphie offers.

If I wasn't so transfixed by my own mistakes, I would have slapped Ralphie by now. Talk about overstepping boundaries.

"Oh—" Tessa's face falls. She's one of those overly nice people. Nursing is a perfect vocation for her, and I often wished I had her empathy so men would find me warmer and less sterile, as my most recent ex, Niles, had so politely described me. Maybe my embryos felt it too, like I was some desolate cavern where they didn't want to nest.

Laurel had told me to envision the embryos implanting, and to think of nothing else but accepting them into my body, and all of that happy positive thinking crap. I didn't do any of that. Maybe that's why Ally is pregnant and I'm not.

"It's okay, sorry to waste your time," I add.

"Emily, why don't we do one anyway? You never know. Your levels just might not have risen yet. I've seen it happen before," Tessa says, encouragingly.

As much as I hate to go through a negative result twice, a blood test will put any lingering thoughts to an absolute rest. It may be the thing I need to move on from this.

"Okay," I concede.

As Tessa sticks me with the needle, she tells me a story about a single woman who went through two egg extractions and eight transfers before she finally got her little girl. Tessa assured me if that woman could do it at over forty, I can do it now.

The only problem is, I have a perfectly viable pregnancy brewing in someone else's belly, and I can't face the consequences of duplicating my efforts before sorting out my first mess. If that's even possible at this point...

FORTY

EMILY

GLUE

When I return home the eggs are stuck to the wall like glue.
Jasper stopped me before I pulled into my driveway because he
said he heard loud banging this morning and wanted to see if I
was okay. I explained that I was, but my walls were likely not.

"Here." Jasper places hot rags overtop the remnants to help
soak them off, but I'm sure there's going to be some paint that'll
come off with it.

"Should I ask what happened here?" He eyes my disaster
with curiosity.

"I'm afraid you'll judge me."

I watch Jasper as he picks up my frying pan, places it in the
sink, turns on the hot water, adds soap. There's something so
sexy about a man cleaning my dishes, and I'm not sure why.

"You saw what happened in my house," he says.

This is very true. I want to tell someone what I've done,
clear the air, try to convince myself it's not as bad as I think it is.
I definitely can't count on Laurel anymore. She's made friends
with the enemy.

But I can't tell Jasper all the dirty details—not about this. "I'm having troubles at work," I settle for.

He straightens a chair that's gone askew. I think of how perfect Jasper's place was and how he's probably one of those people who takes a lot of pride in his home.

"Throw-your-frying-pan-at-the-wall-troubles are pretty severe. Maybe you should think about getting another job."

"I'd probably have to move to a different city if that were the case. There's only so many fertility clinics. That's where I work."

"Well, me and Clem could use a new start if you'd like some roommates." He smiles, and again, what should be unsettling, is somehow not. There's an ease about Jasper, like I know him even though I really don't.

"Is she home alone?" I ask.

"She's at gymnastics. Tumbling." He shrugs. "I have to pick her up soon." He glances at his watch. TAG—an expensive brand. *Is this why you stay with her, Jasper?*

"Well, I don't want to keep you," I say.

Although I do. I want to keep him all night long in the confines of my bedroom. Have him make me pancakes in the morning—clean the pan.

But I've got enough complications to figure out right now. I don't need to add one more. "I'm sure Clementine is still adjusting to the situation. I'm glad she has a sport like tumbling to keep her moving. She's such a smart, active little girl."

Jasper turns to leave and then swings back around. "You know what the real suck of all of this is?" he asks.

"What's that?"

"I got that damn job." He sounds so defeated, I want to hug him. But I don't. Because if I hug Jasper, I'll want to do other things to him too.

"That's great."

"It's not great. I can't be in an office right now with Chelsea in the rehab facility. I didn't want that job. She did. I turned them down. But it's what broke her. Like she was so convinced I was a piece of shit that when I proved her wrong, she... I'm not sure of her intentions."

He was going to say, she *tried to kill herself*.

"She's obviously suffering from multiple diseases," I say, because alcoholism is one; and so is mental illness. Although, people don't often like to acknowledge either of them that way. But what Chelsea had going on is an entirely different level of sickness.

She built Jasper up to be something else in her mind, and when he proved to be just the opposite, she lost her mind.

I think about Ally, and how she trusted me to do the right thing. Envisioned me to be the one person who could help her, and how I let her down in so many ways, and she'll never even know it.

He nods. "Sometimes no matter what you do for someone, it's not enough. How hard you try..."

It's like he can see inside of me with that comment. Maybe he can sense it. I tried to do the right thing, make everyone happy, but I've burned myself in the end. I feel like I'm out of options. Anxious and stuck. Jasper probably feels the same.

"We can only do our best. You're an excellent father," I tell him. At least he has Clementine. I have no one.

However, by the time the gunk softens, I'm too exhausted to scrub it off. The mental deliberation of what I should do about Bemily is driving me mad.

Laurel texted me that she's signed up for the Pittsburgh marathon in May. She said I have six months to train too and that I should do the half-marathon.

Laurel: Make your body healthy for baby.

Only a woman in my current condition would read that text as a knock of failure on my part. It's like sending a subliminal message that if I'd taken better care of myself, I'd be pregnant right now. Meanwhile, she's the one that practically shoved wine and whiskey down my throat.

I know Laurel didn't mean it that way.

She's just trying to find a reason to communicate with me since I still haven't spoken to her after she lied to my face. She can't be serious with the whole marathon talk, though. I want to train for a marathon like I want to march over to Ben and Ally's house right now and announce they're having my baby.

It all sounds so weird in my head that I can hardly process it.

I plug my phone into the nightstand charger with Laurel's unanswered text sitting there, illuminated in the dim lighting. My exhaustion is so heavy it makes my pajamas a struggle to pull on—if you count Niles's old boxers and a tattered Nirvana T-shirt as pajamas.

Then, I fall backwards into my bed and pass out. It's the kind of serene restless slumber I haven't had since they chemically put me to sleep for my transfer.

"*No,*" I scream.

My hands are shaking and I look all around for the syringe and the baby. My hands wrestle in the sheets, searching for a cry, but there's nothing there. Have I smothered her? Have I smothered my baby?

I switch on the lights, and my right thumb is still pushed down on my forefinger like it's stuck to a joystick—or a syringe.

My eyes flicker on my bedroom wall and I think I see Ben's angry painting of El Capitan for a moment howling back at me, but it's just the same eerie framed poster of Picasso's *Girl Before a Mirror* that I thought would make my apartment appear more modern before I had cancer.

Afterward, the abstract painting of the woman with body parts juxtaposed in different positions only reminds me of my misplaced breasts, larger now with the implants. When I examine myself naked, they still don't look like my own, the gap in the middle too vast, the way they hang like overfilled balloons.

My heart races and my whole body feels like it's on fire. I made the mistake of going to bed with my socks on, something I never do, because I often get overheated. I rip them off, sweating so badly I have to throw myself into the shower.

I cry as the water runs down my body. That was the scariest dream I've ever had in my life. I fell asleep with my infant girl and had killed her somehow.

I think this dream was trying to tell me my inability to be present in the moment resulted in my body's failure to receive. My mind splinters at the jumbled thoughts, like the painting on my wall, playing with my fractured mind.

I should take the painting down.

The lukewarm water pours over my scalp and my face, blending in seamlessly with the river of tears that has begun, and continues to fall.

Is this what I'm supposed to do? Find a way to terminate Ally's pregnancy?

Or am I supposed to let Ally and Ben know so they can terminate it themselves? A cold shudder rocks me hard against the plastic of the tub as I suddenly realize the spray from the shower has gone cold now.

I turn it off and sit there nude, arms wrapped tightly around myself. I wonder if it's always going to be like this. If I'll always be by myself and hurting, mundane tasks filling my days, regret filling my nights. Seasons and holidays passing by, with me, and me alone, at my mother's depressing kitchen table, no boyfriend or child to sit along beside us.

Terrycloth envelops my skin as I wrap the towel around myself. I take a smaller towel to wipe my eyes and hair. My head hurts the way it does after an excessive crying fit.

It's clear I am not cut out for the repercussions of what I've done.

I cannot let Ben and Ally have my baby without the knowledge it's really mine. I'm not the type of person who can carry this type of lie with any amount of dignity or sanity. What happened with Cook was an accident. And I injected those drugs in my father's IV so he could die with dignity.

But this... there's no redemption for my actions. I'm in over my head. Living with this lie will whittle me down more every day until it rips me apart, comes out, or eventually kills me.

The horrible part that nags at me—what if I gave *her* the best embryo?

What if that one would've implanted for me too and I just gave it away? If we both would've gotten pregnant, I know I would've fooled myself into believing all was well as long as Ally and I were both happy, no matter whose child it was, but this is not okay.

It will gnaw at me constantly.

Every year that passes, every birthday party for that child that I attend, I know I won't really be able to live with the fact that another woman is raising my child. It will bother me that Ben is the father too, but could I really leave the mothering of my offspring to Ally? Do I know her that well?

I know what I have to do.

The longer I put it off, the worse it will be.

I will tell Ally and Ben tomorrow. If they want to abort the baby, I'll understand. But I know they won't. Ally is deeply religious and it's still Ben's biological child. If they want to press charges against me, they can, and I'll hire a good lawyer.

I'll have to. Ben will most certainly bring up my first medical error—Dr. Cook. He'll use it as evidence of my instability and if he's smart, he could have them reopen the case. But... that would only damn him as well. He's the one who retrieved the pill bottle.

In any case, I'll claim a laboratory error was the reason for the oversight, and hope for a good verdict. I'll most likely be fired, and the clinic will probably get sued, but Batey has it coming. She might even try to file a civil suit against me, but I'll use her secrets as collateral. I bet I could make my lawsuit disappear if I threaten her hard enough. I know a local urologist, Dr. Corini, who might even testify in my defense in that regard.

Then, I'll try to procure rights as the child's biological parent, and hold up the fetal termination process, if that's the route they try to go. And if they choose to keep the baby, I'll fight for custody rights. We'll have to co-parent three ways.

It's the only solution I see for this scenario.

Even though I can't imagine raising a child with two other people who will detest me for what I've done.

I should've known better than to think I could keep this secret. I've watched one too many DVRed episodes of *Days of Our Lives*, and I let my fantasy world blend in with reality, and now it's all catching up with me.

The disaster I've created is colossal and terrible.

If I could take it back, I would. There're two huge mistakes I've made in my life and they both involve Ben Holiday.

Maybe my bright and shiny spot in all of this will be this baby, but its shimmery brilliance will be diminished by the dark ugliness of how he or she was created. It will be branded a monster, a colossal accident, a focal point of disdain.

That's what my dream was trying to show me.

If I lose my job, it might be best to just pick up Bemily and move out of this city and start over. She (if she's really a she because she was in my dream) may not have come into this world under the greatest circumstances, but I can promise the rest of her days here will be nothing short of the best.

FORTY-ONE

EMILY

LOST

After several failed attempts to reach Ally, I decide to extend the olive branch to Laurel.

"No one can find her," Laurel breathes into the phone. She's too close to the receiver.

"What're you doing? You sound like you're trying to eat me," I say. I couldn't have heard her right.

"I'm sorry, I just got done running. Winded."

"It's like forty degrees."

"That's the threshold for running. Any lower than that is bad for your lungs."

"It all sounds bad for your lungs to me. I need to get in touch with Ally. Where did you say she was?"

Laurel stops breathing, and I come to the conclusion she must be holding her breath. "Ben can't find her. It's become a... thing," Laurel says.

"What do you mean? Like she's... missing?" *With my baby.*

"He's not using that word yet. None of us are. What're you

planning on saying to her?" Laurel asks, sounding strangely protective.

"Why?" I ask, equally defensive. The information I'm about to unveil to the Holidays is not something I want to share with Laurel first. It occurred to me Ally and Ben might not want people around them to know about the true identity of their baby. Plus, there's been a breach of trust, and my loyalty toward Laurel is uncertain at this point.

"Ally's been very hyper about this pregnancy," Laurel reveals. "Ben said she didn't react the way he expected when the pregnancy test came back positive."

"What do you mean?" I ask.

"She's had four miscarriages, Emily," Laurel says plainly.

A chill shoots down the back of my wool sweater as I make my way to my mother's house. "Well, her embryos were cultured in the lab this time, and there's nothing physically wrong with her uterus," I reason.

"That's all good and fine, but she's scared to death. She's lost four babies."

The moment of truth slaps me in the face. Ally has had four previous miscarriages for no good reason, and it could happen again. Then, all of this stress will be for nothing. I'll lose a baby too, but it will be a much bigger loss for her, because it will truly be her last chance at having one the natural way.

"Ben doesn't know where she is. He thinks she may have needed some space. He speculated she may be hiking or in the wilderness." *Alone in the wilderness with my baby...*

"That's absurd." All these people training to run, and hiking mountains voluntarily—this time while pregnant. No thanks.

"Emily, why do you want to talk to Ally?" I don't like Laurel's tone. I figured she'd be ecstatic to hear from me again, but that isn't the case.

"It's nothing." The conviction I felt so strongly last evening is wavering again. If Ally can't sustain the pregnancy, there's absolutely no reason I should lose friendships, my job, and possibly my freedom over it. There seemed like no way out last evening.

But maybe I can wait out Ally's first trimester to see if nature takes care of my laboratory experiment itself. It'll be a slow, cruel torture—for everyone involved.

"You're not going to do anything crazy, are you?" Laurel asks.

Done and done. "No, my God, Laurel."

"Well, it's shitty, the way things worked out. Ben moving here, and then he and Ally decide to get pregnant and then you decide you want to try to get pregnant too. Then, they get pregnant and you don't. The whole thing just sucks."

"Thanks for the recap," I say.

Laurel sighs at my sarcasm. "I don't know, Emily. If it were me, I'd probably be going a little nuts, and you've been mad at me, and I'm a bad friend for not telling you the truth, but how are you really doing?" she asks.

The question lingers in the air, and I wonder why she always has to make me think about the most profound things while I'm driving. Just then, I slam on my brakes at the red light that has seemed to come out of nowhere, and come inches from smacking into the back of an old Ford truck. By the looks of the bearded man glaring at me in the rearview mirror, I've nearly escaped a moment of road rage, and possibly murder.

"Laurel, look, I can't talk to you about this right now."

"Just tell me you're all right?" she demands. "Cat's been climbing the walls asking about you." She laughs. It's an old joke for our psych major pal, Cat. If she's been climbing the walls, I don't want to know what I've been doing, exactly. Searching for dead babies in my dreams?

"I'll be fine," I manage. It's the answer my mother used for the first ten years of my life when she holed herself up in the garage and read loathsome books. She asked Miss Sue, my nanny, to take me out into the sunlight and play.

"But don't you want to come out and play too, Mommy?" *I'd ask.*

"Later," she'd answer.

But she never came out. I'd enjoy myself playing outside with Miss Sue. Mother probably thought I'd forgotten about her dark days, but I never did.

Maybe was a dangerous word to say to a child, and one I promised not to use in vain with my own.

"Okay, well, I'm a little worried about Ally, but I feel better about you," she says.

You shouldn't, I want to tell her, but instead I say, "Tell me the minute they find her."

FORTY-TWO

EMILY

MISSING

Ally's status has elevated from lost to missing.

The authorities are searching all of the local parks. A rescue team has been launched, and Laurel mentioned something about cadaver dogs.

The word cadaver makes me want to vomit, even though I live for clinical terms.

She and Zach are joining the search team after work, and she asked me if I wanted to come with them.

Ally's mother is driving up too.

This all seems entirely surreal, and terrifying.

The missing woman they speak of is carrying my child. And I'm the only one who knows it.

Or am I?

Is that what this disappearance is about?

Ally is extremely intelligent. Did she somehow figure out what I've done? Is it all too much for her? Is she pulling a Chelsea and trying to make a quiet exit from this unfair life, or is she attempting to guilt me into a confession?

I was so close to doing just that—confessing.

As if on cue, the police appear, in my lab.

They speak to someone at the front, but I already know they're here for me. *The police.* Facing the law wasn't a scenario I anticipated.

At least not so soon...

"Miss Daugherty, thank you for securing this meeting room so we could speak with you. We realize you're in the middle of a busy workday and won't take up too much of your time. I'm Officer Tina Shire and this is Officer Garrett Macy."

I settle into a chair behind my desk, a place of authority, while they remain in the patients' chairs. We're in the consultation room, but it's my turn to be cross-examined. "It's no bother. How can I help?"

"Thank you. As you know, one of your patients, Allyson Holiday, has gone missing. Shortly after using your services here at the clinic. I hear she was a friend of yours," Macy says.

"Yes, it's terrible. I hope she's found soon. We're all so worried about her."

"How do you know Ms. Holiday personally?" Shire asks, her eyes shrewdly upon me.

"She's the wife of an old college friend." Best to describe him that way.

"I see, and did she contact you in the weeks leading up to her disappearance. After her procedure here?"

"Yes. We had lunch. Once."

The male cop with the military haircut flips through some pages. "Your office manager said she came here three times that week and called incessantly until you saw her. Is that true?"

Lisette! She had to know what a statement like that would

do to me. After all the secrets we've shared, why would she divulge that?

"That's true. Unfortunately I was ill, and couldn't meet with her until mid-week."

"Why did she need to see you so urgently?" Macy asks.

Because her Dead Babies were trying to rat me out. And so are you. The pulse in my neck ticks up a notch. "She was worried about the procedure she'd had done here."

"Why is that?" Macy asks.

I straighten in my chair and try to embody the Emily at this clinic that Dr. Batey has forced me to be—the liar. If the cops suspect anything is out of sorts at this lab it will upend Batey too. I'm not trying to protect Batey, exactly, as I am the missteps I've made for her. "Patients going through IVF are pumped full of hormones. They're emotional. I think it was too much for her knowing she had someone on the inside. In the lab. The poor woman had suffered four miscarriages, previously. That's HIPPA information. Please don't share."

"Of course. What questions did she ask you?" Macy asks.

"Um... they weren't questions, exactly. She was worried there was something wrong with her sample."

"Why did she think that? It says here she was a marketing analyst. What led her to believe this, Miss Daugherty?"

I was trying to steer them away from the lab, but it's hard to answer this question without placing them squarely inside of it. These questions are dangerous. "She didn't pull very many good eggs..." *None actually.* "I think she was just worried this one wouldn't make it like the others, and she thought I had some kind of inside track as to what was going on."

"Did you have concerns about her procedure?"

"I don't do the procedures. That's the doctor's job. I heard it went well, though."

Get out of my lab.

"You'd think someone with her history would place herself

on bedrest, or engage in a less dangerous activity than hiking, as her husband suggested."

Uh oh. They don't suspect Ben, do they?

"You would think that..." I swallow hard realizing the truth —they always suspect the husband first when something happens to the wife. I want to say more to protect Ben. I want to tell them that he couldn't hurt a fly, but then they'll ask why I'd say that. How I know him.

Why I injected his sperm into my egg and passed it off as Ally's.

For the love of God, where're you, Ally?

"We're looking for clues to indicate her mental state. What do you think Ms. Holiday would've done if she miscarried this time?" Shire asks, woman to woman.

Macy might as well not even be in the room, because we both know he can't possibly understand the weight of her question.

"She said... she'd just die if the procedure didn't take."

FORTY-THREE

EMILY

HIKE

Laurel and I have found a good place in our friendship again, although we'll never be in a *great* place until I receive a formal apology. So far hers have been layered with... *buts*... followed by lame excuses. None of which makes me feel any better about the information withheld from me.

As I lace up my barely used sneakers, Laurel stretches her long legs in her spandex pants. I have on many layers for this excursion, but I can't shake the chill, as it's barely thirty degrees.

We'll be hiking the backwoods of Pittsburgh's three-thou-sand-plus acres of North Park in search of Ally.

A five-mile-circumference lake sits in the middle of the park, its outskirts sprawling into horse trails, a dog park, and activities for all walks of life and their furry companions.

It's the largest hike-able area closest to where Ben and Ally live.

According to Laurel, Ben alerted the police that Ally mentioned wanting to check it out.

We start at the boathouse, and as I glance around, I can't

imagine how Ally could've possibly come here unspotted. This park is beyond busy with droves of walkers and runners.

"Laurel, how could she go missing at this park with all of these people milling around?"

Laurel gawks at me. "Well, it's freezing and slippery out here. Maybe she fell. Pregnancy can throw you off balance."

"She's only a few weeks along," I say.

"Your joints loosen up throughout your whole body, and early on. That's why they say to be careful and not to overexert yourself. And not to take on any new fitness regimens during pregnancy. I noticed differences right away," she proclaims.

"Okay..." I pull an athletic fleece headband over my ears trying to drown out her bullshit. That baby is the size of a damn pea. Laurel is running her mouth again. If Ally slipped, it's not because her femoral head became unstable in her pelvis.

It's because her foot slipped on ice and caused her to fall.

Or, because someone pushed her...

I shiver at the thought.

"Is Ben joining us?" I ask. There's a small crowd that's gathered and a news truck parked in the lot. No one speaks to one another, our mission a grave one. We all want to find the missing pregnant woman, yet no one wants to discover her under horrible circumstances.

"No, he's dealing with a lot and wants to avoid the press. The police questioned him today."

"They stopped by my work today too," I tell her.

She looks at me as though I've slapped her. "And you're just telling me this now?"

I glare back at her long and hard. She chose to withhold information from me, and in the future, I'll do the same—until she offers me a decent apology.

"This isn't about you and me, Emily. We need to put aside any grievances we may have and work together to find Ally."

I have a lot more at stake in finding this woman than she realizes, but Laurel needs to understand our trust has been broken and what that means for our friendship now. "You're right. I am worried about her. It's so strange she just disappeared."

"What did the police ask you?"

"They wanted to know about our lunch last week. If Ally was acting strange. If she mentioned anything concerning."

"Well, did she?" Laurel asks.

I inhale deeply, wondering now if there's anything I could've said or done that day to prevent this. "She did. She mentioned she'd... die... if this didn't work out."

Laurel makes an awful noise with her throat. "Did you tell Ben that?"

"No. At the time it sounded like something people say flippantly... Like—*I'll just die if I don't get into med school...*" I rationalize.

Accusation is written all over her face. "This isn't comparable to getting into a graduate program, Emily."

My body flushes hot and cold in embarrassment the way it does when I read the room wrong and say something out of turn. Just like my work HBDI personality profile said, I'm lacking in the relational department. I probably deserve to be alone, and now someone might be missing—or dead—because I failed to recognize signs of distress too late. "She seemed okay, just a little bit nervous about her results."

"She said she wanted to die," Laurel says.

"You're taking what I said out of context." My breath releases a puff of air with it. The temperature has already dropped. If Ally is out here somewhere, the weather could make this situation dire.

A police cruiser pulls up next.

Zach appears out of nowhere beside Laurel. "Hey, ladies. Sorry, had a late conference call. What's the scenario?" he asks, concerned.

"Cops just got here," Laurel says.

I stand in a huff next to my so-called best friend. I can't believe she blames me for this. I shouldn't have entertained Ally's request for lunch. Then, I couldn't have said, or not said, anything to make this situation worse.

But knowing my luck, Laurel would then admonish me for not helping the poor girl in her time of need. Officer Macy, megaphone in hand, begins doling out assignments. The press cameras are rolling, and all of a sudden instead of watching a missing person drama unfold on television, I'm part of the real thing. I just hope I'm not the cause of it.

We're on a mountain bike trail off the beaten path. In agreement with my earlier statement, Officer Macy said that if Ally ran into trouble, it was likely off the main circuit that loops the park. Otherwise, someone would have likely seen her by now.

I do recall Ben and Ally's previous excursions to be of the adventurous sort, so this makes sense.

The cops came prepared with a map of the park separated into grids and assigned pods of five or six individuals to each designated area. Zach, Laurel, and myself are paired with a local couple in their twenties who are treating the search like a first date.

"Do you think she might've wanted to see the waterfall? You can cut through here to get there?" the female asks.

"If you ever want to find the hidden waterfall, you call me. I've seen it before. Trust me, it's not worth all of this," her boyfriend says.

Giggles from the female.

Annoyed eyerolls from Laurel and myself.

The couple shut up and snap to attention. We only have so much daylight.

Guidance from the police officers in charge follows next.

"Take it nice and slow," Officer Macy instructed. "Stay arm's length apart from each other and maintain the same pace as your team so no one is left behind."

"If you come across anything suspicious, tag it with the bright tape in your search bags."

"Take pictures of anything that looks off. Footprints that lead nowhere. A bundle of snapped branches that seem out of place. Pieces of clothing. Hair. Discarded personal items that appear odd... a wallet, etc."

"Watch your step for trees, cliffs, ditches, but don't skip those areas. If they're perilous to you, they may be a danger to the missing person."

"You are in the wilderness. This isn't your natural habitat, but that of wild animals. Be alert."

"Give out the flyers in your search bag to anyone who crosses your path."

The frigidness has seeped into my tennis shoes. I should've worn hiking boots, but I don't own a pair anymore. My life feels a million miles away from Louie and Riggs Moor. I think Laurel feels my pain because I've caught her jumping up and down to warm herself a few times.

It's been almost forty-eight hours since anyone has heard from Allyson Holiday.

I hate what circulates through my brain, yet I can't stop it.

If Allyson Holiday is out here, in these woods—she's dead.

FORTY-FOUR

EMILY

CHANGE

The assigned teams return to the boat house at the scheduled time, each group with hopeful expressions that someone has found something, but no one has. Darkness settles in all around us, and the coffee the volunteers shuttled in has run out.

The press interview Laurel.

She seems to relish it a bit, even offering the reporter an Emmy-worthy performance.

"*Please...* we're just trying to bring our friend home. She's new to town and pregnant with her first child. It's not like her to wander off. If anyone knows anything, call the number at the bottom of the screen."

I cringe at her response.

She and Ally "targeted" together once, but Laurel acts as though she's known Ally all her life. And everyone in the crowd gobbles it right up, some even brought to tears. I want to believe that Laurel's plea is genuine, but neither of us know this woman enough to be truly invested in her life. It leaves me with the awful feeling that maybe I should be, and once again that I'm in an emotionally stunted group all my own.

As we're walking to our cars, Laurel asks me, "Where do you think she could be? This is just insane."

I'm freezing cold by now. The gloves I'm wearing are not thick enough and I think I can feel my bones poking through the knitted surface. "I don't know. But wherever she is, I hope she's not out here."

Snow falls and Laurel glances into the swollen sky absently as if contemplating the truth that filters all around in icy flakes. Ally may not be coming back—ever.

The concept of death is a foreign one to Laurel, a woman who's led a charmed life. Both her parents are still living. She has two siblings who're nearby, a husband who adores her, healthy children. She even has some grandparents who are still around.

She doesn't know Death.

I've dealt with it firsthand. Held the needle that injected it. Watched my father take his last breath.

Stared Death down in the face as they pumped toxic chemicals into my body to fend it off. Beat it.

Held it in my hands. Scrapped it in a biohazard bin, over and over again for the last nine years.

I understand the fragility of life and the real possibility that Allyson Holiday very well may be dead. It's a truth I don't discuss with my best friend, because she doesn't understand it.

"Get home safe," she says, as if we're all in terrible danger.

———

Jasper and I pull into our driveways at the same time. Neither one of us advances into the garage, staring at each other through the windows of our cars like the watchful strangers we are. I exit my vehicle, appearing a wreck, I'm sure.

My nose is probably still red, my body unable to unthaw from the deep freeze of a winterlike hike, even after cranking my heat full blast, heated seats on.

Jasper steps outside of his Lexus appearing like his beautiful self. Nice jeans and a fleece jacket that pull at his broad shoulders. I'm still wearing my warmest winter hat, an extra thick knit number with a giant pouffe on top and matching gloves.

"Where were you? The North Pole?" he heckles.

"No... I was part of a search crew. My... friend... has actually gone missing."

"Oh my goodness, I'm so sorry. Did they—"

"Not yet." I save him from having to ask the question.

I feel my teeth chatter involuntarily. I want to talk to Jasper. My loneliness closed in on me in those woods, hiking side by side with two other couples, one, in the early stage of dating, the other an "old" married couple. But I'm shivering and I need a hot shower more than company at the moment. "I'm still freezing from my hike, Jasper. I'm going to—"

"Come in!" he says. "I'll make you hot tea or coffee, and we can talk a bit? Clementine is with her aunt. I'd like to hear more about this, if you have any energy to discuss it."

I nod, unsure I really should, but then again, talking to someone else might be good for me.

"So, she was just there one day, gone the next?" Jasper asks.

He fixes me a cup of hot tea first and then wraps a colorful blanket around my body until I can barely move. He says it's made out of alpaca fleece, and it sure insulates like something made out of rare fur. The way his muscles flex when he tucks me into his couch makes me want to nestle in and never leave. "Something like that. She's a patient of mine. And she's also pregnant."

Jasper appears surprised. "I'm so sorry to hear that. Was

anything wrong with her before she was in your care? Or are you not allowed to tell me? Patient confidentiality."

I shrug, needing to get some of this off my chest. "She was nervous about her procedure not taking. But then it did. So, she should've been thrilled."

I sink into the blankets thinking about how it didn't work out the same way for me. *I should be the one hiking alone in the woods toward a cliff... not her.*

"Why do they think she was at North Park?"

"Ben, her husband, told the police that she mentioned she was going there to clear her mind. They were outdoorsy people before they moved here from the south. Hiking is something they did often."

I watch as the snow falls gently upon the city outside.

"I wonder why he didn't go with her." Jasper leans in, his own cup of hot tea steaming in his hands.

It's a loose-leaf blend, something spicy and acidic—like orange or cranberry. It coats my throat and radiates my insides in a way that makes revealing these details possible. "I think she wanted to be by herself. She was a high-risk case. It's been a journey for them to get pregnant. She was probably grappling with the idea of motherhood."

Jasper says, "Don't you think it's odd that if she was high risk he would let her go off on her own, traipsing around in the cold forest of all places? In an unfamiliar park she'd never hiked in before?"

I stare at the beautiful, insightful man before me. "Ben's a bit flighty. He probably wasn't thinking about any of that, just honoring her request for space."

"You seem to know him pretty well."

I clear my throat, finally in a comfortable place in my own skin. "We actually dated years ago. When we were in college. They returned to town and requested my services, and now here we are."

"Oh wow. And I thought my life had drama."

I smile at him, because for the first time ever, someone has used the word "drama" in relation to my life. The more appropriate genre is usually a boring tragedy. "Yes, well, I hope our stories both end well."

Jasper looks at me curiously. "This might be too personal a question, but did your ex have a bad temper?"

"No, why? He's a schoolteacher, for background info. A gentle soul."

"Hmm... okay."

"Why do you ask?"

He clears his throat. "In these cases, where the wife goes missing..."

I know where's he's going with this. "Ben didn't do anything to her, Jasper. He's a good guy." Better than Jasper knows. Although, he did cover up an unintentional drug-induced homicide for me.

I remember what he said in his apartment when I broke up with him—*I protected you.*

He resented me, but was he really sorry Professor Cook died, or was it all a ploy to try to control me, reel me back in? What was his marriage really like? Could he have done something to Ally?

Jasper nods. "They'll probably look at him first, even so."

"I have no doubt, but they won't find anything."

"People can change over the course of many years. *Circumstances* can change them."

I inhale deeply. If he only knew how familiar I was with this concept. Until Ben and Ally arrived in town I would've never considered tampering with samples. "I'd agree that people can change in certain ways. Like they can become stronger or weaker, learn new skills. But at the core they're still the same. I think Ben's core is good," I say. I want to believe this.

But then I think back to Ben's aloofness at the hospital.

How he, himself, went missing for a while. The way he quickly hid his phone when he saw me. His threat during his consult before we even got started—*I did things for you that still keep me up at night. Do this for me.* Was there malice behind it?

What would he have done if I hadn't agreed to his demands? Sold me out? I'm sure if he wasn't also implicated in Cook's death, he might've done it a long time ago. Maybe he was just waiting for the perfect time to bring it back up. What kind of man does that?

When Laurel hid her phone she was trying to conceal something. What was Ben hiding?

He seemed discontented in his marriage. His choices. To what lengths would he go to change his path?

"Okay, well, I really hope they find her," Jasper says.

I smile, and wiggle a bit. I'm trying to shake loose the wrapping Jasper has swathed me in with little success.

"Let me help you with that," he says. "I think you're tucked into the couch."

I laugh again as he walks over to unravel me, thinking about his words. *People can change over the course of many years...*

If I've come to a place in my stagnant life where I've made manipulating patient specimens okay in my mind, could Ben have come to a place where snuffing out his pregnant wife was a possibility in his?

FORTY-FIVE

EMILY

MEDIA

The next day, social media is eating Ben alive. I can't believe how on-target Jasper was about all of this. It's like he's been through it before himself. Or maybe he's just one of those quiet people who intently observe everything around him—the news, his child—his neighbor.

The comments people are making about Ben are malicious and ungrounded.

> **Gladysfromtheburgh** The husband has no social media accounts. None. It's not because he's too evolved for the Gram, it's because he knows it makes it easier to hide...

> **LouinBlawnox** Who lets their newly pregnant wife go hiking in this weather?

I look outside and the ground is covered in a fine white powder. It's not fair to make such comments, because the day before yesterday it was all clear skies and twenty degrees warmer. This is the problem with social media and the comments made there—they're often ill-informed.

> **AshleyBrown** She was on hormones from recent IVF therapy, probably has some of that post-partum depression.

Again, not how that works, *Ashley*.

Post-partum refers to after a pregnancy has already occurred. These stupid people are pissing me off, but more so, I'm upset imagining Ben reading them. Then again, if he doesn't have social media, maybe he'll be graced with never seeing them.

Either way, I feel for him.

I want to reach out, but it doesn't seem appropriate.

I also feel strangely guilty about our conversation. I didn't make Ally go missing, but I did perform a medical procedure on her without her knowledge before she disappeared, and it's hard to separate the two events.

Did she figure it out somehow?

What does the bible say about surrogate pregnancy? Because that's pretty much what Allyson is—my surrogate mother—and she's missing.

The social media feed is never-ending. Ally's picture is everywhere. They picked one of her from an old vacation, wide smile, dark hair blowing behind her in the wind. You can see a cropped portion of another person, indicating Ben was also in the picture.

They've cut him out.

Demonized him.

> **DJKaley** It's always the husband. Even when it's not the husband... it's the husband.

I think about this comment, and wonder again if Ben could

actually be involved. It's an absurd concept. He seemed exactly the same person I remember (and loved) at the party, as if time hasn't changed an iota of his personality or mannerisms a bit. But in the hospital... he was different. Antsy. Distracted. Late. He made lame excuses about needing to go for a walk. I didn't believe him. Where was he really going?

It's natural to be uneasy during IVF. It's not a simple process and emotionally taxing on all parties involved.

It makes me wonder if they had an argument. Maybe Ally didn't go for a hike by herself. Perhaps Ben was with her, and something terrible happened...

I might be able to forgive Ben for an accident that hurt his wife, but I'll never be able to forgive him for accidentally killing our child.

ChrisandRebeccaPine A white van of suspicion was just reported at the park at the time Ally was hiking. I wouldn't be so quick to point to the husband. Women aren't safe walking alone anywhere anymore.

NorthHillsCrimeStoppers North Hills crime stoppers is committed to following the lead on the van which is reported to have no license plate on the rear. Van was scene parked, lakeside, beside the playgrounds near the boat house. Anyone with leads, please call 888-NHC-STOP.

JezebelsDaughter The woman's car was found in her driveway. How did she get to the park? Did she levitate there? Maybe the guy in the van gave her a ride. I don't think she was ever at that park... False lead thrown from the husband to toss them off his trail.

Well, now, that's some news.

I never stopped to question if they found Ally's car at the

park or not. I just assumed they did, because why would a police force take the time to form a search party if they weren't at least sure she'd been there?

But if Ally's car was found in her driveway, I can't see how she could've been at the park. Did she have any friends here? Had someone given her a lift? Gone walking with her?

Jezebel makes about the most sense of all of the deluded posters. Ally's missing person case has taken on a life of its own.

I want to concentrate on other things, but I can't stop thinking about Bemily. Freezing to death in the snow as her mother takes her last breath.

Hidden beneath an undiscovered cliff somewhere. Maybe there's still time to save her.

There's only one person who knows what happened to Ally right before she went missing—Ben.

It's time to face him and find out what happened to Ally, and find out where my baby is.

FORTY-SIX

EMILY

PRESS

I snagged Ben's address off his medical chart. There's a press parade set up in his townhouse development. A quick drive-by tells me he isn't home. There's one place I know I can find him on a Sunday afternoon—eating an early dinner at his parents' house in Monroeville.

I hop on the turnpike and take the familiar route. The snow has calmed down and the roads are clear. When I reach the Holiday residence, a large brick house where Ben and his three siblings grew up, I'm shocked to discover there's nowhere to park because there's so many cars in the driveway.

I find a spot up the street and trudge all the way down the road.

I stop dead in my tracks when I see Laurel's Forerunner and what I think is Cat's Audi SUV. *What in the hell is going on?*

I ring the doorbell, already feeling like I've been betrayed before anyone answers. Angela, Ben's older sister, opens the door. "Emily." Her smile curls into confusion. "It's been ages. I guess you're here to join the others."

"Hey, Angie. Yeah... sure."

She welcomes me inside, and the whole gang is sitting around the kitchen table—Laurel and Zach. Cat and Seth. Hooch—and Ben. They wave at me. Laurel motions me forward as if this was all planned.

Ben's three siblings, Angela, David, and Rachel, just gape at me as if they're not sure whether to welcome me in or toss me to the curb. I'm sure when me and Ben broke up they heard a mouthful from him about me—none of it good.

And then, there are the ex-almost-in-laws, weathered and worn over the current events in their family, and not that happy to see the girl who broke their son's heart years ago.

I had a frayed relationship with Marybeth Holiday.

She was a prayer and a stayer, and I wasn't a believer, and a leaver.

"Can I take your coat, Emily, so you can join the others?" Marybeth asks.

"Sure." I hand her my puffer jacket.

"Hello, dear, how're you?" Arthur Holiday asks.

"Great, Art, thanks."

"I guess you got my text," Laurel says, as if trying to throw me a life raft. I'm over her lies and decide to deflate it instead.

"You didn't text me, Laurel," I say. I've never called her out on her bullshit before. It's about time... Her mouth drops open in surprise, and she doesn't respond. "I drove here because I was having trouble sitting at home imagining what you're going through, Ben. I thought I might be able to help somehow."

Ben's eyes are completely bloodshot, and he looks like he might burst into tears. "Thanks, Emily. Come on, we're retracing Ally's steps."

I work my way into the circle beside Hooch because it's the only space around the island that's available. There's a map of North Park at the center. It's the same one the cops gave us yesterday, partitioned by sections. There are two fluorescent marks and a messy drawing of a van by the lakeside.

"Those two pieces of tape symbolize spots on the map that hikers marked on the trail as being possibly suspicious," Seth tells me.

"One was what appeared to be a mud slide, as if someone could've slipped down a hill. Or it could've simply been a disruption from the weather," Cat finishes her husband's thought.

"The other mark is to indicate unexplained broken glass." Zach shrugs.

Ben's eyes flicker toward mine at the mention of the broken glass, and then away.

"The van... is the van that's been on the news," Hooch says.

"I have a question about that. Ally's car was found at your townhouse. Right, Ben?" I ask.

"Yes," he says, solemnly.

"Well, then how did she get to the park?"

"I–I don't know that. It's one of the things we're unsure about."

"Is it possible she just went for a walk around the area surrounding your property instead? That might make more sense. Perhaps we should set up a search team there."

Ben shakes his head. "There's nothing really there besides sidewalks. It's all residential and industrialized. No walking trails. She specifically said North Park. Maybe she Ubered or got a ride."

"From who? Did she have friends here?" I ask.

"No... Not except for Laurel. And you, of course," he adds.

My eyes float over to Laurel who won't look at me after I called her out.

"I haven't seen her since we went to Target," she says, finally.

"It doesn't make sense," I say.

"None of it makes sense. That's why we're here," Laurel says sharply.

"What does her mother say?" I ask.

"She's in town, but she hasn't heard from Ally. She's staying at a hotel. The Days Inn," Ben says.

I don't know why, but I glance at Marybeth. She looks away. From what I know of Ally, she grew up pretty poor. The Holidays should let Ally's mother stay here, both being Christian, God-fearing women, and all.

There're cell phone records spread out beside the map.

"There's nothing unusual in the call record. We already went through it," Laurel informs. I pick the papers up anyway to inspect them.

Each of the recent calls has notes beside it.

"What's ACG?" I ask.

"It's the default number for the Carolina builders' network. They do everything from drywall to building actual homes. We were getting the house ready to sell. Ally was really settling in here, especially once we got a positive pregnancy result. Our house down south needs to be painted. She probably called a contractor."

I nod, and can't find anything amiss in the stack of call log notes either.

"Oh God, where is she?" Ben breaks down and starts crying. Laurel glares at me like it's all my fault. I asked too many damn questions. Ones that were likely already asked, compounding his worries in my attempt to get caught up.

He stops abruptly. "Do you know something, Emily? Is that why you're here? Did you... not disclose something about her procedure, because she seemed wigged out something was wrong?"

Everyone lasers in on me like I'm the enemy. And I know why Ben's asking. None of the other people in that room know what I did in college. If they did, I wouldn't be standing there.

They'd be horrified and one of them would've turned me in—probably Laurel, if I had to choose one. Ben wants to know if I covered up something to do with Ally's vanishment—like I covered up Cook's death.

Forget my father. He doesn't know about that, but I understand the theme. No one else in this room would've had the cloudy judgment to go through with the acts I've committed.

Ben wants to know if Ally's disappearance is one more thing.

Zach places a firm arm around Ben. Marybeth steps into the kitchen to take over, holding her son.

She offers me a harsh up-and-down like this is all my fault too. If she only knew the truth...

"No. I don't know a thing. Her fertility treatment at the clinic was textbook perfect." I step away, out the back sliding glass door, a bit nauseous. *Is this all my fault somehow? Did I do this?*

Or is Ben putting on an act? He's an artist. But is he an actor too? All of that talk about decisions by the hospital elevator. Did he learn of Ally's pregnancy and then decide he could no longer be with her? Did Ben take out a hit on her? He also proved to have a cracked moral foundation by discovering that pill bottle and getting rid of it. He helped cover up an involuntary death. But is committing murder himself out of the question?

I hear her quiet footsteps before I see her. "I'm sorry I didn't tell you we were coming here, but it didn't feel right inviting you. I also wasn't sure what kind of terms you were on with the Holidays," Laurel says.

"It's fine. I hope I didn't upset Ben more."

"He's been doing that. Fine one moment, destroyed the next. He's an emotional guy. This is killing him. Not knowing. The fact that Ally is pregnant. He's a little ticked you didn't share with him what she said about just dying if things didn't take."

I shoot her a look of reproach.

"The cops filled him in, not me." *Lie.* If the cops suspected him even a little they wouldn't offer that information up to him on a platter.

"No they didn't. And I'm going to start calling you out on shit every time you lie to me. Every time you've ever done it, I've known, by the way."

"Excuse me?" Laurel asks.

"The cops didn't tell Ben that. You did. You did it to try to help find Ally, okay. Just own what you say and do."

I'm the pot calling the kettle black right now, but there's only so much a human being can endure.

Laurel crosses her arms at her chest, totally inflamed. "Do you want to know the real reason I didn't tell you we were coming here?"

"Enlighten me."

"Because you haven't been treating this like an emergency. On our hike yesterday, you might as well have been on a different planet. I don't know what you were thinking about on that hike, but it wasn't Ally."

She's right. I wasn't thinking about Ally; I was worried about my baby.

"We all process things differently, Laurel. I internalize."

"Yeah, well, while you're busy doing that, the rest of us are expressing the right amount of concern and support for our friend." She charges away, right after she's hit me in the most vulnerable spot possible. She knows I'm self-conscious about my ability to show emotion. Now she's telling me it's hurting others, which totally sucks. I can never confide in her and tell her what I've done. She'll never understand.

No one will.

Just then, I hear it, even from outside. The strangled cry, the same one Ben expressed when we broke up. Something has happened.

I walk into the living room and turn my attention toward the television as everyone crowds around to listen.

The newscaster is speaking: "An unidentified Caucasian woman, suspected to be between thirty and forty years old, was found along the riverwalk with multiple stab wounds... it's estimated she died sometime between Friday evening and Saturday morning this weekend..."

Ben is inconsolable as his mother rubs his back.

The others stand back and watch the broadcast in dismay.

"Now, we don't know anything for sure, son..." Art reassures, but Ben just shakes and cries.

What're the chances it could be anyone else? Someone abducted Ally, and killed my child. I run out of the house with my hand over my mouth and vomit in the bushes.

FORTY-SEVEN

EMILY

BODY

Everything changes now that there is a body.

I was fairly sure after the first forty-eight hours passed that this is how everything would end, but I didn't anticipate murder.

Someone murdered my baby.

After I left Ben's parents, I drove away in a blind rage that turned into ugly cries.

It's hard to imagine someone could be so heinous as to stab a woman to death. The kind of hate that would have to exist in someone's heart to commit that type of act is unimaginable to me.

At the same time, the fact that the woman was pregnant with my child seems like a sort of sick punishment for what I've done.

I played God, created a life that shouldn't exist, so it was taken away from me. Only the payback came with interest, because they took the mother too.

I'm overwhelmed with terrible thoughts. Why would

someone do something so awful? And it's just my luck that on top of losing my child, I'll likely have to face the legal implications that go along with it.

My scientific brain goes into overdrive of what will happen next.

Ally's body will be transported to a morgue, and the criminal investigators will order an autopsy. Autopsies are usually performed within the first twenty-four hours. They will discover that Ally is pregnant.

Because they are looking for motive, they may test the unborn fetus. Even though the baby was created via IVF, the authorities may not stop to consider this and follow all the normal tests and procedures that are required for a pregnant female homicide victim.

And after they perform the tests, they will come to realize that somehow, the woman who's carrying this child is not the biological mother.

They'll ask how this can be...

Which will irrevocably point the finger back to me.

Even though there's no real motive for why I might want to kill this woman, they'll also discover that she's the wife of my ex-boyfriend.

The medical files from the clinic will be unsealed and they'll learn that me and Ally were going through IVF at the same time, and that Ally conceived a child.

And that I did not.

My mind switches to viewer mode, like I'm watching this story through a television screen. My brain does that sometimes when I want to escape reality.

The setting presented in my mind's eye is a typical courtroom procedural backdrop.

The prosecutor struts confidently to present his case to the jury.
"It's hard to believe that a woman could possibly make the

mistake of implanting her egg, with her ex-boyfriend's sperm, by accident.

"Come on, people... we weren't born yesterday.

"A single woman. Who hasn't found anyone else since she broke up with the victim's husband...

"She works at a clinic that has one of the highest success rates in the country.

"Are we to believe that Ms. Daugherty's first mistake involves her own specimen? Wouldn't she be even more cautious with that one, and that of her friends'. No, I don't buy it and neither should you.

"This was no accident. Ms. Daugherty produced her own children without the male counterpart's consent, and then signed off on them to be implanted in someone else's body. This action right here shows instability, terrible judgment—mental illness?

"When both women underwent the procedure and she learned that Ally Holiday became pregnant and she did not, that had to have driven her absolutely crazy, right?

"Crazy enough to kill?"

Fuck. I am in big trouble.

I sit in the parking lot of the Days Inn, waiting for a glimpse of Ally's mom. I checked with the front desk, and they rang her room for me, but it didn't appear that she was there. It's probably because she's still at the county morgue identifying her daughter's body.

I shouldn't be here.

If Laurel were standing over me, she'd ask me what the hell I was doing. This woman just lost her daughter. Why am I bothering her?

But I'm curious as to why everyone's left her all alone. At this time, shouldn't the Holiday family welcome Ally's mother into their home? I can't imagine what it must be like to go through this by herself. Perhaps talking to me will bring her comfort.

These are the fallacies I feed myself to hide the real reason I'm here—to protect my own ass.

There's still time to convince Ally's mom not to do an autopsy.

I researched Catholicism and autopsies, and while it is allowed, it's reserved for legal inquiries and scientific research, like organ transplants.

We know Ally's cause of death—stab wounds.

Will it really bring her mother any relief in knowing all the dirty details—how many times her daughter was stabbed, where? What happened to her in the moments before and after the murder occurred.

A dissection of the body won't change the outcome of events, and especially that of the embryo. Those destined for Heaven will still reach their destination.

Why carve up the groupings of cells that are to become a baby?

And find out what I did...

Maybe Ally's mother will also know something about why her daughter was acting so erratically in the days before she went off with God Knows Who and got herself and my future child killed.

I have a right to understand these details. My future baby's last moments.

The embryo is only a bunch of cells right now, but it's what it represents. My heart is so heavy I can barely sit here in one piece.

I wipe a tear away, knowing that I can't tell anyone about my loss. I must grieve in solitude. I actually had fantasies of watching this kid grow up. I didn't realize how much I was anticipating this small slice of happiness in an otherwise impossible situation until I thought about the fact that I won't be able to sneak onto the bleachers of a stadium and watch Bemily play sports from afar like I'd dreamed of. I'm not athletic, but Ben is, so maybe there was a chance.

It's possible it's not just a delusion and my make-believe attorney in my fake on-screen dilemma was right. Maybe I *am* mentally ill.

———

After what feels like an eternity, an old Honda Accord rattles to a standstill in the parking lot. The driver's bob of dark hair tips out of her car, and I see Ally's mother trudge to the front door. I slip out of my vehicle and walk quickly behind her.

She heads for the elevator.

"Excuse me."

The woman whips around, startled. But she doesn't appear as devastated as I expected.

"I'm Emily Daugherty, the embryologist on your daughter's case. I met you briefly in her hospital room."

"Yes! Emily. I'm so sorry. It's been a trying few days. Caroline." She outstretches her hand to introduce herself, and then drops wearily into a lobby chair. I sit down next to her.

"I can only imagine... I'm so sorry about the news. I wanted to reach out. I saw some of Ben's family earlier and I was surprised you weren't with them. They told me you were here."

"Yes, I called Marybeth, and we've texted each other with updates, but she hasn't called me back or invited me over." I tilt my head to the side at this information, taking it all in. I always thought Marybeth didn't like me because I was career-driven and headstrong, but perhaps she's just a snob.

Caroline's phone lights up and she looks at it annoyed.

"What is it?" I ask.

"It's nothing... Dollar General is going to force me into early retirement if I don't return soon. They've been trying to for years. Maybe it's time."

"That's too bad." I take her hand in mine.

"Yes, it is... I shouldn't have left Ally. She was having troubles in her marriage, missing home. Now, it's too late."

Too late. Those are the words I need to capitalize on here. "Did you... were you at the coroner's? Did they have..."

I can barely articulate my thoughts. Caroline shakes her head at me, apparently at a loss for words.

I say, "I'm so sorry. I know in your religion autopsies aren't the first request if there's no reason for investigation. I think we know what happened here. Lord knows that baby doesn't need to be—"

"Emily, what're you talking about?" she asks. "My heavens, haven't you seen the news?" Her southern accent has grown thicker. "It wasn't Ally. I went down there to identify her, and it was another woman in town on business. Her husband didn't know anything was wrong because she'd checked in with him right before it happened. It was a robbery gone wrong, apparently."

I stare at Ally's mother in disbelief, a tidal wave of emotions from relief and hope to fear and wonder.

Allyson Holiday is—alive?

FORTY-EIGHT

EMILY

NARRATIVE

I sat with Ally's mother a while last evening as she lamented to me about her lost daughter. I can't help but think there's much more to the story here.

Ramblings of *she doesn't really like Pennsylvania,* and *tension in the marriage,* kept creeping into the conversation.

These aren't facts I knew before, nor ones they shared on the news. The broadcasts made Ben and Ally out to be the all-American golden couple.

They're important details to me now.

Especially since Ben's account of Ally's acclimation here was different. He said she was preparing the house to sell because she was finally "settling in."

As I sit on my lab stool and peer through the microscope, picking up the slightest defect in a patient's specimen, I realize that's the difference maker in sensitive cases. Sometimes it's the smallest discrepancies that can affect the outcome.

So which is it—Ally liked it here, or she didn't?

Ally was content in her marriage, or she wasn't?

Was Ben trying to sell himself on a false narrative because he wanted his wife to be happy here—or were his intentions more sinister? I pull away from my scope at the thought.

Ally's car was in the driveway...

Ben led the cops to the park—away from his home.

Ben said Ally told him she wanted to hike North Park because she needed space. Did she really say that? Ben said something similar to her in the hospital. That he took a walk because he needed space. What would he do to get it?

Or did Ben purposely lead the authorities away from his home because he had something in there—evidence—he didn't want them to see. The police have probably done a thorough sweep of their home by now, but his theatrics—if that's what they were—might've bought him some time to get rid of whatever he needed to. Just like the pill bottle. It's hard to think of Ben this way, but if there was tension in the marriage, who knows what was going on behind closed doors.

Ben's sweet, but he has a nervous energy about him, a hyperactivity that's always thrummed at a low level—instability? It makes me wonder how he'd channel it under the wrong circumstances.

In the face of adversity. With an unstable, hormonal wife screaming in his face...

Ben also wasn't a part of the search party. Laurel said it was because he was *going through a lot*, and—he wanted to *avoid the press*.

It seemed like reasonable logic at the time, but it doesn't now.

"What're you noodling about over there, Em? Looks like you're going to bust your slide with the high-focus beams coming out of your eyes. Did they find Ms. Holiday yet?"

I flinch, forgetting Ralphie is even here. I don't think I said hello to him this morning. "They haven't. That's what I'm thinking about. Something doesn't make sense to me."

"What's that?"

"If your wife went missing, and you thought you knew the proximity of where she was lost, wouldn't you lead the charge to find her?"

"Hells yes."

"Ben wasn't with us, Ralphie. He didn't come to the search party. I'm fine with the possibility that he was in shock, but I also heard he was trying to avoid the press."

"You'd think he'd want to use the media. He could've made a statement. People love to feed on the sympathies of others, but it can also make them invested in the search. They might be more liable to keep an eye open, make a concerned phone call," he says.

"Exactly."

"Although that dude couldn't even produce a sample... so that leads me to believe he might not be the strongest of character. Might've been too much for him."

"Ben's led a mostly easy life. I imagine this could break him."

"I'm sorry about your friend. I will say this... the way she called here after her procedure made me think she was nuts. She isn't the first patient you've known personally. None of the others did that. It's like she suspected we were up to something in here." He laughs, and I'm unable to join in, because if Allyson Holiday decided to take off because she thought we somehow tampered with her sample, she's exactly right.

And if that's the case, she's probably somewhere verifying her hunch right now.

It would make sense to tell no one of her suspicions and flee, even her own husband, because he would try to stop her.

I'm petrified right now, because I've just convinced myself this is what happened.

Allyson Holiday was our most educated IVF candidate.

She asked more questions than any patient before her.

She's made her career as a marketing analyst. She thrives on facts and figures.

And if she had her doubts after we performed our services on her, she probably did research to calm her fears, and maybe she found something.

I inadvertently gave away at our lunch that one of the embryos was deformed. She probably read into that, and assumed they were all bad, and that it was highly unlikely one would be perfect in that case.

Allyson Holiday is an educated woman who I vastly under-estimated.

An educated woman who's going to get me thrown in jail. And if I go down, we all go down.

I peer at Ralphie, sadly. I've taken him for granted lately, and I'll truly miss working here.

One thing I've learned from this experience—I can't continue to work here and lie to the patients. I'm going to need to take some time off to follow my suspicions about Ally, and if I do that with no notice, Batey could fire me.

And if that doesn't do it, what I'm going to lay on her next will.

"You want to take how much time off?" Batey asks.

"Two weeks," I say.

"Emily... we'd have to cancel twenty scheduled transfers. Now, I know you've been through a lot recently, but I don't see how that's the best care for our patients. You just went through the process. You know how potential mothers-to-be count down every minute until their implantation day. This will cause a major disruption." Her white teeth shine at me as she spits out the last words with vigor.

"Not so. Just bend your rules and let Ralphie and Ellen or Tawny assist you."

She snipes at me, "Telling me how to do my job, are we?"

"About that..." Something this situation has taught me is that the only thing I can truly control is my own actions. The very best I can do for myself, and my future child—if I locate him or her—it to set a good example and hope they follow suit.

Hopefully, when they look at me one day, they'll see that Mommy was a highly motivated scientist who created families for people who otherwise might not have been able to have them. And I can feel good about that.

But if anyone were to dig deeper, right now, they'd see that I allowed myself to be led by a tyrant who took advantage of my kindness and used me as a tool to procure higher numbers for her own personal interests. And I can't let that be my life story any longer.

"I had something I wanted to talk to you about." My voice sounded sterner in my head when I thought about this speech earlier.

"What's that, dear?" Her gold jewelry glints beneath her oxford shirt.

"This situation with my failed transfer and missing friend has made me realize that life is fragile. People are delicate. My picture of the world is different now. In a good way..." I say.

"Go on..." Batey flips through charts, impatiently. "So what bright idea did you arrive at?"

"Dr. Batey, I will not consult your patients for nine-one-ones anymore. Not a single one. If you aren't here, I'm telling Lisette to cancel them. It's not my job. I'm not comfortable doing it, and I'm not trained to do it. It isn't fair to me. And it isn't fair to the patients."

My head swims with dizziness.

I grab onto the end of her desk. She looks absolutely flummoxed and needles her fingers through her fine gold chains. I could find another job at a different fertility clinic, but the only place I want to work is here. It's the best clinic in the country, and if she tells me to get lost, I'll be heartbroken, but I need to do this. It's not just about me anymore.

"Very well," Dr. Batey says gruffly. She pounds away on her keyboard.

My breath is raggedy and my palms are sweating so badly I think I might slip right off her desk into the trashcan. "I'm glad we could come to an agreement on this matter. I'd also like my vacation approved."

"Well, look who found her big girl pants. Good for you. Very well, then. You have to give me at least two weeks to get everything sorted, and then we'll figure it out until you get back." Batey is typing furiously on her keyboard now, steam practically rolling out of her ears. And that's it—I did it. I stood up to Batey and got my way. A rash of hot prickles wash down my face in relief.

Why haven't I done this before? I'm the best embryologist in my field. She needs me just as much as I need her.

FORTY-NINE

EMILY

CLUE

The news released a statement that the unidentified van at the park spotted at the exact time Ally was presumed to have taken a hike has been verified as a vehicle for a new pest control company. The driver was taking a dinner break during his work-day. He had a temporary tag taped on the front of his wind-shield. That's why there was no plate on the back.

False lead, which just gives me all the more incentive to believe one of my two other hypotheses is correct—Ben murdered Ally in a fit of rage and is trying to cover it up with a false alibi about her taking a hike in the park, or—Allyson is on a research mission to prove I've made her a guinea pig in a much bigger scheme.

Ben's strangled howl in his parents' house when they released the news about the murdered female was not unlike the one he expressed when we broke up. It's also a sound I could've gone the rest of my life without hearing again.

But I know this—it's a sound of pain, and it's also one of love.

At one time, Ben Holiday loved me.

And he loves Ally.

It's hard to believe, even at his worst, that he'd harm her.

I need to find Ally.

No one can discover what she knows about her procedure. What I've done.

I've corresponded with Laurel, only so that I can get information on Ben.

After I fled the Holidays she texted me.

Laurel: I can't believe you just took off.

One of the biggest losses of this entire tragedy is that I no longer have a best friend. I'm not sure what transpired exactly, but Laurel is no longer on my side. Maybe she senses it—that I have something to do with Ally's disappearance.

That I caused this.

That Ally is on the run because of something I did.

My phone shakes in my hand as I sit on my laboratory stool, nausea rising.

Me: Is Ben still at his parents?

Laurel: Of course. He can't be alone right now

Me: Give him my best, I reply, but really I just want to know where he is while I look for his wife.

The headlines on Ally have slowed the way they do when a case drags on beyond five days—on to the next hot story. Ally's picture is still flashed on the screen every so often, a tip line and reward included, but as far as I can tell this woman vanished into thin air.

As a person of science, I find this conclusion impossible. I also find that this situation has drastically increased my appetite.

"Jimmy John's for lunch?" I ask Ralphie.

"Again? You might have it worse than me," he says.

"It's their peppers. I think I'm addicted."

"I think it's more than the peppers." He raises an eyebrow at me.

"What're you saying?" I ask.

"I'm saying, I'm placing bets on who tests for high cholesterol first, you or me?"

"No way, you've got years of binge eating this stuff on me. I just discovered it."

Ralphie is one of those tall human garbage disposals that never gains weight.

"You've got ten actual years of living on me, woman."

"Good point," I say, sadly. Just another reminder of me and my aging body.

"Yeah, I'm down for a little cold sammy, though," he says.

"Sweet. Give me ten minutes to put this sample in the incubator."

I eat my submarine sandwich with the force of a saber-toothed tiger that's just come out of extinction. To my embarrassment, Ralphie has barely scratched the surface of his Italian hoagie. When he glances up to engage in conversation, I'm sitting back in the uncomfortable plastic seat burping up peppers.

"*Girl.*"

"I know, I know. I was hungry. Actually, I could eat another one, but I'm just going to get a bag of chips and a cookie instead," I comment, as I rise from the bench.

I feel Ralphie's eyes watch me questioningly as I near the counter.

As I return to the table with my extra snacks, he asks, "Anything you want to tell me?"

"Like what?"

"Like why you're eating like you're trying to grow an extra ass. Like why your face is puffed up like you're getting ready for another transfer."

My hand instinctively flings to my face, now hot and flushed.

"My face is fat? Stress makes me hungry." I let my oatmeal raisin cookie remain on my tray in its cute little white envelope. I have one of those small heads people often mistake for a child's from the rear. When I attempted softball in high school I was the only girl on the team who took an XS helmet. Extra weight on my face is not a good look.

"Not fat, just glowing," Ralphie teases, pressing his hands together and smiling smartly.

"Well, that's unfortunate, since I haven't taken any hormone shots in over a month."

"Oh, well, uh, maybe we should try like Panera or even the cafeteria salad bar next time or—" he fumbles with his words.

"I get it, I've gained weight."

"Em, you know I don't like my girls thin. You look good to me," Ralphie muses, smacking my thigh under the table.

"Very funny. Be a real friend, and just tell me I'm getting fat and that I need to go on a diet."

"Could've been a low hCG read. False negative on the blood test?" Ralphie jokes.

Low hCG is bad. If the levels initially showed up as low after the thirteen-day mark and then got higher, the pregnancy often ended in miscarriage.

"Unlikely. I'm just fat, let's be honest."

"I got friends, Em... who like thick girls. Your hips probably wouldn't even qualify."

"Uh huh, and are they also in their twenties?"

"Well, yeah, but—"

"Ralphie, no thank you. I want to date men not boys."

"Well, suit yourself. You might want to lay off the cookies, though."

I laugh and throw a chip at him. He dodges it and ducks dramatically, brightening my mood. It's nice to work with good people and I know I'll be okay, just as long as I can keep it together.

It's been almost a week since Ally has gone missing—no leads.

Where is she—*with Bemily?*

"Yo, I heard Lisette complaining that she's tried to call Kelly Amstead three times for her follow-up with the twins, and she hasn't responded." Ralphie makes his expressive gossip eyes at me, and I wish I could go back to when all we had to talk about were noncompliant patients and our obnoxious colleagues.

"Maybe Marx is out of the country fighting and she went with him. They also live in Philly. That's a haul." I shake my head.

"You would think that if you repeatedly saw the switchboard number for the hospital on your voicemail and you were pregnant with twins, that you'd return that call. Do you think they'd ditch us?" He raises his eyebrows at me, mischievously. "Like they'd start the process here, and now that the babies are all up in her womb, they're going to see a different doctor close by. Batey would lose her shit. Might not be able to legitimately count them in her success rates."

I giggle, but something about Ralphie's statement makes me stop mid-chew. Ally started her shots in North Carolina and finished them here.

If Ally was going to take off somewhere to have herself tested, she'd probably go back to her original doctor. She could claim she wasn't happy with her level of care and ask if they would take her back. I remember her saying, "I liked Dr.

Williams..." There can't be that many Dr. Williams who are fertility specialists in Charlotte. I'll find him or her. And then, I'll find Ally.

It's a longshot that she ran home—or is it?

What I'll do with her when I find her is still a big unknown.

I'll come clean for sure. Tell her my good intentions. She doesn't need to know I used Ben's sample to create mine. That can go untold. But still, how do I convince her not to ruin my life? I can't imagine what her church would say about what I've done, but I'm sure they'd advocate for keeping the baby.

After my lunchbreak, I realize there's something about my conversation with Ralphie that bothers me and it isn't the fat jokes. Well, maybe a little of it is the fat jokes, but as I prattle through our lunch convo in my head, it's the words "false negative."

Of course, in science, there can always be false positives or negatives when it comes to a test. There's human error, but there's also the different chemical makeup of each individual patient. Every human metabolizes differently, and while it isn't unheard of for a negative pregnancy blood test—which I officially received—to later yield a positive one, it's extremely rare.

A slushy rain has begun to fall on my journey home, making the Pittsburgh skyline look like steel bridges crying long white tears. As cold as it can be here, I don't think this view will ever get old. It's lovely in all its seasons. It would be hard to leave this place.

And my clinic. I can't let anything compromise all the work I've done there. It's my legacy. If Ally doesn't turn up, it's the only one I'll ever have.

Thanksgiving is right around the corner. Soon, I'll be seated at my mother's lonely table, pretending to be interested in our ordinary conversation, wondering if this is as good as it gets until the day I die. However, today is the first time I've questioned whether Bemily is the only child I'll be leaving behind.

FIFTY

EMILY

VACATION

Two Weeks Later

They still have not found Ally. I let everyone know that I'll be headed to Mexico for a few days to destress. I don't mention which part of Mexico.

I don't say for how many days.

I only offer up the information so no one thinks I went missing along with Ally.

That would look very poor for Ben, who I heard was asked not to come back into work until all legal matters with his wife were cleared up. If Ally took off on purpose, she's really messing with a lot of people's lives here.

Laurel said that the school district told Ben they were looking out for his mental health in the absence of his wife, but I don't buy it. They just don't want the whisper network that goes along with a new teacher and his missing wife in their well-to-do district.

He's a new employee, and they're probably deciding what to do with him in this situation.

The only response I heard back from Laurel is: *I can't believe you're going on vacation right now...*

Much like the way my skin adapted and toughened after my first few fertility shots—Laurel's jabs don't hurt anymore.

Only my mother seems to be in support of my fake vacation.

Bring back some sunshine for me!

She hasn't said much about Ally's disappearance. Only that she hopes the girl is found. After Dad died, she seemed to reach a maximum threshold for losing people. She doesn't attend funerals anymore, and she doesn't have much to say when people pass away. Or perhaps she just doesn't communicate those thoughts to me considering how Dad lost his life. I can still hear her voice in my head some nights when I sit alone with the city skyline.

Emily, what have you done?

What, indeed, Mama? What would she say if she heard about my most recent blunder with a needle? I've got to fix this.

I reach the airport and buy my one-way ticket to Charlotte, North Carolina, in cash.

No return flight.

I have no idea how long this will take or if my entire trip will be futile. As I wait in the airport, I research all the different ways Ally could be plotting against me right now.

If anything, I have time on my side.

In order for Ally to prove that anything untoward had been down to her sample in my laboratory, she would need to undergo an amniocentesis, a procedure where they inject a needle into the fetus to remove amniotic fluid and cells and test it, usually for genetic abnormalities.

First, she'd have to convince her physician that something was wrong with her baby.

This could be problematic if she's trying to remain hidden and doesn't want them to contact her previous doctor. They'll want to swap records… talk… conduct the typical correspondences in this situation.

But if she knows this physician. Like… it's the same one she's been going to since she started her period, and she begs the doctor not to follow these protocols, it's within the realm of possibility that they'd comply. Patient confidentiality and all that jazz.

I put the situation in viewer mode for a moment.

The doctors did something to me there. I just know it. Something's wrong. They didn't want me to meet the head doctor for some reason. I think I asked too many questions. They didn't like that. And then, I didn't feel right after it was all said and done…

I swallow hard at this likely scenario. It's been a long time coming. Why she had to be the patient to take us down, I'll never understand. They'll drink her right in with her sweet dimples that she's probably had since infancy, and accept her unconventional requests.

Even so, an amniocentesis cannot safely be performed on a fetus before the fifteenth week, but I've heard it can be done as early as the tenth week in an emergency situation. Ally is at about week five at this point. I can't imagine she'd want to take the risk of having the procedure early, considering the slight chance of miscarriage.

Could she be down south somewhere, waiting it out?

Seems implausible considering all the ways she's knowingly causing her family to worry in her absence. Perhaps she's rationalizing that Ben is the one who really wanted her to undergo the treatment, so he should suffer. It's all so speculative, I can't get my head around it.

I have to see her for myself. But I'm half certain that I'm just chasing a ghost.

I've rented a car and have mapped myself to the only physician I could find with the last name Williams who specializes in fertility. It's a giant medical park in North Charlotte, a nice suburban area, that I'm guessing Ben once called his home.

It's so pretty here, it makes me wonder why Ben really left.

Was it truly to pursue a new career, or was he running from something? Or someone? Laurel never made it clear what spurred Ben's temporary separation from Ally. How long had they been having trouble before they left this place?

I taste the stagnant air when I step out of my rental. It's cool, still November, but twenty degrees warmer than home. The reflection of the sun billows off the paned glass of the medical building in waves. There's no great way to approach the practice or the doctor. Patient files are sealed. I'll have to get creative—not my strong suit.

The elevator carries me up to the sixth floor. I was sure to bring my credentials with me, but I'm not sure what I'm going to do with them exactly.

Hi, I was treating Ally in Pennsylvania, and I'm so dedicated to her health, I drove all the way down here to confirm records...

That's absurd. This whole idea was a bad one. I'm getting cold feet. Maybe I should drive back to the airport, buy that ticket for Mexico, and never come back. Because as soon as this thing blows wide open, I'm going to need to pack up and start over anyway.

The only person I really feel bad about leaving is my mother—and Jasper. Our ice cream date last week went good—too good.

We're a constant for each other, and when Chelsea came

back from rehab right before I left, and the screaming started back up, he needed to see my comforting glance from the balcony. We fulfill each other's needs, but we'll never be able to do it fully with Chelsea still around.

Jasper told me he was going to try again with Chelsea for Clementine's sake. Chelsea threatened to take Clem away if Jasper leaves her. I heard her harsh words through the open window.

I believe she would do that to him, and get away with it too. Money talks.

I pat the cash in my pocket, a withdrawal from my safe. That way I can't be tracked by bank withdrawals or charged airplane ticket purchases if this all goes poorly. I think about bribing Dr. Montgomery Williams, but given the sternness of his practice headshot, salt and pepper thinning hair, straight line for a mouth—indicating he's no nonsense—I have a feeling he's a man who cannot be bought.

A receptionist greets me. "Can I help you?"

"I hope so. I treated Allyson Holiday, a former patient of yours, whose whereabouts are currently unknown. I was a personal friend of Ally's as well as her embryologist. There's... a dire concern with her mother, up north, and I was hoping I could talk to someone, her previous physician or nurse."

The receptionist apprises me with doubt. "She's that missing woman, ain't she?"

"That's right. I was hoping her previous doctor could shed some light on a few things. Here're my credentials." I pull them out, but the receptionist barely looks at them.

"Ma'am, could you please have a seat?"

I sit in the waiting room with patients. After a few wayward glances from the staff, I'm half-convinced they've called the cops, and I'm just waiting here for them to cart me away. *As they should.*

After what seems like an eternity, a woman emerges in

scrubs, but she's not Dr. Montgomery. She motions me into the back, and I follow her. I don't know why, but the soundless exchange makes me worried there's a surprise attack at the end.

But she just leads me back to a conference room.

"Gail says you're here about Ally. I'm Annette, a nurse here. Dr. Montgomery is tied up, but I treated Ally for years and know her family. What's this about her mother?"

Uh oh.

"Nothing. She's just broken up about her missing daughter and didn't want to leave Pittsburgh where she went missing, but thought she might've come back here. To see you all." I throw in a southern accent, but it doesn't land, and Annette looks at me unconvinced.

"We haven't seen or heard from Ally since she moved, ma'am. I have no idea where she is. Surprised she moved in the first place, to be honest. She loved it here. Loved her house. Spent years fixing it up."

"Oh... well, that should give her mother some peace knowing she didn't come back here. One place she can cross off her list."

"A simple phone call would've suited," she says. "What's this really about?"

I don't want Annette making any concerned phone calls, so I add, "I'm here on business. A conference. Told Caroline I'd check in here. That's all."

Annette nods at the mention of Caroline's name, somewhat satisfied, and sees me out.

And I'm no closer to finding Ally than when I arrived. At least I know she isn't trying to persecute me... here.

Well, if not at this clinic, then which one?

FIFTY-ONE
EMILY

HOLES

It doesn't take a lot of effort to locate the address for the Holidays. Annette's mention of their home prompted a visit. If Ally's house was a cherished piece of her old life, one she had trouble leaving, perhaps there're clues in there. I'm sure those realtor boxes with the special code will make it impossible to enter, but, as I cruise past, I notice there is no "For Sale" sign posted in the yard.

Ben led everyone to believe that their house was being prepped to sell.

Maybe it wasn't at a point it could be shown yet.

At second glance, I notice that the grass is a bit overgrown. The landscaping in general is brown and unkept.

The house itself is farmhouse style—large and white with a wraparound porch, two rockers out front. Big blue shutters flank the windows. A country star hangs at the top, but the whole structure could use a coat of paint.

If Ally was getting this place ready to sell, she hasn't done such a great job.

Or the vendors she's hired have taken her money and run.

Or it was all a lie, and she wasn't getting the house touched up to sell. It doesn't jive with Ben's story. Yet another thing, just like the one he fed the media about Ally settling nicely into Pittsburgh. What's he hiding? Does it have something to do with his mystery phone call or his extended walk? I'm wondering if the answer is inside that house.

I contemplate breaking and entering. What's the sentence for a first-time offender, really?

Is it more or less than the amount of time I'd go to jail for medical fraud?

I see a glimmer of something move in the backyard. At first, I think it's the tussle of a bouncy animal, a dog or another southern creature I'm not familiar with—a fox?

Upon exiting the car, I creep along the property to inspect closer.

It's not an animal at all. It's a person, digging holes in the Holidays' backyard. What in the world?

It's broad daylight, so surely this person has been hired to do this.

As I get closer... Nope.

It's Allyson Holiday, frantically shoveling beneath a tree. There's a madness about her, like she's digging for gold down there. I'm almost afraid to approach the scene, but it's not like I can leave now that I've found her. I walk toward Ally, but she doesn't seem to hear me.

"Ally? What're you doing?"

She looks up slowly, her dark eyes lifting to meet mine. Her gaze is wildly frantic—like an animal caught in a trap. Her hard stare holds blind obsession.

Then she glances all around me, shovel drawn, as if she's waiting for others to come out of the bushes for her.

"It's just me. It's okay, Ally." I approach her slowly, fearful a mental breach has occurred. Her clothes are dirty, her face tear-streaked. She looks unwell. "No one knows I'm here..."

Her face contorts into something ugly, and she charges me with her shovel. I almost don't know it's happening until she starts swinging. She catches me in the shin and I howl in pain. "Ow! Stop, Ally!"

"You did this to me!"

"I can explain," I say. "This was never supposed to happen. We can fix this."

She raises her shovel to strike again.

I lift my arms from my bloodied leg, hopping on one foot. "Everyone is so worried about you. Your mom is going to lose her job. Ben too. Everyone is a wreck. Think about who you're hurting!"

"My mom lost her job..." She lowers the shovel.

That's what makes her take pause? Her mother's job at Dollar General?

"Yes, but if you reappear soon, she'll be able to keep it." Just then, I see a knapsack, and its contents sprinkled on the lawn.

A passport is flipped open. It has Ally's picture on it. I pick it up. The name says—Layla Hendricks.

"Who's Layla Hendricks?"

Ally picks up the passport with her shovel and tosses it in one of the holes. "He never came for me. I've been waiting for days."

"Who, Ben? He doesn't know you're here." I glance behind me, contemplating if I should run. Ally isn't right in the head. I'm afraid she's going to hurt me—more. But if I don't stay, I'll never be able to work out a reasonable compromise here. Not that there's much hope for how to make this right.

A garden hoe sits beside one of the open holes. I could lunge for it, fight back. But I have to remember, any harm to Ally could potentially hurt my unborn child. If she's still even pregnant...

"No, not Ben. He expected too much from me," she sputters, wipes her face. "I know it's only a matter of time before I lose this one. I'm already digging the grave. See." She points at the hole.

Oh, my Dear God. She's digging her baby's grave. But what about the other holes in the earth? Why're there so many of them?

"Ally, why don't you let me help you..." I reach my arm out, still balancing on one good leg.

"I'm sure you've helped yourself while I was gone. I know you had something going on with Ben the day of the transfer. Don't lie to me." She points the shovel at me.

"No... I didn't." Is that what she's mad about? Does she even know I tampered with the samples?

"Bullshit!" She throws a shovel full of dirt at me, and some gets in my mouth. I swat it away and spit. I think about screaming, hoping a neighbor will hear me. "You're all full of shit. You and your backstabbing little friends. You were lying to me about something."

She raises her shovel to take me out again, and I say it, "You're right! I was hiding something from you. Me and Ben both were."

"I knew it!" She wails now.

"But it's not what you think it is. Ben couldn't produce a sample the day of your procedure. A fresh sample is needed."

"What?"

"It's true. It's why he was delayed. He couldn't get... what he needed in that room."

"So, you helped him?" she asks, incredulously.

"Yes." She swings and misses. "I mean, no, not like that!" *Shit.* Me and my big mouth! "We couldn't even find him for a while, but he finally came through. He just didn't want to alarm or worry you, and... I think he was embarrassed."

"No, no! I did all this..." She points at the passports. "I was so sure... And then the one good embryo out of all the bad ones. The whole thing..." She sniffles again, and I'd feel a lot better if she'd release that shovel, but she's brought up the good embryo, and this is the moment where I have to decide if I should tell her or not.

In her current state, she might murder me. And dig me an adult-size hole. It all comes down to one question. "Ally, are you still pregnant?"

Because if she's not, then none of this matters. She doesn't need to know a damn thing, because there would be no sense in revealing information that could get me in trouble.

"Yes! And he said it didn't matter. I waited at the bus station for a whole week!" she wails. "His text message just said, 'I can't do this with the kid. I'm sorry. I thought I could.'"

The bus station. That's how she got away. She must've gotten a ride and used that fake-ass passport. She probably disguised herself to hide from the cameras, but I wasn't sure the police were looking hard into buses.

And she was running off with... a man? Ally was cheating on Ben?

Well, then, in that case, she doesn't really deserve to know the sacrifices I've made for her, and her family. A family she was planning on abandoning anyway. "I can't believe you would leave Ben."

"Why? You did."

I hobble backward. She's right. I did. "I was really young. You're married, but look, you made a mistake. I think if you go home, he'd take you back. Everyone just wants to know you're okay. Ben wants to raise that baby with you."

"He'll never take me back if he knows I was going to run off with some other guy. I just couldn't take the pressure anymore. He wanted a family I couldn't provide. Then he wanted me to adjust to a place I hated."

Ben lied about Ally's fondness for Pittsburgh. Poor guy

probably wanted that for the two of them and made it up. Anything not to blame himself for causing this.

"Don't tell him," I say.

Because if she doesn't, we'll both have a secret. Ally might not know what mine is, exactly, but I'll keep hers to preserve my error in judgment and so I can keep a close watch on her—and my biological child.

As much as I want to give Ally reassurance this baby will survive, I don't. Although, I do think this baby will make it because Ally's eggs were defective and mine are not.

"You'll tell him. How could you not?" she asks.

"Tell him what? You never ran away with the guy. He didn't show up. There's nothing to tell. Unless he's someone Ben knows."

Ally stiffens. "No, he's not. He was a contractor... working on the house."

A contractor... that's why his number didn't show up in Ally's call log. Much like the hospital, his work phone probably showed the parent company on the caller ID. Ally had a nice little runaway plan here. Too bad it backfired on her.

"I don't need to know anymore. Everyone thinks I'm in Mexico. I figured out you might've gone home and wanted to check here first. Just return and say you had a mental breakdown and had to go home. Your real home. Then, let Ben take care of you and your baby for the rest of your lives and forget whoever the hell this guy is." I point at the passports. "Because if he left you like this, he'll never love you as much as Ben does."

"Don't you want Ben for yourself?" she says. "You could probably have him now. After what I've done."

"I don't... I'm in love with someone else."

Ally finally lowers the shovel.

FIFTY-TWO

EMILY

SIRENS

Two Weeks Later

When I return home two weeks later after a solo jaunt to Hilton Head, so I'd have at least a tint of a tan after my faux trip to Mexico, there're police cars lined up the street.

It's nighttime on the weekend, and who knows what kind of shit is going down. Usually it's relegated to the backside of the mountain.

I'm assuming it's rowdy traffic from the local bar, until I see a patrol car on the inside of my gated property.

My heart ratchets up; I really did let myself relax on my mini-vacation.

My knee still throbs from where it was gashed as I pull out my suitcase. The police are at Jasper's. Oh no, this isn't good.

There's caution tape around the front of his townhouse. *What happened?*

I pull my car into my garage. The police glance at me as if I'm disturbing them as I shut the door. I run inside and use the bathroom. The unopened pregnancy tests glare at me like a constant reminder of my failed transfer.

I dash to the balcony next and that's when I see it. Jasper is crying. He has bruises on his face. Clementine is wailing too, and reaches for me across the railing.

She, too, looks as though she's experienced an assault of some kind.

"Jasper?" I shout.

He looks over, stunned. He shakes his head—*No.*

No, what? I wonder.

He's crying and it breaks my heart. I see now that Clementine has scratches on her face.

"Clementine, what happened?" I ask.

She looks at me, so sadly. "Mommy went over." She points over the balcony, and I clasp my hand to my mouth.

I see it now—the crag of the rock, the very tip, the sharpest one—stained red.

I've imagined her falling in that exact spot. It feels like a premonition of sorts.

Did she survive?

There's no one left on the balcony. They've retreated inside and closed and locked the doors.

FIFTY-THREE

EMILY

ODDS

The next day I sit on the doctor's exam table, a paper-thin blue gown rustling at my twitchy knees, waiting for some confirmation of the thing that cannot possibly be true.

After the type of chemotherapy and hormone therapy I endured, the chances of conceiving a child without IVF is less than five percent, the impact on my ovaries irreversible.

But the risk of breast cancer before age thirty is less than one percent, and I got that too. I've broken statistical records before.

Maybe this one just happens to be in my favor for once.

Dr. Menen enters the room next, temporarily halting my wild stream of consciousness. She's my sleek, young OB with a face that strongly resembles Kirsten Dunst.

"Well, it looks like you're definitely pregnant!" She clasps her hands together excitedly. I've gone through IVF. Obviously, I very much want this baby, and her reaction is appropriate, but none of it feels right.

"But my hCG was really low—" I begin, scooching up on the table.

"Well, it's not anymore. I don't know, maybe you tested too early, but your blood results are in, and they look great. Now, let's take a look at that little bean in there."

My feet are in the stirrups already when Dr. Menen whips out a wand and looks behind her as if she's waiting for someone. It's a good thing she glances away, because I'm pretty sure my mouth opens wide enough to eat a canary.

"This is a trans-vaginal ultrasound. You're likely too early along to see anything with a regular ultrasound, and we want to know what's going on in there given everything you've told me."

But I haven't told her *everything*.

Dr. Menen instructs me to relax as she passes the wand to her ultrasound tech who's just entered the room.

"My name is Paula, sorry I'm late," she says as she jams the probe into my body. They both just sit there smiling at me as if one of them hasn't just thrust something the size of a microphone staph inside my vagina.

I'm tense. Until I see a little blip jumping on the screen.

"Is that—?" I ask, pointing.

"Yep. A heartbeat. Good sign," Paula says, but she has a questioning look on her face. She begins taking measurements of the *said* bean. Dr. Menen points out the beating heart, and I'm just amazed this is actually happening.

The transfer didn't work. I knew it didn't, and my meds are supposed to prevent me from ovulating. And my maternal clock is... old(ish).

It's *elderly multigravida*.

It couldn't have started ticking again that fast, could it? My ovaries are supposed to be scorched with chemo. I did have a period since my IVF treatments, so it's not completely out of the realm of possibility.

Oh my God, I can't believe this is happening. It's a miracle.

Or a mistake. It's a good thing that monitor isn't attached to my chest because my heart is beating so fast it might barrel through.

However, Paula's expression worries me. Something is wrong.

"What is it?" I ask.

Paula stares at the paperwork from the doctor's clipboard, her cropped hairdo tucked neatly behind her ears. She keeps glancing back and forth from the clipboard to the black and white blob on the screen.

"The dates aren't exactly adding up, but everything looks good otherwise," she affirms.

"What do you mean?"

"Well, it says your transfer was the first week in October, which would make this baby about eight weeks old, but it's measuring closer to five weeks," Paula puzzles.

Even Dr. Menen scratches her perfectly done-up platinum hair.

"Well, could it just be measuring on the small side?" I ask.

"Could be. It's too early to tell. The important thing is, the baby's got a strong heartbeat, and everything looks great," Dr. Menen says, with her perma-grin again.

Paula hands me a black and white grainy photo of a fetus and leaves the room.

Dr. Menen starts going through the rundown of prenatal vitamins and additional testing and blood work, and my regimen of increasing doctor visits that would occur in the future. Her eye contact is great as she explains the instructions quickly, but she isn't picking up on the fact that my mind is a thousand miles away.

She obviously can't see my fingers slipping through each other as I ball my sweaty fists and clench my breath. I can't hear a word she's saying, and accept each pamphlet and prescription blindly, hoping I can play catch-up later.

Because this baby wasn't created through IVF.

This baby was created...

Five Weeks Ago

I place my empty earthenware mug of drunk tea down as Jasper stares at me with wonder and desire. "You're the smartest woman I've ever met. That's probably why you're single, you know? Most men are intimidated by a girl as pretty as you that has it up here too." He points to my head. My hair is tied up in a messy knot after my wild goose chase through the woods looking for Ally.

I grin at Jasper, but I don't argue with him, because I've actually found this to be true.

When I attempted dating and mentioned my job and level of education, if the man wasn't of the same breadth of success, they often found reasons not to call me back.

"Well, I think you're a brilliant creator. This place is gorgeous," I tell him.

Our townhomes have the exact same layout, but the inside of Jasper's looks as though it's been snagged from a swanky interior design magazine. A lot of the pieces, like the fireplace mantel, is made of reclaimed barnwood. There's brightly colored, refurbished turquoise pieces that look as though they were absolute labors of love.

"Thanks. I've tried to add lots of color, but I'm still tired of being sad and alone here," he says. The fire crackles with heat.

He walks over and unwraps me from my blanket, his desire all-consuming. My lips part as he brushes my cheek with his lips, and I don't want to say it, but I'd be a terrible person if I didn't. "Me too, but... you have a wife," I say in a whisper.

"I haven't had one of those in a long while. She's sick. And horrible to us. And I'd like to try to see if she gets any better for

Clementine, but I don't think she's going to. I don't think I can take it here anymore. But I don't want to leave you."

His honesty rocks my world. "What?" I look back at him, the gentleness in his eyes. He deserves to be loved.

"Do you have family you can let Clementine stay with? Until she gets better?"

"Not in this country. I don't have anyone here, and Chelsea will never let me take Clementine overseas. It isn't safe... where I'm from."

All I know about Jasper's heritage is that he's from somewhere in the Middle East. I don't question where. I'm hoping there will be time for that... later. "I'm sorry."

"Don't be sorry." He nuzzles against me again. After seeing him at a slight distance all those years, his closeness is intoxicating. His cologne overpowering, a delightful spicy scent, his lips plump and soft on my neck. "Seeing Clementine... and you... is the only thing that's kept me hanging on all these years."

Jasper stays... for me?

He kisses me on the lips then, and I let him.

Maybe it's because I've always wanted someone to pine over me, desire me in a way they can't contain. Or perhaps it's because I'm cold, and when Jasper peels my shirt from my body, his bare chest against mine is solid and warm. But it's not enough.

I need more. So does he.

Any wanting and needing of anything is fulfilled in the next couple of hours as we roll around in his silk bedsheets.

We left it open-ended. Chelsea was returning from rehab. They were going to try to work it out. It probably wouldn't. And then... maybe we could talk.

Now, things are even more out of balance. Chelsea is back in the hospital. She broke her back when she fell.

In my mind, I can see her leaning over that damn balcony too far, likely after a relapse.

It's a familiar, morose story. Seventy-five percent of addicts relapse in the first year.

Jasper didn't say much after it happened, and I haven't seen him at the house in days. I'm not sure if or when he's going to return with Clementine, and I have no idea how to tell him he's the father of my child.

FIFTY-FOUR

EMILY

POSITIVE?

My mother is the first person I call.

She'll be my test pilot for the believability factor of my failed transfer—that has suddenly decided to work. Will people who aren't science-based question this methodology? She's a nurse, so she'll be a good trial run.

"Hello, Emily," she answers in the hushed way she often does.

"Hello, Mom, I've got great news for you," I announce.

"I'm late for pickleball, what's up?" Mother asks.

Did she miss the part where I said I had news? I never have news.

"I had a doctor's appointment. So, turns out my pregnancy results from the transfer were a false negative," I say, with an edge to my voice that rarely exposes itself in the presence of Mother's normal bouts of complacency.

"A what?" she asks confusedly.

Now, I am the one who's sighing. The fabricated explanation of my failed-transfer-turned-good could prove to be more exhausting than the pregnancy itself.

"The early testing didn't show the right levels. This happens sometimes in people who have naturally low levels of hCG, or in instances where the dating isn't correct in relation to conception," I blurt out.

"Oh. Well, how can that be? Didn't your lab do the procedure?"

Ugh. This question isn't expected. My ignorance is going to make me look incompetent at my own job.

"Well, I didn't do my own blood work, and they don't test for hCG before your transfer. It's the hormone that shows an elevated level after conception. I must be one of those people that have a low showing."

"Low showing." That's not even a real medical term. I'm a shitty liar, and I'm never going to pull this off.

"Oh, that's interesting," Mother muses.

I tell her she's going to have her first grandchild, and that's her response—*That's interesting*. Not, when are you due? How are you feeling? When do you find out the gender? Do you want me to go with you to the next appointment? She's provided none of the motherly commentary I expect to hear. Is it because she doesn't believe me or because she has a heart the temperature of a meat locker?

"Can you believe it?" I ask, fishing for happiness.

"It's very surprising."

"Very surprising that the transfer worked or that I'm pregnant in general?" I ask.

"I never heard of a false negative, only a false positive, but I suppose it's possible. And the pregnancy more so," she says, dully.

That's all I needed to hear. The word—possible.

As long as people think it's possible, they won't question it.

It wouldn't be the most terrible thing to reveal Jasper is the father—if he wasn't married, that is. My baby will immediately be cast as a product of a dirty affair. It's better people believe he or she was created in my lab.

"Yeah, I am shocked," I continue in the same boring monotone as my mother. Why feign for her attention?

"And you didn't do an additional transfer with the one embryo you had left, and you're just not telling me?" my mother asks, still confused. So, this is the source of her awfulness. She knows I lied to her. Well, she's precisely right, but it isn't about the transfer.

"No, Mother. I would've told you," I say.

"How did you know to test again?" she asks.

"I've gained a little weight and a lack of a menstrual cycle," I reveal. A little weight is the understatement of the year. I've gained twenty pounds already and I'm not even all the way through my first trimester. Some people only gain twenty-five pounds their whole pregnancy, so I'm doing poorly in that department. A pamphlet on nutrition is among the ones Dr. Menen handed to me.

"Well, those are definite indicators," she says dryly. "I have some things I bought for you when you were going through IVF," she says. "It's a diary to track your pregnancy. And a special surprise. With this news... I'd really like to give it to you. Can you stop over?"

"Not today. I need to go to the pharmacy and get my prenatals. Maybe this weekend?"

"Okay, if you can't make it to me this weekend, I'm coming to you." She finally sounds a little excited.

"Deal," I tell her.

As I wind up the hill to my house, I see Jasper pushing Chelsea into theirs in a wheelchair. The scene is grim, as she has on a neck brace that holds up her head. She stares blankly ahead.

Clementine is not with them. I wonder where she is.
This is not the day I can tell Jasper about the baby.
I wonder if and when I'll ever be able to.

FIFTY-FIVE

ALLY

SECRETS

Sebastian is fantasy.

A secret I kept from everyone, because deep down, I think I knew he wasn't real. Before I left for college, he tried the same thing—to derail my plans. It's a game with him, I think.

I should've known after all these years that if he hasn't coupled up with anyone else, I could never be his one and only. He just liked dangling the promise, but holding on to Sebastian is like trying to grab the wind. As soon as he wraps his warm arms around you, the minute you hug back, he slips right through your fingers.

It likely wasn't about the baby. He just wanted to see if I'd really leave my husband for him.

Marriage is hard, and Sebastian was temptation.

I gave in, but I see that now, and I won't let it happen again.

I'm foolish to have taken Ben for granted. The father of my child. The one who's stuck by me through thick and thin. I see how I made up reasons to leave him when things got tough.

How I blew up his small idiosyncrasies into monstrous acts.

Everyone has taken me for the woman who went on the run after the pressures to become a mother. I've been given the same sympathy as those who have PPD, and it feels undeserved, but I take it so I can gain Ben's trust back.

Women's groups have come out of the woodwork to support me online, while others have vilified me.

I know which side of that fence I really belong on—villain.

The only other person who knows has a dark secret of her own.

I don't like that my secret is bigger than hers.

She knows that I more-or-less cheated on my husband.

That I was going to trade the beautiful life I made with Ben for one with a different man I built up in my mind to be something he's not.

And... I know the baby she's carrying was fathered by a married man.

She didn't ask me explicit details about the man she refers to as *the contractor* and I didn't ask her who the married man is that she slept with—only verifying it's not Ben.

It's not.

It still makes me feel filthier. I'm the one who broke vows. She's just the girl who made another man compromise his. The temptress. We'll never be friends, Emily and I, but we have come to a special understanding.

She's dead set on keeping her secret that her baby was made in the lab. Even though the birthdates won't line up, she's asking me to back her up. In exchange, she won't breathe a word to Ben about what happened in Charlotte.

Ben thinks I got on a Greyhound bus in a fit of delusion and rode around on it for a week. That's the story Emily helped me concoct as I bandaged up her knee, which I bashed open with my garden shovel.

I did apologize for hurting her, but you shouldn't sneak up

on people, and especially at their home when they're in the middle of a nervous breakdown.

Apologies went all around—Ben, his family, my family, his friends.

Everyone said the same thing, "I'm just glad you're home."

And that's when I decided I needed to stay—here.

Abandon that old life and the old hurts I left behind. Even what's buried in the ground.

Our exchange, mine and Emily's—seems somewhat even.

That, and the fact that the baby she procured for me in her laboratory has miraculously hung in there so far.

Maybe Emily Daugherty is the answer to my prayers.

Tonight is the first of many where I'll join her friends for a joint homecoming celebration. Things between Ben and myself are still tense, but we're in counseling now.

They've also prescribed sertraline for me, even though I've secretly refused to take it, because I'm not depressed. I was just confused. I'm just glad to be back on the righteous path, with good people, who're on my side and would never, ever lie to me or lead me to believe things that aren't true.

FIFTY-SIX

EMILY

INJECT

"Are you sure it's mine?" he asks. Jasper holds the wonder of a man who's just been handed the world.

"Yes," I answer. But our joy is drowned out by the stillness that overcomes his house and the woman responsible for the quiet. She sits in a wheelchair just a few feet away.

Chelsea had a bilateral fracture of the C2 vertebrae which has left her paralyzed from the neck down. Brain trauma has left her mostly unresponsive. Home health has set up a bed so that Jasper can take care of her, but he looks as though he's hanging on by a thread

It seems the baby news has brightened his disposition just a bit, though. "I can't decide what's worse. When she was abusive and would yell at us endlessly... or this."

It has to be *this*, right?

Although I don't fully understand what Jasper's really been through up until this point. All I know is that when Chelsea came home from rehab, she drank three-fifths of a bottle of vodka while Jasper ran to the store—for something she'd requested—and lost her temper with Clementine when she'd spilt milk.

Clem was trying to pour her own milk for her cereal because her mom was too drunk to do it for her.

Jasper came home to a house of spilt milk and blood. Chelsea went after Clementine so hard, she'd broken skin with her long nails.

Then Chelsea went after Jasper. He tried to hold back her swatting hands. She scratched his face and punched him, darting for the balcony—where she fell over the edge.

I'll never ask Jasper if he pushed her.

Frankly, after seeing Clementine's face, I don't care if he did.

"I have to pick up Clementine at gymnastics. Can you watch her?" Jasper nods at Chelsea.

"Sure. Do you mind if I move her to my house in the wheelchair and watch her there?" I ask. I kiss him on the mouth.

"No problem," he says.

He doesn't resist me. This is going to become our life—me and Jasper and Clementine. None of it is normal, but Jasper's felt right from the minute he opened up to me on that balcony. We've known each other for years, even if it was a courtship by osmosis. I love this man, and I'm determined to make this family mine.

I watch Jasper leave, knowing what I have to do.

In order for it to work, it has to be completed soon after Chelsea's accident. We're running out of time.

I know for a fact Jasper doesn't want Chelsea here anymore.

Clementine may want her around, but it's heartbreaking watching her retell the stories to her mother that she heard in pre-school that day. "Those are the stories they tell us before nap," she says. "Maybe Mommy will wake up."

But Mommy is never going to wake up from her nap. Or walk again.

I see myself in viewer mode. This is like a movie where the clinician is the hero. The one to make the pain go away.

Just like I did with my father.

Everyone will be better off.

Pre-dusk light filters through the blinds like an unwanted houseguest.

But light is where the truth lives.

No one can find out what she's done.

It's the right thing.

The patient sits listless and broken in a chair.

Nothing but a life of pain in their future.

This will all be over soon, she whispers to herself.

She pulls the plunger back on the syringe, taps the barrel.

And smiles at how much better everyone will feel once she's done.

She positions the needle close to the crook of the patient's arms.

A green vein presents itself at the surface.

She's about to inject her patient.

But movement behind her in the shadows...

Freezes her in position.

Someone's... there.

I inject the patient—with the high dose of ephedrine I snagged from the hospital that will most likely be the cause of a brain hemorrhage—and sudden death.

It will be copesetic with the type of brain injury Chelsea experienced during her fall, and easily explainable. I'll ask Jasper not to request an autopsy.

He'll understand why.

We've discussed this.

It'll be fine. Our little secret. Like all the other ones I keep to myself. In my lab, there are checks and balances. In my home, there are none.

I turn slowly at the noise, probably just city street noises, and then see that my front door is open.

My mother stands there, something in her hand.

It's the baby journal and the gift she mentioned on the phone. I recognize the present. It's something my father made for me when I had my eggs extracted. A special piece of welded metal with colored glass, a mosaic that makes—a butterfly—intended for my future baby.

My mother nears me, a ghostly expression on her face. "Oh Emily... what have you done?"

A LETTER FROM CARA

Dear reader,

I want to say a huge thank you for choosing to read *The Clinic*. Please note: although there was a ton of research that went into the more clinical aspects of this book, there were creative liberties taken in its completion.

If you did enjoy it, and want to keep up-to-date with all my latest releases, just sign up at the following link. Your email address will never be shared and you can unsubscribe at any time.

www.bookouture.com/Cara-Reinard

I hope you loved *The Clinic*, and if you did I would be very grateful if you could write a review. I'd love to hear what you think, and it makes such a difference helping new readers to discover one of my books for the first time.

I love hearing from my readers—you can get in touch on my Facebook page, through X, Goodreads or my website.

Thanks,

Cara Reinard

KEEP IN TOUCH WITH CARA

www.carareinard.com

 x.com/carareinard

instagram.com/carareinard

ACKNOWLEDGEMENTS

Some novels take longer than others to complete. This book was a labor (no pun intended) of love for me. I finished the first draft of *The Clinic* nearly eleven years ago. It was originally called *A Tiny Secret* and marketed as a women's fiction novel, and unfortunately it did not sell to a publisher. *The Clinic* sat on my hard drive for over a decade. It's the only book I refused to shelve, and one of my favorite projects because it combines my love of science and writing.

After spending twenty-plus years in the pharmaceutical industry, my last seven in oncology, I was finally able to edit *The Clinic* into the version it was always supposed to be—with the help of my wonderful editor at Bookouture, Natalie Edwards. I typed the last word of the revised draft and thought to myself—this is it. This is why it took so long. It wasn't ready yet. And I'll be forever grateful that my readers finally get to enjoy it.

So many people have read early drafts of this novel and given valuable feedback that it's hard to thank them all, but I'll try (if I missed anyone, I'm sorry!): Savina Cupps, Dana Falleti, Nancy Hammer, Lori Jones, Kim Pierson, Carolyn Menke, Vickie Reinard, Lisa Coulson, Kathie Shoop, and Janice Sniezek. A special thank you to Sarah Hardy, my publicist, as well, and the whole team at Bookouture with special props to the cover designer for *The Clinic*, Emma Graves, on a stunning job.

And of course, I'd be remiss if didn't mention my family—

my husband, who is my biggest support to our two not-so-little bundles, Jackson and Charlotte, who were toddlers when I started this novel and are now pre-teen/teenagers. I hope they've learned from the publication of this book, that there is no expiration date for realizing your dreams.

PUBLISHING TEAM

Turning a manuscript into a book requires the efforts of many people. The publishing team at Bookouture would like to acknowledge everyone who contributed to this publication.

Audio
Alba Proko
Melissa Tran
Sinead O'Connor

Commercial
Lauren Morrissette
Hannah Richmond
Imogen Allport

Cover design
Emma Graves

Data and analysis
Mark Alder
Mohamed Bussuri

Editorial
Natalie Edwards
Charlotte Hegley

Printed in Great Britain
by Amazon

55636116R00187